Text copyright © Alan MacDonald 1998
Illustrations copyright © Sally Anne Lambert 1998

First published in Great Britain in 1998
by Macdonald Young Books
an imprint of Wayland Publishers Ltd
61 Western Road
Hove
East Sussex
BN3 1JD

Find Macdonald Young Books on the internet at http://www.myb.co.uk

Designed by Triggerfish, 11 Jew Street, Brighton, BN1 1UT
Printed in Hong Kong by Wing King Tong.

British Library Cataloguing in Publication Data available

ISBN 0 7500 2596 4

D1759214

ESCAPE
Dead End

David J Antocci

This novel is a work of fiction. Names, characters, places, and incidents are the product of the author's imagination or are used fictitiously. Any resemblance to actual events, locals, or persons, living or dead, is coincidental.

ISBN-13: 978-0692406199

ISBN-10: 0692406190

For information about permission to reproduce selections from this novel, visit the author's website, www.Antocci.com

Books by David J Antocci

ESCAPE, A New Life

ESCAPE, Past Sins

ESCAPE, Dead End

CONTENTS

Acknowledgements

While it's my name on the cover, I have a great team behind me that I want to thank for donating their time, expertise, and brutally honest opinions of my writing. My beta-readers and proofreaders keep me on my toes and help to whip the story into shape. Lisa Antocci, Nicole Andries, Lindsay Russo, Christine Souza, and Cindy Fogarty, THANK YOU for all that you did to help me make this book a fitting ending to the trilogy.

Throughout the ESCAPE series I have had the pleasure of working with an extraordinary editor, John Briggs of Albany Editing. Over the course of working on this project he has taught me a great deal about the craft of writing, and his insights have been indispensible.

Finally, a HUGE thanks to you, the reader! Your encouragement and support throughout the release of the first two novels gave me the confidence to keep moving forward. As a boy I dreamed of being a writer and telling my stories to anyone who would listen. You have made that little boy's dreams come true, and are more important to me than you can imagine!

Thank you for reading my books and spreading the word to your friends! - Dave

David J Antocci

...

1

ABBY BREATHED SLOWLY, trying to calm her pulse. She sat with her legs crossed under her in a small clearing in the forest. A bead of sweat trickled down her brow despite the crisp morning temperature.

This is supposed to help? she thought to herself.

It did when she was moving. Forty-five minutes of intense yoga occupied her mind and forced her to concentrate on her breathing, on getting through the pain.

Although her bullet wound had healed several months ago, each time she stretched her arms above her head it felt as though the muscles in her shoulder might tear all over again. The pain alone was enough to make her break a sweat.

The pain was good. The sweat was good. It kept her mind occupied more than yoga ever could.

Sitting on a bed of fallen leaves, birds chirping all around her in the early dawn, she closed her eyes and let her mind momentarily wander. As it often did, it wandered to Eric.

She saw him smile as he told her, "I love you, too. Now go!" That was the last thing he ever said to her.

Almost, she reminded herself.

The absolute last thing he ever said came just a few moments later as he desperately screamed her name, "ABBY!" seconds before her ex-husband's car slammed into him as he shoved her out of the way. The car had been gunning for her. She should have been the one taking the full force of the hit. Thanks to Eric it only clipped her and broke her leg.

Just breathe, she reminded herself, counting her breaths and attempting to clear her mind. *It will help.*

And yet, she watched helplessly in her mind's eye as two tons of steel slammed into the love of her life at sixty miles per hour. His head smashed into the windshield and his neck snapped in slow motion.

In and out. In and out. Feel the anger leave your body.

His body sailed over the roof of the car, thrown ten feet in the air by the impact.

Breathe out, Abby... breathe out...

He seemed to float in the air for an eternity as she watched, horrified, unable to do a thing.

Breathe...

His body struck the earth with a thud.

Finally Abby gasped for air. She had relived this scene a thousand times, and the pain in her heart never eased no matter how many times she saw it. Her eyes snapped open, confused for a moment, forgetting she was meditating in nature.

Bursting into tears, she slapped herself hard across the face and scolded her weakness, "Get a grip on yourself!"

Closing her eyes again, she listened to the birds sing their morning song. A woodpecker worked on his latest project near the top of a tall pine. A squirrel nibbled on acorns at the base of the oak to her left.

Eric smiled at her, "I love you, too. Now go!"

As her tear-filled eyes forced themselves open, she lifted her face to the sky and let out a scream that silenced every living thing it touched. The birds fell silent and the squirrel scampered away as her cry echoed through the forest.

Abby put her face in her hands and screamed again, "THIS IS BULLSHIT!"

Jumping up, she grabbed a thick branch from the ground and slammed it into the trunk of a tree over and over again. She ignored the fire building in her shoulder and battered the tree until the branch shattered in her hands, leaving her palms cut and bleeding.

"Fuck this," she said as she threw the remnants of the branch to the ground and marched back to her cabin.

Abby was as surprised as anyone about this place she currently called home. Like most visitors to the region, she thought of the American Northeast as densely populated, with city stacked upon city. Massachusetts, New York, and New Jersey were home to some of the most packed cities in America.

3

However, it turned out that there is far more country than city in the Northeast. Vermont, New Hampshire, Maine, and most of New York lay beyond the city lights, with huge expanses of forests and farms. Millions of acres worth of forests and farmlands spread across the region. Massive swathes of Maine remain as foreign to some Northeasterners as the deltas of the Mississippi.

Nestled deep within a few hundred acres of privately owned forest was the facility Abby called home. *For now,* she reminded herself.

Once the hospital stabilized her, after having nearly died from the gunshot wound and having a severely broken leg, Robert arranged to have her moved to a private rehab facility in the middle of nowhere. Discretion was the law around here. Without it, the facility would quickly go out of business, and it was too profitable a business to surrender.

It was where people who didn't want to be bothered went to get better. The massive private fees paid by its patrons bought not only the best care possible, but also the guaranteed silence of everyone they met.

If anyone Abby came into contact with actually knew who she was, they never let on.

The leg break was a tough one, but Abby was determined to work through it as fast as possible. Her tibia was broken in two places. They were both clean breaks given the car's high speed, but it was still six months before she could walk comfortably without feeling significant pain. She continued to push herself hard, and at eight months, was back to running every morning.

The leg was nothing compared to getting shot, however. It felt like it was yesterday, a pain much worse than she had ever imagined it could be. It was like being punched incredibly hard as a searing, white-hot fire engulfed the wound.

She had been lucky in that the bullet missed major vessels and organs, but it still severely impacted her left side. It hit above her left breast, an inch in from the shoulder. Given the angle, the surgeon said she was lucky it didn't shatter her shoulder blade. Fortunately the 9 mm round didn't make it all the way through. It did a number on her muscle structure, though.

The rehab staff was impressed with her commitment – she just about lived in the gym, weight training, stretching, doing everything she could to move things along. Doctors expected Abby to stay in residence for about a year, half as long as an average person, thanks to her work ethic and strict regimen. Abby, however, was not motivated by the idea of getting better. She pushed herself because she never forgot what was at the end of it all for her: Revenge.

And the time for that was drawing near.

2

AS SHE HIKED through the woods back to her accommodations, she felt that her physical readiness for confrontation at last matched her mental readiness. Had she been able to leap from her hospital bed ten months ago and hunt down Bryce, she would have. A few hours after Robert had told her that Bryce escaped across the Canadian border and disappeared, she actually tried.

She left three nurses incapacitated in her wake before two beefy orderlies held her down while a doctor administered a sedative. Three hours later he gave her another dose and ordered her placed under twenty-four hour watch. Anything to keep her from getting up and hurting herself or the staff. It would be eight weeks before Abby could put any weight on her leg again.

She spent a great deal of those eight weeks thinking about how her life had changed so drastically during the past few years. She replayed the first time she saw Eric on *Trial Island* in the middle of a storm. She didn't know who he was, or who he would become. He was just a person, unconscious, out in the rough surf, who needed her help. She acted quickly, jumped into the water and saved his life, a debt he ultimately repaid by saving hers.

ESCAPE
Dead End

All of their time together struggling to survive on the island brought them closer together. They owed their lives to each other, and after escaping the island, intended to spend the rest of their lives with each other.

The year following their escape from *Trial Island* made Abby the happiest she had ever been. Living in their own little piece of paradise on another out-of-the-way island made each day feel like a dream. The friendships they made with the local people, the small villa they constructed with their own hands on the beach, and the love they had, came as close to a sappy romance novel as real life could get.

At least until JJ found them. Then there was another decision to make, one that would change the course of her life yet again—the decision to get her memory back.

Her heart remained torn over that decision. On one hand, getting her memory back led her to the first true love of her life, the beautiful daughter she didn't know she had. On the other hand, it led directly to Eric's death, the second true love of her life.

Would I make the same decision now, knowing what I know?

Robert had been coming to see her at least once a month since she arrived at the facility but had left a few days ago. She asked him, "Would you make that decision, knowing how it turned out?"

After some thoughtful silence, he locked eyes with her, "We all have to make decisions. Sometimes it's easy, sometimes it's hard. You can spend days mulling over these things, weighing the pros and cons, trying to take the absolute best course of action, but there are no guarantees. You would do well to stop second-guessing yourself and look to the future. Eric is dead, my dear. I miss him, too. Not a day has gone by in the last ten months that I haven't thought of him. But nothing will change the fact that he is gone. And you know he wouldn't want you to spend your life mourning his loss."

Abby nodded. "I know, but it was my decision that led to it. My decision. If it weren't for me, he would still be alive."

He reached out and held her hand. "No, Abby, that's where you're wrong. We all make our own decisions. We decide the course of our own lives. Eric made a decision, too. When he saw that car barreling toward you and Ava, he made his decision. Someone was going to die, and he decided that that someone would be him. He shoved you out of the way and saved your life. That was his decision, not yours. His."

"But…" Abby was immediately cut off by Robert, impatience in his voice.

"No buts, Abby. It was his decision. Your decision to get your memory back did not lead to his death. His decision to save your life and Ava's life did. Don't take that from him. He chose for you to continue living. If you want to honor his memory, that's what you have to do!"

She leaned on her hand, propping up her head as the tears flowed. "You always know how to put it into perspective."

He smiled.

"But how… how can I move past it? The monster that killed him tried to kill me and Ava… the monster that tortured me for all those years, who drove my daughter and I apart… he's still out there. I can't rest, Robert. I can't live my life with him out there, never knowing when he might show up, always living in fear and looking over my shoulder. What do I do about that?"

"That is your decision to make."

She found that the decision was not a hard one. Yes, Robert was right. She had to move on. Eric would want that. He would hate her living her life this way. He would hate her living a life full of sadness because of what he did for her.

She knew she needed to move on. She needed to continue living. Before she could move on, however, she needed to extinguish the beast who had plagued her for the past ten years.

Abby liked simple plans, and this was no different. Find Bryce and kill him. That was the extent of her plan. The trouble was finding him.

Bryce was well-connected in the underworld. When he showed up on her sister's lawn, he had already been "dead" for a year. He was a ghost, with no records or trail of any kind. When he escaped that night, so did any knowledge of his existence.

JJ was on the case and confident he could track him

down eventually. As far as Abby was concerned, he seemed to be dragging his feet as if he didn't want her to find him. Was he worried about her? More likely Robert was, and had asked JJ to take it slow for her sake.

Her patience was wearing thin, though, and she would soon take up the hunt for Bryce herself. Abby felt she had one advantage: as far as the world was concerned, she was dead. The news reported that she had been gunned down by a mob hitman ten months ago and died at the scene. It was a story Robert went to great lengths to make sure everyone believed. If the word got out that she was still alive, Bryce would come find her, and that simply would not do.

Abby did not intend to be the hunted. No, this time she would be the hunter—and the element of surprise was her greatest asset.

Finally arriving back at her cabin, she smiled a little at thinking of her accommodations as a *cabin*. It would probably be more accurately describe as a luxury villa, but this was the backwoods country of Maine and luxury villa didn't seem right. It didn't exist in the vernacular for this area.

To look at it from the outside, it was a modest, twelve hundred square foot cabin, but after the thumbprint scan allowed her access to the interior, it was anything but. The entire interior was hardwood. Not simply the floors, but the walls and ceiling. It had a wide-open floor plan with the well appointed kitchen and dining areas opening up to the living space and a massive stone fireplace that took up an entire wall.

The locking mechanism secured the door in place behind her as she kicked off her shoes and walked down a small hallway toward her bedroom, where she deposited her clothes in the hamper and turned on a steaming shower in the large bath.

While the water was heating up, she took a good look at herself in the mirror. The scar from the bullet hole just below her shoulder had healed over though it was still red and a bit sunken despite the surgeon's effort. The rest of her body looked great, in her opinion, the best it ever had. When she had woken up on *Trial Island*, she had been impressed with how she looked and felt, but thoughts of revenge meant she continued to push herself harder. Most striking was her straight, jet-black hair that hung down past her shoulders. Her loosely curled brunette locks that she wore on *Trial Island* had turned into a shorter blonde cut while she and Eric had been in hiding. Both were gone now, in hopes that she would be less recognizable.

Enjoying the hot steam of the shower, she was thankful to have her current accommodations, especially after her time on *Trial Island*, where she spent her days fighting for her life and her nights sleeping on whatever pile of leaves she happened upon.

Her cabin was more than comfortable. No one ever bothered her, and she was getting her mind and body back into shape. Even so, Abby was tired of living this life of solitude. She wanted to be with Ava. Not visit with her but *be* with her.

Once a week Abby left the facility to drive six hours northwest and visit her little girl who was living with

Abby's older sister, Sarah. Abby had enjoyed becoming reacquainted with her daughter over the past ten months or so. However their time together was limited to the weekends, when Abby checked out of her anonymous rehab.

Ava was nine years old now, so still of the age that she idolized her mother. Their weekends were filled with as much regular mother and daughter time as they could fit; doing each other's hair, baking brownies, watching movies, doing crafts with beads. She even still enjoyed being silly, playing with dolls, and hide and seek, in the house, of course.

They never left the house.

Their entire relationship existed between the four walls of Sarah's home. Abby would sneak in under the cover of darkness, and leave the same way. She worried about the danger that Ava would be in if anyone found out that Abby was alive and word got back to the wrong people.

She longed to be a mother again, to dry tears after a skinned knee, to go shopping together at the mall, or go to the park. It was the simple things she missed the most. She needed to get back to living the life that a mother and daughter should live, not this life of clandestine visits.

After she toweled off, Abby sat on the thick comfortable sofa and called JJ. She always had a difficult time reaching him at his office, but she hadn't heard back from him in weeks. She figured he could use an early morning wake-up call.

"Do you have any idea what time it is?" his groggy voice said from the other end of the line.

"It's time to get to work."

He sighed as he sat up in bed. "How have you been, Abby?"

"I'm good. I'd be better if I knew where Bryce was hiding so I could end his life and get on with mine."

"Abby, please, you know you can't say stuff like that to me. I can't track him down knowing that you're going to kill him."

She stifled a laugh, "But you will. Unless you have some sort of strict moral code you're living by these days."

Silence.

She smiled and said sweetly, "I won't kill him, I just want to tell him to leave me and my little girl alone. Forever."

"Yeah, right."

"Seriously, where are we with this?"

"I've got other cases I'm working on."

"For ten months? What kind of a fool do you think I am? You found *me* faster. If you wanted to find him you would, so what's the deal?"

"There's no deal, Abby. He's long gone. I've tapped every resource I have. I've even got a couple informants that my brother, Ace, met with personally. No one has any idea if he's even alive, never mind where he's hiding."

"Someone has got to know something!"

"If anyone does, you're talking about his inner circle. Gaetano Rosso, the head of the family, maybe a few others. I don't have anyone who can get info out of someone that high up in the food chain."

"Well, keep trying, I'm running out of patience."

3

ABBY GLANCED AT the screen of her ringing phone to
see that her sister, Sarah, was calling. "Hi, Sar."

Her sister whispered as she peeked through the drawn
curtains of her dining room window, "They're back."

"The same guys?"

"Yes."

"You're sure?"

"Yes, I'm sure. I'm looking at them right now."

Abby immediately felt a sinking sick feeling in the pit
of her stomach. *Who the hell are these guys?*

Sarah and Ava had never moved after what had
happened on the front lawn of her house so many months
ago. Abby had wanted them to, but Sarah didn't want to
pull Ava out of school. Abby wasn't a huge deal in Canada
like she was in the States, and even the Stateside media
interest disappeared a few weeks after she had been
"killed".

Everything had been quiet and ordinary, until the past

15

few days.

Sarah called Abby several times over the course of the week. She had noticed them for the first time on the way home from the grocery store with Ava at the beginning of the week—two large men sitting in a late-model American car at the end of the street. She didn't think anything of it until later that day when she saw the same car on the other end of the street, and then the next afternoon they were parked in front of her house. They weren't even trying to be discreet.

Abby ticked through the options in her head. "You've called the police?"

"Yes, and they said there's nothing they can do. An officer went over to talk to them the first day, and they told him they were on a lunch break and just relaxing and talking in the car. He tells me there's no law against that and to have a nice day."

"There's no one else that will listen?" Abby asked, agitated.

"I've tried, Abby. I've called every afternoon for the past four days. Yesterday, the officer didn't even go over to the car. He just came and pounded on my door, told me that no one is breaking the law, and I've become a nuisance. He said the next time I call they're going to cite me for wasting the officer's time."

"That's a thing?"

"In Canada, yes."

Abby thought a moment. "You know where my box is downstairs?"

"I'm not going to bring a loaded gun up here. I don't even like having it in the house."

"Well, I wish you would, for Ava's sake."

"She's nine years old, Abby. I'm not going to teach her that guns are the answer to trouble."

"No, they're not the answer, but an even playing field is always nice. In case you forgot, her father tried to shoot her—through my chest—on your front lawn less than a year ago. He's still out there, and so are all his friends, and they've all got guns."

"You said she's safe now that he thinks you're dead."

Abby sighed. "She is. Or she should be. He had a reason to kill me, to keep me quiet. Killing her would just have been icing on the cake. He's a sociopath, but he's not an idiot. He's been in hiding for what, almost two years now? He showed up only to tie up some loose ends. He'll stay 'dead' if he's smart, but that's not my point. At least consider keeping the gun handy, OK?"

"No, Abby, I won't consider it. I don't even like it in the house."

Then it's a good thing you don't know what else is down there, Abby thought. Over the past several months that she had been sneaking in to visit Ava, Abby had amassed a small arsenal of handguns and other trinkets.

17

"Ava gets her report card next week," Sarah said, changing the subject. "She says it should be all A's. Isn't that great?"

"It is," Abby said vacantly.

"You OK?"

Abby was silent a moment, "Yes, I'm fine. Tired, that's all. It's a lot of work here; a lot of physical work."

"Well, Ava is looking forward to seeing you this weekend. Are you still coming tomorrow night, as usual?"

Abby stared at the calendar hanging on the kitchen wall. She usually left after therapy was done in the afternoon, reaching her sister's house around midnight. "Maybe I'll come tonight instead."

"No, Abby, we'll be fine."

"They're waiting for me, you know. They've got to be Bryce's guys. Why else would he have them there? Could he know I'm still alive?"

"We buried you, Abby. It was all pretty convincing—and it was all over the news."

That it was, Abby thought. There had been a full-fledged funeral and burial. All the news outlets covered it. It was a pretty huge story, and elaborately orchestrated by Robert and his money.

"At least tell me you'll keep a gun by the bed tonight?"

Sarah smiled. "Yes, Abby, I'll keep a gun by the bed

tonight."

"You're full of shit."

"I am. We'll be OK one more night. Tomorrow night, just come as usual."

"I'll be there. And I'm hoping those two fat bastards in the car are still hanging around, too."

Sarah thought a moment before admitting, "Me, too, Abby. Me too." She knew what her sister was planning, and knew there was no alternative.

*   *   *

"Rinse your dishes and put them away if you're done," Sarah reminded Ava as she cleared the pots and pans from the stove.

"Yes, Auntie," Ava said, smiling, but almost rolling her eyes.

As was their typical ritual, they both cleaned the kitchen table after dinner. Ava didn't help to get dinner ready, as she was usually completing her homework, but Sarah expected her to help clean up after.

Sarah looked out various windows of the house over the course of the night but saw no sign of the men in the car. *Maybe they're taking the night off,* she thought, amused— albeit morbidly—at the thought.

After the dishes were put away, teeth brushed, and pajamas put on, Sarah and Ava sat on the couch to watch a little television before bedtime. Ava's therapist had advised Sarah that organization and structure would go a long way toward helping Ava feel safe again and get through what had happened. "Knowing what to expect, and when to expect it, helps put the mind at ease," she had advised. Despite Ava's traumatic upbringing, nothing can prepare a little girl for seeing her father shoot her mother in the chest only a few feet away from her.

Sarah did the right thing, and they were in a psychologist's office not forty-eight hours after the incident. Maybe it was her young age, or the fact that her father's psychotic actions were not unprecedented, but Ava worked through things fairly well and was a relatively well-adjusted girl.

Still, Sarah rarely deviated from structure and schedule. At eight o'clock sharp, she announced, "Time for bed, little girl."

"I'm not a little girl. I'm almost ten! Can't I stay up just a little while longer? Please?" *A test,* Sarah thought.

The therapist told her, "Especially in the face of a test, it's important not to give in. Stay firm. Asking to stay up longer is a test of the boundaries, and it is important for a victim like Ava to know that boundaries are there."

Despite wanting to give in, Sarah fought the urge and resisted. "Not tonight, sweetie. You still have school in the morning. When your mom is here, we'll talk about having a new bedtime for you. How does that sound?"

Ava, as always, lit up with the thought of seeing Abby.

"Sounds great! I'll see you in the morning!"

Sarah gave her niece a kiss on the cheek. "I'll be up in a little while to check on you. Have sweet dreams."

As she walked away, Ava chuckled a bit at that expression. "I will, Auntie. You know, you don't have to say that every night. I'm really not a little girl anymore."

Sarah smiled as Ava turned and trotted out of the room. "No," she said to herself, "you're certainly not."

*   *   *

Something woke Sarah just after two a.m.

Like every other night these past few days, it took her a few moments to realize where she was. Sitting up, her neck a little sore from having fallen asleep in an awkward position on the couch, she stretched before turning off the TV.

She checked the front-door locks, and then peeked out the dining room window to make sure that neither the car nor the two men were anywhere to be seen. Satisfied that everything looked in order, she sleepily walked up the stairs in what had become a nightly ritual over the past week.

She opened Ava's door to look at the lump under the covers. She smiled to see Ava sleeping peacefully though she was a bit shocked at how cold the room was. Fall always came a little early this far north, and notwithstanding Sarah's constant reminders to shut her window before bed, Ava insisted otherwise.

Sarah shook her head and rubbed her arms as she crossed the room and shut the window. It had to be just above freezing outside, and the chilled air gave her goose bumps as the breeze fluttered over her skin when she pulled the window closed. The poor girl must be freezing, Sarah thought, seeing that Ava had pulled the covers up over her head.

As she leaned over to adjust the covers and give Ava a kiss on the cheek, a hot wave of panic washed over her as Ava's body completely compressed. Ripping the sheets off the bed, a wave of nausea overtook her. Nothing more than pillows lay stretched across the bed, arranged in the rough shape of a small body. Ava was gone!

Overcome by panic, Sarah raced around the house, throwing open closet and bathroom doors, "Ava?!"

After tearing through the house in mere moments, Sarah realized the worst and grabbed the phone with her trembling hands.

*   *   *

Abby sprang into action and was racing through the backwoods of Maine at a breakneck speed in her little import inside of two minutes after her sister called her. She had barely dressed, and her hair was a mess, but none of that matter to her. Two hours into her six hour trip, and she had been cursing herself the entire time. *I knew I should have gone tonight.*

As the gray light of dawn started to threaten the horizon in her rearview mirror, Abby told herself to get a grip. *If I go crazy and do something stupid, Bryce wins, and who knows what happens to Ava.* She had to stay sharp and think clearly.

Even though Sarah had promised to call her with updates, and they had just gotten off the phone twenty minutes ago, Abby dialed her again. She needed to stay calm, to keep focused, and to feel like she's part of the situation.

"What's the status, Sarah?"

"Nothing has changed here, nothing new."

Abby cursed the steering wheel.

The police were not taking the situation seriously, and this frustrated Abby and Sarah to no end.

"This happens all the time," a female officer had assured Sarah an hour earlier. "Kids run away. We'll keep looking, but she'll turn up by breakfast, as soon as she gets hungry."

The police were doing pretty much that—just looking. They were searching the neighborhood, knocking on doors, the usual first steps when a child goes missing.

Abby knew that by the time the police got around to it, Ava would be long gone, hidden deep in the Canadian wilderness or flown out of the country on a private plane. She slammed her fist into the steering wheel and pushed down harder on the gas pedal.

*　　*　　*

The fatter of the two men secured the duct tape around Ava's wrists a bit tighter once they found a safe place to pull over a couple miles down the road. With her arms bound behind her and a gag in her mouth, she looked up at her capture helplessly, with terror in her eyes. He felt bad for her, he really did, but business was business. He stroked her soft brown curly hair with his meaty hand and spoke through labored breathing. "Don't worry, honey, we're just bringing you to your daddy. Everything will be fine."

At the mention of her father, Ava's eyes became as wide as saucers as he slammed the trunk shut.

4

SARAH WATCHED ABBY pace the kitchen like a caged animal as she poured two cups of tea and set them down on the island. "Abby, why don't you sit down and have some tea? Wind down a little."

"I'm not having fucking tea," Abby shot back.

Her mind was racing and immediately started making connections. Tea always made her think of Robert. The first time she met him on the island, he made her peppermint tea. Of course, Robert, the island, and damned near everything else brought her thoughts back to Eric.

She stopped, body tense, and closed her eyes trying to push his image from her mind, but it was no use. It didn't help that she was at the scene of the crime. There he was, smiling, crashing broken to the ground, body jerking as Bryce put two bullets in his chest.

Sarah watched her poor sister, her body wound tight and rocking slightly. She wanted to hug her but was a little scared. Abby had thrown a fit when she arrived fifteen minutes ago. She punched a hole in the foyer wall before breaking down in tears on the floor. Sarah worried that, mentally, her little sister was becoming unhinged. Years of fighting just to stay one step ahead of Bryce and his mob family were finally catching up with her. With Ava gone, Abby appeared to be going over the edge, and Sarah didn't want to wind up collateral damage if she did.

Abby concentrated on her breathing and pushed Eric from her mind. She needed to think about Ava, no matter how much it drove her mad. She'd be damned if her daughter suffered the same fate as Eric. She needed to find a way to stop Bryce because the police never would.

She thought about how she would exact her revenge on that bastard, and sooner rather than later. She could picture herself shooting him or breaking his neck. No matter what steps she took to end his life, the image of his dead body calmed her and allowed her to sigh her first easy breath in hours.

Sarah smiled and gestured to the tea. She smiled again when Abby nodded and took a sip.

Abby stared at the flower garden in the back yard through the French doors. "It's been almost seven hours. She's gone. Long gone."

Her lip quivered a bit as she was about to speak, so Sarah simply nodded her head as her eyes glassed over.

Abby was emotional but had moved past crying. Tears weren't going to get Ava back. She was calculating, trying to determine exactly what Bryce's next move would be. At last Sarah broke the tension. "The detectives will be here in a half hour. They'll help find her, right?"

Abby laughed. "Just like they found Bryce after he

murdered Eric and shot me on your front lawn?" She shook her head, "I'll be gone before they get here. Don't tell them a thing. Useless, Sarah—they're useless. Crimes get solved either when someone confesses or the facts drop in their lap. We tell the police everything and my face becomes the lead story on every news station in North America. Bryce may think I'm alive, but he doesn't know it for a fact. I still have surprise on my side, and I have to go after him. Alone."

"How? Do you know where he is?"

"No," Abby shook her head. "But I know who does, so I'll go after them. They're hiding him, and they're going to pay, too."

"Abby," Sarah's hand shook, and she had to put her tea cup back on the saucer, the china rattling upon contact. "Abby... these are dangerous people."

She smirked, "Not as dangerous as me."

*   *   *

With some effort, Abby pried open the storage bin under the basement stairs. Inside sat a large metal box with a combination lock. After dialing in the code, it popped, and she smiled.

She took out what had become her favorite handgun at the shooting range—her Combat NCO .45. It was a big gun made to finish the job. *Not like that little 9 mm Bryce shot me with*, Abby thought. JJ let her borrow his when they snuck off to the shooting range together a few months back, and she immediately fell in love. It was about as accurate a gun as you could get, and its silencer meant her victims would never hear death coming. She loved the feeling of power in her hands when she held it.

It had a hell of a recoil, though, and being a small woman she had to be well-set and braced to handle it. It wasn't a gun she could whip out unprepared and fire one handed if need be. The thing would send her whole arm flying backwards if she tried that. She knew this from a rather embarrassing experience at the shooting range. The old-timers had gotten a kick out of it, though.

She holstered the .45 against her body under her left arm and took out the smaller .22 she reserved for close combat. Also silenced, whomever she hit within twenty feet would be dead as a doornail if she wanted them to be, and never hear it coming. She holstered this weapon in the small of her back and smiled at her old friend in its leather sheath at the bottom of the box.

"Well, hi there," she smiled as she slid the seven-inch blade from its leather scabbard and inspected the gleaming metal finish. She thought about all the times this knife had saved her life. It hadn't seen action in quite some time, but she knew it was up to the job. *There are a few more bad guys for you to take care of,* she thought. She secured the sheath around her right thigh and felt as complete as she had in months.

Checking her watch, she figured another ten minutes until the detectives arrived, and she wanted to be gone with her small arsenal by then. She grabbed a few more items from the box: a small pouch—similar to a coin purse—that contained a few quarter-sized discs numbered individually, a palm-sized case containing a powerful night-vision monocular, a small canister that looked like an asthma inhaler, and a larger four-by-six-inch case that contained five small, dull gray tubes each about the size of a roll of quarters.

The discs and grenades were presents from Ace, JJ's brother. The first were small discs of plastic explosives that she could remotely detonate by phone, or by clicking in a code on the small button on the back. The second were homemade flash-bang grenades, designed to blind, deafen, and generally disorient anyone for ten to fifteen seconds with their combination of bright explosive and concussive sound. She clipped the packages to her belt and pulled on her thigh-length, black leather jacket.

Checking herself in a dusty, full-length mirror in a corner of the basement, she was satisfied that the various arms strapped to her body were well-concealed. She grabbed a disposable flip-phone, a billfold with a few hundred dollars in American currency, and a fake driver's license and passport JJ had procured for her.

Abby hurried upstairs but froze when she got to the top and heard a man's voice. She stood listening through the cracked door.

"Sorry, we haven't come up with anything on your daughter."

"She's not my daughter," Abby heard Sarah say. "She's my niece. Her mother passed away last year."

"I'm sorry to hear that," the detective said.

"It's OK," Sarah said louder. "I'm going to pour myself a coffee in the kitchen. Would you like one?"

"No, thanks. Trying to cut back."

"OK, wait here in the living room, I'll be back in a moment."

Sarah knew that Abby's presence might raise some questions. Abby had to get out of there without being seen, so Sarah was letting her know where the detective was. He was in the living room, so Abby could sneak out through the French doors at the back of the kitchen without being seen. Quietly, she eased through the basement door as Sarah entered the kitchen. Abby held her finger to her lips.

Sarah nodded and gave a slight smile as she hugged Abby. There was no mistaking the hard bulges she felt under Abby's coat. When Sarah backed away, she mouthed, "Be careful" to her, with a tear in her eye.

Abby nodded and mouthed back, "I will" before slipping out the French doors and through the back yard, where she had snuck into the house so many times before.

Sarah watched for a second as her sister disappeared, and was wiping tears from her eyes when the detective's voice came from behind her, "Everything OK?"

She whipped around, surprised, with tear-filled eyes and nodded her head.

"I'm sorry," he said. "I'll give you a minute to compose yourself, then we'll go over the questions, OK?"

Sarah nodded and stole one more glance out the back door, wondering if she would ever see Abby alive again.

*   *   *

Abby cut through a neighbor's yard, behind a house that had had a For Sale sign on it for at least six months, heading toward her vehicle to get on her way. Just before she turned the corner of the house, she heard men talking. She stopped in her tracks and listened closely. After a moment, she realized she was going to have to find a new getaway vehicle. The officers were running the tags on her vehicle. It made sense. A car from outside of the country, parked in the driveway of a vacant house, they'd be remiss not to take a good look at it with a child missing in the neighborhood.

She was at least happy that they were trying to do something; though she also knew it wasn't going to get them anywhere, and certainly wouldn't lead back to her. The car had been purchased, registered, and insured all in a fake name that wouldn't lead anyone back to Abby. All the exercise was going to accomplish was to delay her.

Easing away from the corner of the house, she looked around to figure out a plan. She briefly considered stealing a car, but that would get red flagged pretty quickly and she would never make it across the border back to the states in it. Not to mention cars were much harder to steal than the movies made it appear. Almost every car made in the last thirty years had a little transponder chip in the key, without

31

it the engine will not start. "Hotwiring" a vehicle was a thing of the past, but it didn't stop Hollywood from continuing to use the convention.

For now, she decided that she would have to travel on foot. She cut through another couple of backyards before coming out on a fairly main route near a shopping complex. A few miles later she procured a rental car under a fake passport, paid for in cash, and was quickly back on her way.

She would have preferred to go back to the border crossing that she had been using weekly over the months that she had been sneaking to Canada to visit Ava and Sarah. It was small, normally not very busy, and staffed by a rotating handful of agents willing to flirt with her, who never once had even glanced in her back seat.

Abby liked to think it was because she had a trustworthy way about her but was sure it had more to do with the cleavage in her black tank top. Either way, as long as no one was asking questions, she was fine with it.

Unfortunately, that border crossing was back in Maine, and to cut back in that direction would have turned a ten-hour trip into more than a day. Ideally she would be on a plane, but that was out of the question with small arsenal she was traveling with, so she decided she would head through Toronto into Michigan.

"It'll be fine," she told herself.

Traveling with the flow of traffic, she made good time. To ease her mind she had found a classical music station and concentrated on her breathing. She had to stay calm. Five hours later she pulled into a rest stop to stretch her legs and grab a drink. She also took the opportunity in a deserted corner of the parking lot to stuff her various arms into a black messenger bag and stow it under the floor in the trunk of the rental car.

While she paced around stretching, she looked at an oversized map laid out on the wall of the rest stop. She figured she was a little more than halfway there, and also realized that while she had a general idea of where she was going next, she needed just a little more direction.

As she hit the highway again heading south, she spent the next hour thinking about how she was going to find Bryce. She had spent the last ten months thinking about the time when this moment would come, that she would finally set off to right the wrongs that had been done to her. She wanted to plan a specific attack that wasn't some idle fantasy of hers, and she needed some hard information.

Hitting the number two on the throwaway phone's speed dial, she waited to hear the familiar voice.

"Who's this?" he demanded.

"That's how you answer your phone?" Abby asked in a mocking tone.

JJ smiled. "I had a feeling it was you."

"Oh? Why is that?"

"I'm an investigator, remember? Sorry, Abby, nothing

new to report. I'll be honest with you—I'm at a loss here. I don't think we're getting any further with this."

"You said the inner circle would know, right? Gaetano Rosso and his top men?"

"Yeah, but I can't get to them."

"Where do I find him?"

JJ was quiet a moment, processing what he just heard. "What?"

"Where do I find Rosso? Give me an address."

JJ knew better than to laugh. She sounded pissed off and would probably come after him next. "Abby, you can't just knock on his door and ask him where Bryce is hiding."

"Watch me," Abby shot back. "The game is over JJ. Ava was kidnapped last night."

"Are you serious?"

"As a heart attack."

"Holy shit Abby, when? Last night?"

"Yeah, in the middle of the night. The police have nothing. They're not even trying."

"Why didn't you call me Abby?"

"I don't know, I wasn't thinking real clearly, but I'm calling you now. I know it was Bryce. It has to be him."

JJ agreed, "Why would he do that though?"

"Maybe he's trying to draw me out. He wants me to find him, so the least you can do is help me here. If you think Rosso knows where that scumbag is, then I'll start there. Just tell me where to find him."

"Abby, it's not that simple. He's old and sick. He's barely left his house in years, and that's the only place you're going to find him."

"The address, JJ."

"It's not a house, Abby, it's a fortress. You're on a suicide mission. You're not going to be any good to Ava dead."

"Well, I'm not doing her any good alive either if I can't find her. Now, you've got a choice, JJ. I'm in my car, crossing the border any minute now. Once I cross, I can head west to Chicago and beat Bryce's address out of Rosso, or I can head east to Boston and beat Rosso's address out of you. Either way, I'm ending up in Chicago, so save us both a lot of trouble and give me his address."

Abby and JJ had spent quite a lot of time together over the past ten months. He spent a day or two a week up north working at the rehab center with her, improving her hand-to-hand combat and firearm skills. Many years ago, he himself had been in special forces and served overseas. He knew what he was training her for. He also knew her resolve, and there would be no talking her out of storming the castle.

"Can I at least help you? You can't do this alone Abby. Give me a day. I can be in Chicago tomorrow."

"And I can be there in four hours!" Abby yelled back. "He has my daughter. Now give me the fucking address, or so help me you're next on my list."

They were silent as her words hung in the air.

"I'm sorry," she said. "I didn't mean that. But JJ, please. I need to do this now. It's my little girl. It can't wait a second longer."

"OK. Do you have something to write with?"

After she jotted down the address, she said thank you and promised to call later, or if she needed anything else.

She thought a great deal about what she was going to do when she reached Chicago. How would she gain access to Rosso and what would she say to him when she faced him? To that end, she had to make one more phone call, one she had been putting it off. Hesitating, she hit speed dial number one and waited to hear the English accent on the other end.

He was not a man who often answered his own phone. With an astounding wealth somewhere in the billions and corporations across the globe, he had assistants on six continents who answered his phones for him. Abby was in possession of a personal number that few others had, though, and it always rang directly to him.

"This is Robert. To whom do I have the pleasure of speaking?"

Abby smiled. His voice always brought her comfort, even at a time like this. "Hi, Robert."

"Abby, my dear! How are you?"

Still smiling, Abby said, "I've been better Robert. How are you?"

"Who cares about me, my dear, what's wrong? I can hear it in your voice."

"It's Ava. She's gone."

"What do you mean 'gone'?"

"She's been taken Robert. Someone went into Sarah's house and took her."

"What? When did this happen?"

"Last night, sometime in the middle of the night. It's got to be him, Robert."

"I agree, but the question is why? You've been off the grid. Very few people even know you're alive. He can't have any idea. It's impossible."

"But he has to be sure I'm dead. I know his deepest, darkest secret. He was willing to murder me in front of our own child to make sure it never got out. He has to be sure I'm dead, so I can never talk. This is how he'll make sure."

Robert thought a moment. "I know I'm suggesting the impossible, but hear me out. Suppose you do nothing."

"What?"

"Hear me out. Do nothing. Don't make a move. If you don't come for your daughter, then he'll be convinced you're dead, right?"

"Then what happens to Ava?"

Robert sighed. "I don't know."

"I'll tell you. He's hated that child since she was in the womb. Once he's satisfied that she no longer serves a purpose, he'll kill her, plain and simple. It's not like he hasn't tried before."

Robert quietly said, "I won't try to talk you out of it, Abby."

"Thank you."

"Is there anything I can do? Have you spoken with JJ? You know, he's much more than he leads on. He can help you. He's just as sore about Eric's death as you are."

"I have spoken with him, and he wants to, but I told him no. I'm on my way to get answers right now, and I don't have time to wait for him."

"What are you planning, Abby?"

"You'd rather not know. Trust me."

"Please be safe."

Abby nodded. "I'm willing to sacrifice my life for Ava's, but I don't know how this is all going to wind up. If the worst should happen, please do what you can to look out for Ava and Sarah. Where I'm going, there's no turning back. If things go the way I plan, the fallout is going to be monumental. You're the only man I know who can move mountains, Robert."

"You know I will, Abby. But let's pray it doesn't come to that."

"But…"

"No, I don't want to entertain the thought anymore. I can't bear to think of anything happening to you. But if it does, rest assured I'll do whatever I have to in order to protect your family. Stay in touch with JJ. We can't help you if we don't know what's going on."

"I will, Robert. Thank you."

5

AGENT EDDIE VINES had given all of his good years to the FBI and was up for early retirement in his mid-fifties, full pension. That was a bit misleading, though. To say that he was up for early retirement implied that he elected to participate. The reality couldn't be further from the truth.

He always wanted to be in the Bureau since he was a kid, and had been in since his mid-twenties. More than thirty years later he was on the high end of the pay scale for a senior agent with a salary nearly on par with many of his superiors.

He saw the writing on the wall two years ago when the agency announced significant cutbacks. After the debacle last year with the "Mob Massacre" (as the media called it) when his team gunned down those eight mob guys in an alley only to have forensics show that not one of the dead men had fired a single shot, he knew it was only a matter of time before he was asked to step aside.

At least they had the decency to make it appear voluntary. He held a lot of clout within the agency, and they didn't want to make it look like he was forced out. But his director made it clear he was leaving one way or another, so why not save some face?

He lived a modest life, alone in a Cape-style house in the suburbs outside of Chicago. He used to have a wife. He also used to have a condo and a fishing boat in Clearwater where he planned to retire and spend his days fishing along the Gulf coast. The wife was gone and, of course, took the condo and the boat. Last he heard she sold the boat for a new set of tits, which he was sure her new husband was enjoying just fine—in his condo.

Sitting on the small back porch of his home, looking over the remains of what was a beautiful flowerbed leftover from years ago when his wife had been around to tend to it, he was struck with the thought that he had no idea what he would do in two weeks when he left the office for the last time.

Eddie Vines was a man married to his job. He had no real friends, and when his wife left, the kids followed—a boy and a girl, now in their twenties with no use for their father unless they needed money. His work was everything, and for the last ten years, since his family went south, he had adopted a new family: The Rosso Family. The family he had spent a decade trying to take down.

He came close a couple of times. A few years back when old man Gaetano lost his son, things really went to hell. There was infighting for control of the family. Sure the old man was at the helm, but his son, Nick, was going to be his successor. When Nick was unexpectedly murdered, spats surfaced between the various lieutenants and their crews. The Bureau turned up the heat on their informants. They just needed to turn a couple of guys to get the big fish, Gaetano, and then the whole family would come toppling down.

Then Bryce Haydenson happened. This blond haired, blued eyed German kid was just some low-level guy in Nick's crew and the furthest thing from an Italian in the whole bunch. His file was an inch thick, but the short story was that his parents came over on the boat, mom left when he was real young, and his alcoholic dad raised him with a hand as heavy as the drinks he poured. He spent more time on the streets than at home, got friendly with Nick when they were kids, and was adopted into the family for all intents and purposes.

Eddie took another sip of his bourbon and shook his head. The Bureau was on the brink of breaking up the family and this guy comes out of nowhere and takes control. Nick's murder was never solved, but the Rossos blamed a rival family, the Patrizios, and Haydenson got to work dismantling them one butchering at a time.

Of course, neither Eddie nor anyone else in the Bureau could put together a compelling case to prove it. Just like that, within a month, the Rossos weren't just solid again, they were the only major family left in the city. The Midwest was theirs to run with Gaetano at the helm and Bryce as his number two.

For years after that, things were relatively quiet, then the bank debacle happened. "FBI Shoots First, Asks Questions Later", one headline screamed. *Since when are lawless thugs glamorized by the media and embraced by the public?* Eddie thought. But they were, and it was a black eye on the Bureau.

Eddie finished his bourbon, refilled the ice in his rocks glass, and buried it in Kentucky gold again. There was another side to that story the media never got ahold of, and Eddie had dedicated every waking moment to it for nearly a year and a half.

Vines was sure Bryce Haydenson was still alive. He sure as hell knew he hadn't been in the alley that day. Everything happened so fast—there were bullets flying everywhere—but Vines was sure of it. He saw all eight faces, and Haydenson wasn't among them. His director told him to keep his mouth shut; that they were taking enough heat. It was already all over the news that forensics had confirmed Haydenson was among the dead. If it got out that the mob had someone on the inside falsifying records in the forensics lab, they'd look like complete boobs.

"Do your own investigation quietly," his director said. So Eddie did. He had it narrowed down, but couldn't get any support from the higher-ups who were terrified of it coming out that the mob had someone on the inside right under their noses and they didn't even know it. *Either that, or they're on the take, too.* What he wouldn't let go was the fact that Bryce was still alive and out there. Vines only kept his mouth shut because if the higher-ups were on the take, he'd be dead, not retiring. They just wanted him out of their hair and off the payroll.

The nice thing about his senior status, however, was until he was off the payroll, he still had the ability to get work done. Even though he only had two weeks left, he had one more shot. He was sure of it.

He set his glass down on the desk in his home office and hit play on a recording one of his agents had from a conversation with a snitch two days ago.

"The old man is as good as dead."

"What do you mean? Someone's going after him?"

"No, man, he's dying. Rumor is it's his pancreas. They're saying another week; ten days max."

"Then Franco takes over?"

The snitch laughed. "That's what the old man wants, but we'll see. Not everyone likes Franco. Some of the guys are sayin' he's weak. I got a buddy on Monte's crew. He says Monte's thinking of makin' a move. I don't know, man. It's gonna get messy when the old man kicks it. You got my back, right?"

Vines smiled, sipping his bourbon, listening to the recording. He had three more just like it, all from different snitches, all telling the same story. As far as they could tell, the family was split and Franco didn't have the clout to hold everyone together. There was going to be a struggle for power, and that's when Vines would move in.

Eddie had the warrants drawn up and a small team of agents ready to move. All reports were that the old man didn't have much more than a week. Vines slugged back the last of his drink and smacked his lips. He couldn't prove Bryce was alive right now, but if anyone knew where he was, it was the guys at the top. He smiled. Once he had the top brass in the family locked up and looking to strike some deals, he'd nail Bryce Haydenson too. Nearly ten years of trying to nail the bastards would finally come to an end. He'd retire a hero, the higher-ups be damned.

He hit the lights and crawled under the covers, alone, dreaming about Agent Eddie Vines, the national hero. There would be a book deal, a media tour... he wouldn't just be a hero, he'd be a star. *Screw it. I'll buy a new boat and get a newer wife with even newer tits.* He drifted off, smiling at the thought.

6

ABBY MADE TWO PASSES by the house, snapping photos and video each time. She didn't dare make a third. It wasn't a very populated neighborhood. There was the giant Rosso estate, surrounded by a half dozen or so smaller but still substantial homes, all of which were likely owned and occupied by the Rosso family. An unknown car cruising up and down the street would certainly arouse suspicion.

Sitting in a busy shopping center parking lot a few miles away, she reviewed the photos and video and was satisfied that she had a pretty good lay of the property from the front.

Rosso lived in a large mansion made out of gray slabs of rock. The place looked like it could withstand a direct hit from a tornado. A six-foot-high stonewall, topped with another two feet of wrought iron fencing, surrounded the four-acre property. Growing up in Southern California, Abby was no stranger to large mansions and knew that oftentimes homes were concealed by clever landscaping to hide the celebrity owners from the paparazzi.

There were no such landscaping measures taken with the Rosso property, though, and Abby imagined that his vanity worked to her advantage. There was a large wrought-iron gate across the front of the property, probably twenty-five feet long, and through that gate her camera was able to catch a perfect view up the long driveway and the front of the home.

She saw three guards out front on her first pass. On her second, an hour later, there were four. She had no idea how many might be in the back, but she would find out about that later. The video hadn't caught it, but during her second pass she heard the faint distant bark of at least one dog, which she assumed wouldn't be very friendly.

Abby grabbed a quick sandwich at a café, where she used the internet to pull up satellite images of the neighborhood. The Rosso estate appeared to be surrounded by the same stone wall all the way around, butted up to a large forested area at the back of the property. The forested area ran for a quarter of a mile until it met up with a deserted road that appeared completely undeveloped.

After making the fifteen-minute ride up the undeveloped road, Abby found a little path out of the way to park her car about a mile from the back of the Rosso property. She hiked through the woods the rest of the way.

Abby figured many a federal agent had trekked this trail, and she had no doubt it was at least half watched by the family. To stay concealed, she moved slowly toward the property, approaching from the side. She found a tall tree a hundred feet away and figured that would be a good spot.

These are thugs, she thought. *I'm not dealing with*

sophisticated masterminds. But still, she figured better to be safe. She imagined there was a video surveillance system in place, likely being watched by some half-asleep lackey. She didn't see any cameras but decided that, for now, she would stay out of the path where they would be.

Abby settled into the tree about twenty feet up, with a nice clear view of the back of the property. She now noticed that barbed wire extended along the top of the six-foot-high stonewall and the two feet of wrought iron fencing above it.

She adjusted the focus of her monocular for a clear view of the rear patio a few hundred feet away. It was a large patio at the center of the home. Several men rotated in and out of a single door now and then as if changing the guard. There were always two men outside. One stood on the patio, trying not to look bored, while the other walked the perimeter of the property along the wall with the dog. Occasionally a third would pop out the door to chat for a few minutes, then head back in.

One of the men occupied his time chain-smoking cigarettes. Abby couldn't hear them, but the other guy didn't seem to appreciate this. He was constantly drinking from a plastic water bottle, whether he was on the patio or walking the perimeter. *His own nervous habit,* Abby thought. *At least it's better than cigarettes.*

The smoker took his time circling the perimeter. By Abby's watch, it took him fifteen minutes each time. The other one did it in half the time.

Planters down the center of the patio separated the

right side, where the guards were, from the left side. The left had a set of French doors that led into a gourmet kitchen with a large granite island in the center. There was far less activity on that side of the patio. With the large table, and an outdoor living set, Abby figured the left side was for the residents and the right for the guards.

Occasionally a tough-looking guy in a nice suit came through the French doors on the left to chat on his phone for a few minutes. Another man came out less frequently to sit on a comfortable chaise lounge to drag on a cigarette for ten minutes. Otherwise, it was quiet.

Directly above the patio, in the center of the home, was a large balcony that interested Abby. She peered through the glass door, adjusted the focus on her monocular, and smiled. The old man lay in bed. Gaetano Rosso, head of the most powerful crime family in the Midwest, rested on what looked like a hospital bed. He was clearly connected to an IV and a heart monitor.

That's where I need to get, Abby thought.

The guy who kept coming out to make phone calls looked important. So did the guy dragging on the cigarette on the lounge chair. They didn't pull guard duty or walk the perimeter. Maybe they know where Bryce is. Maybe. But Abby wasn't here for maybes. She was here to get answers and didn't intend to waste her time with anyone who *might* know something. She was only interested in the one guy who *did* have the information she wanted.

After an hour in the tree, her ass was starting to get sore and a foot was falling asleep. She decided she had done enough watching; it was time to get things in order. On her way back through the woods to her car, she thought about Rosso sitting helplessly in his bed on the second floor. Now she just had to figure out how to get into this suburban fortress to question him. She wouldn't show him mercy. She doubted he'd ever shown it to anyone on his deathbed.

Guards in front and in back and a half-dozen cars in the driveway made it difficult for Abby to know exactly how many family guys were inside. Even armed to the teeth, she couldn't just storm in and expect to wind up anything but dead, which would suit Bryce just fine. No, she needed distractions.

Surely an FBI agent or two had once pondered the same thought. If the authorities searching for her daughter knew what she knew, they would be trying to figure out a solution to the same problem.

The trouble with the authorities is that they need a reason to get into the house, but I have my reason: my daughter has been kidnaped, and these felons can tell me where to find her. They don't play by the rules, and neither will I. The cops need warrants to take thugs in for questioning, but I have the only warrant I need. Abby tapped the .45 in its holster.

But the firepower wouldn't do Abby any good if she didn't have those distractions.

She checked the clock as she turned on her car. She figured it was a little more than an hour before sundown and probably a couple hours away from complete darkness.

Taking a hit from her water bottle, she had a flash in her mind of watching the guard sip his water as he walked the perimeter and was struck with an idea for one hell of a distraction. She almost chuckled.

She spun the tires as she turned around to drive back to the shopping center and get ready to enact her plan.

7

MIKEY G., AS HE WAS known in the family and around town, stood on the front steps of the grand Rosso mansion surveying the grounds and taking the last few drags off his cigarette.

The family was made up of many factions and elements, but he saw his as the most important. He oversaw security for Rosso himself and had for the past decade. Back in the day it was an exciting gig. Going into the city, he had a veritable army at his disposal and commanded entire city blocks wherever they traveled. Rosso used to joke that Mikey G. took his job so seriously that even the Secret Service didn't keep the president as protected as Gaetano Rosso.

The old man had slowed down over the past few years, and over the past six months hardly left the house. When it became obvious that there was no longer a need for such an elaborate traveling entourage, the various crews started taking Mikey G's best men to work for them. Rosso was fine with this. He knew he didn't have much time left. After the last trip to his doctor six weeks ago, he knew he wouldn't be leaving home again until it was in a casket.

Mikey G. made do with what he had left. Ten men on

rotating shifts protected the estate. At any given time, he had two patrolling in back, two in front, one in an oversized closet monitoring the closed circuit television feeds, and, of course, himself making sure everything was running smoothly. He ate, slept, lived, and breathed within the confines of the estate, never leaving his post.

He had just checked in on the old man before he came out for a smoke. *Guy looks like hell,* he thought. He shook his head. He had admired Rosso all of his life. He worked his way up the ladder in the family to earn the trust of such a great man, and then continued to work hard until he was ultimately trusted with the life of the man who ran the Midwest. He considered it an honor, and the pay was exceptional, too. Mikey G. was young when he took his current position, and it meant he had a promising future in the family. What he didn't know was what that future held for him now.

He snuffed out his cigarette and walked into the house where he could hear the raised voices of the five captains drifting toward the front of the house from the open French door leading from the kitchen to the rear patio.

They are the future, Mikey G. thought, and he didn't know where the chips were going to land.

Rosso had named Franco to be his successor and take over the family, but not everyone was satisfied with that, and a couple of the captains didn't mince words when they told Rosso that he was out of his mind to think Franco could lead the family. Ten years ago, had someone raised their voice to Rosso, never mind told him his judgment was wrong, he would have had Mikey G. bury him out in the forest behind the estate. But the old man had softened in his old and sick state and had the crazy thought that he could talk some sense into them.

That's what brought the five captains here tonight. Rosso wanted just them. No crews, no nonsense, no pissing contests, just his five most trusted men to sit down around the table and hash things out.

The table wound up being Gaetano's bedroom, as he was too sick to move. There was much head nodding when Gaetano asked them to trust him and his leadership this one last time and respect Franco as the new head of the family. He instructed the men to put aside their differences, and stick together, for the sake of keeping the family unified.

As much head nodding as there was, Mikey G. couldn't miss the glances that Monte shot the others, as well as the little smirks that some of the other captains had with their eyes cast down to the floor.

As far as Mikey G. could tell, Monte had the support of three of the five crews, and Franco only two. He shared this with Rosso after the old man had dismissed the captains.

Rosso sighed. "Mikey, Franco is the one. He has to be. Maybe he is a little soft, but Monte is an animal. If he had the power to run the family..." Rosso's voice trailed off as his eyes drifted away before he came back. "Mikey, what do we do these days, huh? We've got a piece of God-knows-how-many businesses in the city. We've got real estate; we've got sway with the politicians; we've got the city contracts for half the public services through our business fronts. Mikey, we're as close to legitimate businessmen as we can be. Granted, with the money laundering we might as well be printing it... but my point is, we're in good with the right people. Franco won't just maintain that, he'll grow it. Hell, maybe in another generation, the Rossos will be legitimate businessmen.

"You put Monte in charge and that's all going away. You know he's got his crew dabbling in drugs. You put him in charge, and he'll be running drugs through the city— hell, through the entire Midwest. You think the feds will look the other way on that? The politicians, we can grease their wheels every election and they'll make sure the feds and the police look the other way on all the stuff we got going on right now. But you bring drugs in there, Mikey? For some reason, every politician has got a fucking bee in his bonnet over the drugs."

Rosso was lost in thought for a minute though Mikey G. waited patiently as he hadn't been dismissed yet. When Rosso came back, he stared hard into Mikey's eyes and was as lucid as he had seen him in weeks, "Mikey, you protect Franco. He is the future. Monte will ruin everything I've worked for my whole life."

He motioned for Mikey G. to come closer. As he leaned in, Rosso grabbed his collar with a weak hand and looked him sharply in the eye. "Mikey, you've never doubted me. Don't doubt me now. Protect the family and *take care* of Monte."

Take care of Monte.

With that, Rosso ordered what would likely be his last hit.

Mikey G. poked his head into the oversized closet where his youngest crewmember, Randy, was half dozing off in front of the closed circuit television monitors.

"Hey!" Mikey shouted, startling him awake. "Look alive! We've got a houseful tonight."

"Yes, sir," the young crewman said, sitting up straight.

Mikey thought a second, "Everything looking quiet out there?"

"Yes, sir, the usual."

"I'll watch these a minute. Go get yourself a coffee and wake up."

"Thank you, sir."

After the crewman left, Mikey G. took a seat and looked over the eight monitors. "The usual" as the young man had indicated, was a whole bunch of nothing. There were no big rival families anymore—*not since that German nut job took out the Patrizios a few years back.*

Two cameras by the front gate gave him a view of anyone approaching from either end of the street. In this case, a small, dark import drove slowly by the house before making a right at the end of the street. A plastic water bottle it had probably just hit rolled to a stop at the front gate, and he made a mental note to have one of the guys pick it up later.

ESCAPE
Dead End

Two cameras in the front yard let him watch anything going on there, which was nothing at the moment. Two in the woods out back showed mostly darkness as the sun had gone down, but would switch over to night mode soon so they could watch the local raccoons walking around. Lastly, the two in the back yard let him watch the fat guy, Tommy, walk the dog around the perimeter while the captains sat on the rear patio smoking cigars.

Mikey G. stared at the monitor, watching Monte.

He didn't particularly care for the man. He never worked for him, or with him, but knew him to be rough on his crew. He was selfish and thought with his dick and his wallet. Rosso was right, and Mikey knew it. Monte was not the man to lead the family, and if he was going to make waves, he had to be dealt with. Mikey just had to hammer out the details. It would take a couple of days, but it would be done, hopefully before the old man passed. Mikey wanted the satisfaction of his boss's approval one last time.

The young man's voice from behind startled Mikey out of his thoughts. "All set. Thanks, boss."

Mikey stood up, his back to the monitors. "No problem. I'll swing back in a few hours, OK?"

"Sounds good, sir. Thank you, again." The young man got a concerned look as he finished speaking, and Mikey saw him looking over his shoulder at a monitor.

Mikey G. turned around to look. "What is it?"

"I don't know, boss. I thought I saw something run by on the woods cam."

Mikey studied it, not seeing anything. He joked at the young man's expense, referencing an embarrassing incident from a few months back. "Probably just another opossum."

The young man shook his head and laughed. "Those things are freaky looking. Don't pretend you wouldn't have lost your shit if one came running at you."

"Well, yeah, but I would have taken out my gun and shot it, son—not screamed and ran like a little girl." Mikey clapped him on the shoulder as he left. "I'm going to duck out back to check on Tommy and Pat. I'll see you later. Stay sharp."

Had Mikey G. not been blocking the view of the monitor, they might have both clearly seen Abby dart through the woods before hiding against the bottom of the stonewall.

* * *

Abby had been gone a couple of hours, grabbed some dinner, and made a fruitful trip to the shopping plaza before circling back and settling into the same spot about twenty feet up in the tree behind the Rosso estate just as dusk fell.

The same two guards patrolled the grounds. One circled the property with the dog while chugging his bottled water, and the other waited and watched, puffing on his cigarette. Then they would swap the dog and the other one would circle him around the perimeter. It was like clockwork. On her way back, she had driven by the front of the estate just slow enough to see that there were still two guards in front, looking bored, with no dog to keep them company.

On the left side of the patio—the family side as Abby had come to think of it—five men puffed on cigars and chatted in the dim light being cast from the open French doors. She peered through her monocular to get a better look.

Most of them looked familiar, but there was one in particular she knew: Monte. Her skin crawled just at the sight of him. He used to run with Bryce's crew back before Abby disappeared. Abby was usually in the dark about Bryce's dealings, but she was pretty sure Monte was his number two guy. He was essentially Bryce 2.0. All of Bryce's worst qualities, amplified by a complete lack of awareness for consequence. She knew this all too well.

She wouldn't be surprised if he had taken over Bryce's crew when he disappeared. All five of them were the right age, late forties to early fifties, dressed in nice suits, and relaxing at Rosso's estate. Abby figured it was reasonable to assume that these five men were on the inside. They must be fairly important in the family, and any one of them—if not all—could probably tell her where Bryce was. But her money was on Monte if no one else.

Abby had planned to go directly for Rosso, and intended to stick with that plan, but if the opportunity presented itself to isolate Monte, she would gladly extract the information from him.

Looking up at the center of the house, she could no longer see Rosso but assumed he was still upstairs. He wasn't outside, or in the kitchen, and the flickering of the television in his bedroom was a giveaway.

Abby sat still, contemplating the men on the back porch. She could picture Bryce sitting there, relaxing on that very patio among those men. His men. He had been there, planning, colluding, and laughing… now roaming out there somewhere as a free man, while Eric was in the ground.

As darkness completely fell, there was only the glow of their cigars, until one by one they went inside to escape the slight fall chill in the air.

Abby felt calm. Confident. Unstoppable.

It's time.

Abby checked down her list. The large zip ties and small roll of duct tape she purchased at the shopping center were ready to be used. She slid the roll of tape around her wrist and stuffed the zip ties into her back pocket. She then placed two small bottles of water inside the pockets of her black leather coat.

She secured the small canister of sedative to her belt. Ace said he got the idea after his fight in the airport last year trying to stop Abby from being abducted. The man following her put a powerful sedative in her coffee. Abby fortunately never drank the coffee, but the man did wind up throwing it in Ace's face. Despite Ace's large stature and the relatively small amount of coffee that hit him, he was incapacitated in minutes.

Ever resourceful, he had taken the idea and made it into a very effective weapon. The device operated much in the same way as an asthma inhaler. It even looked like one. The liquid sedative was under extreme pressure, and when released with the propellant, shot out and vaporized. It was so powerful that it wasn't necessary to take it like an inhaler, though you did need to spray it directly in the victim's face from no less than twelve inches away, and you'd better hold your breath. That was the tricky part.

If that didn't work, her Taser was sure to do the trick. It was strapped to the other side of her belt. If that didn't work, her .45, .22, and knife were all at the ready, though she had decided those were her absolute last resort.

Maybe the men in the compound deserved to die, and maybe some of them would, but Abby was only looking for one man to die at her hands, and he was not here. She would not become a heartless killing machine like Bryce, even if the men inside deserved it. She only intended to get her daughter back. How much force she used was up to the men inside.

Abby scurried down the tree and sprinted fifty yards through the woods to the left corner of the rear wall, quickly pressing herself against the bottom of the wall to hide. She was sure there were cameras in these woods, and just hoped that her head-to-toe black attire did enough to mask her mad dash.

On her shopping trip, she had grabbed a small package of meat, cut and prepared to make a stew or find its way onto a kabob, but she had other plans for it. Turning her head away, she gave it a couple of sprays with the sedative then tossed it over the wall. She wasn't sure it would work, but hoped for the best.

Despite the chill in the air, a bead of sweat ran down her temple as she held her crouched position, waiting. Finally, almost exactly fifteen minutes later, she heard it: the jingle of the dog collar on the other side of the wall.

"What's that, Maxi?" the guard asked.

The dog started barking right on the other side of the wall. *Did it even see the meat?* As the barking intensified, Abby began to panic a bit. Did it know she was here? Had she been found out before she even breached the wall?

As she braced to run, she heard the guard again. "Come on, Maxi. What the hell is wrong with you?"

The barking stopped, but the dog's heavy breathing and slobbering indicated they were still there on the other side of the wall.

"What the hell are you eating? Are you eating your own shit again? Come on, that's fuckin' gross. Let's go."

She heard the dog let out a whimper as the guard yanked on its collar to move him along.

Finally, Abby breathed a sigh of relief and started counting down the minutes slowly.

A few minutes later, satisfied that enough time had passed, she braced herself.

Now or never.

Abby leapt from her squatted position to grab the top of the six-foot wall with her fingertips. The toes of her boots found traction between some of the larger stones, and she hoisted herself up to the top to see the dog moving very slowly behind the guard near the patio stairs.

Being a few hundred feet away, Abby never would have heard them, save for the fact that they spoke in such loud and stereotypical Italian fashion.

"I don't know what's wrong with him," the guard said. "He was fine two minutes ago, but I had to practically drag him back here."

The guard stood at the top of the steps, leash in hand, pulling on the dog. For his part, the dog didn't seem to care. It lay comfortably at the bottom of the steps already fast asleep.

"Must be tired," the other guard said. "It's getting late, let him sleep. I'm gonna walk."

As he descended the stairs, Abby momentarily stripped her black leather coat from her shoulders and laid it over the barbed wire to swing over it, then lowered herself to the ground, crouching behind some ancient overgrown shrubbery.

Abby waited patiently in the cramped space behind the shrubbery and was thankful for all of the time she had spent in awkward yoga positions at the rehab. Were it not for that, her uncomfortable squatted position would have been unbearable after a few moments. In this case, the burning sensation in her quads was almost a welcomed reminder of her training.

She heard his footsteps before she could see him, the soles of his feet crunching the leaves underfoot. She didn't dare turn her head for fear he would see the movement. Abby held her station, knowing that his path would take him directly past her position.

As he walked by unaware of her presence, she silently eased from her hiding spot and hit him in the solar plexus with the Taser. There was a short yelp as he dropped to the ground and twitched for a moment. When Abby tried to roll him over, she regretted not having waited for the skinny one to come back. The big man was a challenge but by squatting low and using the strength of her legs to push, she was finally able to flip him over. She quickly bound his wrists and feet with the zip ties, and sealed his mouth with a strip of duct tape. She hadn't been timing herself, but no more than a minute could have passed.

Sitting back in the grass, she slowed her breathing and thought a moment. That was fine for one man, but how many could she take down like that? She thought about retreating and re-evaluating, but it was too late now. With the guard hogtied in front of her, she had committed herself to getting to Rosso.

Do I run in, guns blazing? She reached for her big gun, the .45, and wrapped her fingers around the handle. A frontal assault like that was suicide. These men were trained killers. She would pick them off one by one, or a couple at a time if she had to. It was the easiest way. It would increase her chance of being detected, but it also increased her chances of surviving this fight. Having spent so much time at the range with JJ, she was a great shot.

There had to be another seven or eight men in the house. One on one, she could probably take each of them, but real fights don't happen like they do in the movies. They weren't going to line up and wait their turns to fight her. She would be quickly overwhelmed by large men out for blood. Out to protect Rosso and Bryce.

So let's not allow that to happen.

She knew what she had to do, and the time was now.

Abby set out on a sprint up the left side of the property, sticking to the shadows along the large stone wall. Reaching the patio opposite the guard smoking his cigarette, she jumped up on the side of the patio in the darkness, hidden by the shrubs lining the center of the patio, and willed her breathing to get under control as she pressed her body against the house just to the left of the doors leading to the kitchen.

She quickly peered through one of the glass panes, then just as quickly backed away. There were three men in the kitchen, backs to the door. Not wasting any time, she dashed past the door toward the other side of the patio. As quiet as she tried to be, the guard must have heard her footsteps.

"Who's there?" he asked the darkness, reaching for his

gun.

Abby froze behind the shrubbery separating the two sides of the patio, waiting for him to come to her.

"Who's there?" his voice came again, getting closer.

The sound of his loafers on the pavement grew louder as his pace picked up.

"Monte, is that you?" he asked.

As he turned the corner around the shrubbery, Abby sprayed him directly in the face with the small canister of sedative from her belt.

"What the fuck?" he was momentarily disoriented and staggered to wipe his face with his sleeve.

Abby used this to her advantage and deftly grabbed the gun from his hand and smashed the butt end down on the back of his head, sending him crumpling to the ground. The sedative gave her about an hour to work with, but Ace warned her it could take thirty seconds to a minute to take effect, and she wasn't about to get into a fistfight when she didn't need to.

Looking back at the French doors, she confirmed that no one inside heard the brief scuffle. At least no one was looking outside. If they had, they could not miss the incapacitated guard lying on the ground. Abby had to act quickly.

Taking the water bottles from her coat pockets, she checked to see that each still had a plastic disc attached securely to the bottom before placing one in a large shrub in the center of the patio. Then, making sure no one was watching out the doors, she sprinted across the opening again to place the other on the coffee table in the middle of the outdoor living room set.

Going back to her position pressed against the house just to the left of the French doors, she pulled her .22 from its holster and unscrewed the silencer. She wanted them to hear the gunshots. Hopefully, they would run in the other direction, seeking safety. With her left hand, Abby slid a cell phone from her pocket and typed in a three-digit code.

She took a deep breath. She was at least twenty feet from each bottle, and was fairly confident that was sufficient, but still crouched down and enveloped herself as best she could in her thigh-length leather coat.

God, I hope this works.

She hit the *send* button on her phone, exploding the plastic discs on the bottom of the gasoline-filled bottles.

8

SHE HAD BEEN SURPRISED the first time Ace had shown her this little trick. A gasoline explosion doesn't have much of a shockwave, like the bigger bang of dynamite or plastic explosives, *but it sure does put on one hell of a show*, she had thought.

The way Ace had explained it, in slow motion you would first see the small explosive disc destroy the bottle, quickly followed by the gasoline droplets expanding into a cloud until just the right mixture of air and fuel was reached, at which point the gasoline erupts into a fireball. While survivable to anyone not right on top of the explosive, it would look very imposing to anyone who saw it. A perfect attention getter.

Of course it was not slow motion; it all happened in a split second and a bright golden flash lit up the patio and yard. The fire rose in two perfect mushroom clouds, with a loud *whoosh* that momentarily sucked all of the surrounding air into the erupting fireballs. Flames enveloped everything – shrubs, furniture, etc. – on the porch.

Just in case that wasn't enough to get the attention of everyone inside, Abby started screaming at the top of her lungs.

Within seconds, the men from inside were running out of the French doors just a few feet to her left, guns drawn, searching for a target. In the shadows, dressed in black, they never saw her coming.

Abby dropped the first two with one shot each to the meaty part of their upper leg, just below their buttocks. Her small caliber gun meant neither of her targets should suffer the same leg damage that she had. The third gunman figured out what was happening and dove to the ground, causing her to miss. The last two out the door stumbled backward and fell over each other trying to scramble into the kitchen and take cover behind the island.

"We're under attack!" one of them screamed.

In the confusion, Abby leaped onto the one she had missed just as he was trying to stand up. In the orange glow of the firelight she saw the bewilderment in his eyes as they toppled backward onto the patio, his gun went clattering off the edge. He landed on his back, the wind knocked out of him momentarily, and as he gasped for air, she shot him in the face with a quick spray from her canister.

She turned to the other two, who were clutching their backsides in pain. As she did, the man she was on top of grabbed a handful of her hair to yank her off. He climbed to his knees but wobbled, weakened by the sedative. Abby rose with him to avoid injury to herself, knowing the man couldn't have more than a few seconds until... *wow, that was quick.*

He teetered just for a moment on his knees before

falling back to the ground. To her shock, he never let go of her hair, and as he tumbled to the ground unconscious he took her with him, her face smacking into the paving stones under them. She tugged her head to free herself, but the unconscious man had a fistful of her hair in a death grip and wasn't letting go.

Neither of the two men whom she had shot was having any luck getting to their feet, but they were starting to figure out what had happened. The one just a few feet to her right raised his gun, but before he could get off a shot, Abby twisted around and kicked it from his hand, sending it flying to the other end of the patio. Managing to get to his knees, he lunged toward her. At the same time, she produced her knife from its sheath and slashed across his face, gashing his left cheek.

As he tumbled backward she continued to struggle to release her hair from the unconscious man's grip, but it was a losing battle. It was laced through all of his fingers and his clenched fist was not coming undone, it would take forever to untangle the mess and get herself free.

Out of the corner of her eye she saw the second man dragging himself toward her, his gun lying between them, and the man she had just slashed was coming back around. She was out of time and needed to make a move. Taking a deep breath, she used her knife to slice through the hair that was in the first guard's grip and leaped to her feet just as the man on the ground grabbed his gun. She jumped on top of him and grabbed his arm as he fired wildly into the air.

They heard the scream together as a bullet hit the

other man in the chest just as he was getting to his feet and he collapsed back to the ground, blood now spilling from his chest as well as his cheek where Abby had gashed him with her knife.

Abby used the momentary shock of the gunman to her advantage and grabbing the canister she gave him a spray in the face. He lost the grip on his gun, pawing at his eyes, which had taken the majority of the spray. He couldn't figure out what was going on, but he attempted to buck her off. As soon as he did, he screamed as the pain in his ass intensified. Abby gave him another shot from the canister before jumping off and watching him pass out.

Five down, she thought to herself.

Suddenly gunshots rang out from inside the house, and Abby hit the deck as bullets tore through the glass panes of the French doors. She rolled to the side and came up on one knee, firing a half-dozen shots from her .45. The huge bullets shattered nearly every glass pane in the French doors, exploding the dark oak cabinets in the kitchen beyond. The men inside dove behind the island for cover.

By her calculations, there were the two men in the kitchen, two more out front, and probably a couple more in the house. Rosso upstairs wouldn't put up a fight.

It was about six to one.

I've got this.

The orange glow from the fire on the other side of the

71

patio was starting to fade, but it was enough light for Abby to see that the way was clear for the moment. She would have to get past the wide-open French doors in order to make it to the other side. The two men inside the kitchen yelled for backup. Guessing it was just the two of them, Abby sprinted past the open doors, firing wildly into the kitchen with her .45 as the recoil kicked her arm around. The heavy slugs shattered the wood, showering the kitchen with the splintered remains of what had been beautiful, dark-wood cabinets just seconds ago. She arrived at the other side of the patio unscathed, but breathless.

Next to the door that the guards had been using was a large picture window. She hurled herself away from it the moment she saw a slight movement through the window. Abby hit the ground a second before bullets shattered the glass and sprayed the air around her. Holstering her .45, she grabbed two of her flash-bang grenades from her belt, armed them, and hurled them through the now gaping window into the darkness beyond.

With bullets still slicing through the air, she grabbed her Taser from her belt and army-crawled toward the guard door, counting down in her head.

10…9…8…7…6…5…4…3… cover… your… ears… BOOOM!

A flash erupted from the dark room that could only be likened to a lightning strike, blinding anyone in the room, as the concussive blast also momentarily deafened the men inside.

Abby sprung from her crouched position, dashed

through the open door, and went for the first man she saw. She wasted no time dropping him to the ground with a hit to the gut with the Taser. Knowing the voltage wouldn't recharge quick enough to hit the second guard right away, she swept his legs out from under him, knocking him to the ground. Before he could push himself up, she grabbed her canister with the other hand and gave him a spray to the face.

As she turned to the other guard to spray him, the one whom she just knocked down grabbed her leg and knocked her to the ground. He was a big man, slowing the effect of Ace's concoction. The added seconds brought his sight back enough for him to cause trouble. He managed to get a solid grip and wrestle himself on top of her. Thinking quickly, Abby slammed her forehead into his face, disorienting him as she rolled to the side and he collapsed to the ground, the sedative finally taking effect.

Voices from the other room were shouting.

"What was that?!"

"What the fuck was that?!"

Abby smiled at the sound of Bryce's two friends screaming from the kitchen, trying to figure out what was happening. Especially Monte. She allowed herself time to enjoy the panic in his voice. *Maybe the same panic he heard in my voice that night all those years ago.* She tried to put it from her mind, but couldn't. When he showed up late that night, looking for Bryce, she either let him into the house or he forced his way. She couldn't remember. The details were foggy, as were most things from that time in her life when she was first with Bryce, but she had no doubt he took advantage of her. As she lay there crying, cursing him, swearing Bryce would kill him, Monte told her that Bryce would never believe her. Monte would tell Bryce that Abby came onto him. "Who's he gonna believe?" he asked. Still, he threatened that if she ever opened her mouth about it, he would cut her throat. She had believed him on both counts and never spoke a word.

Thinking about that now, her rage rose up and drove her forward.

He continued shouting from the kitchen, "Mikey, are you OK?"

She couldn't stand to hear his voice anymore and fired three more shots in anger. They harmlessly struck a bookshelf. The other side of the house went silent.

Two more down, she thought. *Keep it together.*

The room where she stood was in the rear right of the house. Hundreds of books lined the walls, opposite to the kitchen she had just shot up. The voices were coming down a small hallway that she assumed led to the kitchen. Abby tiptoed her way toward the hallway, past the guards she had just relieved of their duties.

She stopped just off to the side. There was a large picture mounted halfway down the hall. Not a nice painting on canvas, but a print of a painting mounted in a frame with a glass front. Its placement perfectly reflected one of the remaining men in the kitchen, who was crouched behind the large island. She did not recognize him.

Monte was nowhere to be seen.

*   *   *

Mikey G. had just opened the door to the patio to check in with his guards when the explosion rocked the other side of the door. He backed up and drew his gun, looking out the large picture window to find that his guards were not there and the patio was engulfed in flames. Seconds later, a commotion down the hallway indicated that men ran from the dining room at the front of the house, through the kitchen and out the rear door.

Just a moment later there was gunfire, more yelling, and screaming, "We're under attack!" he heard.

Mikey ran to the foyer at the front of the house, crashing into Randy who came running out of the video closet. "I'm going for Rosso. Take the kitchen—they're coming in the back." Randy took off as Mikey yelled for the two front guards who were already bursting through the front door. "Head to the library!" he yelled, pointing toward the back. "And don't let anyone through those doors."

Mikey took the stairs two at a time and burst through Rosso's bedroom door. The old man was already sitting up in bed, his Rosary beads clutched in his left hand, his right supporting his weight with an IV stand. His heart monitor beeped wildly.

Rosso managed a weak voice. "What's going on down

there Mikey?"

"We're being attacked. I'm getting you out of here." Mikey went to pick up Rosso but stopped to look at the IV drip and monitors attached to his chest.

Gaetano Rosso smiled at his trusted guard. "I'm not going anywhere, Mikey. I'm done. I'm history. Get down there and protect Franco. It's probably Monte's crew, here for him. He's your man now, Mikey." Rosso lay back on his pillows and repeated himself quietly. "He's your man now."

Mikey was at a loss for words. He had spent the majority of his adult life protecting Rosso, who now lay helpless in bed as thugs raided his home. He stood not knowing what to do, while at the same time knowing exactly what he had to do.

Rosso stared at him, and out of nowhere managed to summon a voice of authority. "Don't worry about me, Mikey. Get the fuck down there and protect Franco!"

Mikey nodded and ran back downstairs, hitting the foyer floor as a bright flash and another explosion rocked the library. He ran the opposite way, toward the dining room, but stopped before entering. He could see the long table that had a plate of pastries in the middle and steaming coffee cups in front of several chairs. The men had clearly just sat down to continue discussing the family situation when they ran toward the commotion.

He eased forward just enough to see through the large opening that led into the kitchen. He could see Franco, crouched behind the island, gun drawn. He saw Monte, as well, in the dining room, hiding behind the wall of the opening to the kitchen. His gun drawn, he stood behind Franco and to the left.

Seeing Monte behind Franco made Mikey nervous. *Where is Randy?* he wondered.

Three more shots rang out from the library. *How many of them are there?*

No matter, Mikey thought. He realized that the raid, presumably by Monte's crew, offered him a perfect opportunity to carry out his boss's final order.

Raising his gun carefully, he eased forward so the barrel just cleared the doorway. He set his sights on Monte standing thirty feet away on the other side of the dining room, who had no idea what was about to happen.

Just as he squeezed the trigger, out of the corner of his eye, he saw a small gray tube roll along the kitchen floor into the opening, and then he was blinded.

*   *   *

Abby eased back from the hallway opening and pulled another flash-bang grenade out of her pouch. She clicked the fuse and rolled it down the hall, counting down in her head. When she hit five, she crouched low, closed her eyes, and covered her ears. Whoever was left in the kitchen would be blind and near deaf, allowing her to charge in and take care of those last two before going upstairs to Rosso.

Three… two… Suddenly she was grabbed from behind as the count hit one. She didn't open her eyes, but her ears were exposed as she instinctively reached behind her with her hands to try to grab onto whoever had seized her.

Although it was fifteen feet down the hall, the blast knocked out every sound around her. Her assailant, however, had his eyes open and let go of her momentarily to grab at his face, his pupils burning as if he had looked straight into the sun. Now free, Abby spun, using her momentum to land a solid kick to Randy's midsection, knocking the wind out of him. He fell, clutching his stomach. As he landed, Abby planted her boot to the side of his face, connecting with his jawline and bringing a cry from him that she heard through the ringing in her ears.

Apparently his shrieks also reached the men in the kitchen. Franco and Mikey came running into the room and tackled her from behind. The three landed on the floor in a heap. Her .22 fell from her hand and clattered off to the side, just out of reach. Her small canister rolled away, out of sight.

Despite the surprise attack, Abby twisted from Franco's grip and landed an elbow to his windpipe. With him disabled, she sprung to her feet to find the second assailant.

She didn't see Mikey behind her, but saw Monte charging down the hallway toward her. Like a flash of lightning, she grabbed the .45 from its holster and aimed it at Monte, squeezing off two shots. The first hit his shoulder; the second missed entirely as the recoil of the huge gun jerked her shoulder back and off-target. She never had a chance to get off a third shot as Mikey chopped her arm from the side, right at the wrist, sending the second weapon to the floor just a few feet from where Monte landed. Abby was caught off-guard, and Mikey used that to his advantage. He slammed his fist squarely into her face, disorienting her.

Mikey had a gun in his hand. The ringing in her ears had died off, and Abby could hear him screaming at her, inches from her ear.

"Who sent you?"

Abby spit blood and tried to twist away, but he still held her tight.

Pressing the gun to her head, he screamed at her again, red-faced, shaking. "Who sent you?"

Franco now had his gun on her, while Monte climbed to his feet. Abby scanned the room for a way out, but all she saw were the three bodies on the floor.

Three to one.

Two of the three remaining had guns trained on her; she had only her knife, still strapped to her thigh.

Mikey used his hold on her to force her to her knees. She grabbed at his hands to free herself from his grip, but it was futile. He pressed his gun into her flesh harder. "This is the last time I'm going to ask. Who sent you?"

Abby stared straight ahead, eyes darting, her mind searching for a way out. She had to buy time, say something, but as she opened her mouth to speak, she heard another voice.

"Get the fuck outta town," Monte said with a smile, almost laughing.

Mikey looked at him, confused at first, but then understood. "You know her?"

Monte bent at the waist to meet Abby face to face. He smiled as he wrapped his meaty hand around her jaw and lifted her face so their eyes met. "You fuckin' bitch! Are you serious?"

Abby shook her head to get away from his hand, and then spit in his face. "Burn in hell, Monte."

He slapped her hard across the face, laughing as he reached into his pocket for a tissue. "Whoa, look who grew a pair!" He looked at Mikey and Franco. "You don't recognize this bitch? This is Bryce's girl."

Mikey and Franco both looked at her, and after a moment, recognized her.

"Oh, the boss will love this," Mikey said.

"Get her up," Franco said, and then looked at Monte, who was inspecting his shoulder. "You alright?"

"Yeah," Monte said. "It grazed me. Bitch can't aim for shit."

Franco held his gun on her while Mikey took her knife and inspected it. "Is this the one you had on *Trial Island?*

The same knife? Seriously? You think this is a fuckin' movie or something? You think you're a tough girl from TV, so you can walk in here and mess with us?"

Monte bent over to pick up the .45. "This is a big gun for a little girl, don't you think?" He pointed it at her square between the eyes, smiling, then dragged the barrel along her skin, tracing an outline around her entire face and then down between her breasts. He laughed, slid the gun into his beltline, and then retrieved the .22 that had skidded into a dark corner. "You and me are gonna have fun with these later." He looked at Mikey. "Let's bring her to the boss."

Franco and Mikey each took an arm to follow Monte up the stairs to Rosso.

For her part, Abby didn't resist. At least they were bringing her to where she wanted to go.

*   *   *

On their way up the stairs, Monte thought about the movement he saw out of the corner of his eye in the doorway to the foyer that had caused him to look away a split second before that flash-bang grenade went off. He also thought about the smoking bullet hole in the wall just inches in front of his nose after the blast. A second later, Mikey came running from the foyer. It was obvious to him what happened.

As they climbed the stairs toward Rosso's room, Monte made up his mind what he was going to do about it.

9

ROSSO WAS SITTING UP in bed. "Eight men?"

Mikey nodded his head.

Rosso looked at Abby, standing between Mikey and Franco, each with a hand on one of her arms. Mikey casually held onto her arm with his right hand, holding Abby's knife in his left.

Rosso shook his head. "You came into my house and took down eight of my men before anyone got a hand on you?"

"The dog, too… if that counts for anything." Abby gave Rosso a wink and offered a coy smile. She wasn't being sarcastic; she was being flirty. She was also very impressed with herself. It had taken her just under fifteen minutes to cripple one of the largest organized crime syndicates in the country. *Not bad,* she thought.

Rosso eased back into the pillows that were propping him up. "Eight…" He shook his head. "You know, you should come work for me."

Abby smiled at him, the way a child smiles at her daddy when she's trying to get out of trouble.

"Now why are you here? Obviously you want something."

"Bryce," Abby said. "Where is he?"

"What?"

"That's why I'm here. I'm looking for Bryce."

Rosso shook his head. "He's not here, sweetheart."

"I know, but you know where he is. I know you do."

Rosso shook his head again. "Six feet under." He stared into her eyes, trying to read her. "You didn't hear?"

Monte spoke from his position behind her, Abby's .22 still in his hand. "Bank robbery gone bad. It was all over the news." He leaned in close, groping her backside with his free hand. "I would have thought you'd have heard. Where have you been anyway? I've missed this sweet little ass."

She couldn't see him behind her, but Abby could hear the smile on his face and the sarcasm dripping from his voice. Of course, he knew she had heard. *Son of a bitch probably helped Bryce plan the whole thing to get me out of hiding.*

She wanted to turn around and lunge for his throat but wasn't sure she could take all three men at once, being unarmed. For the first time since entering the room, Abby acknowledged just how panicked she was.

Stay cool, Abby. Stay cool. You can do this.

Abby looked at Rosso. "Everyone in this room,

including me, knows that Bryce is alive. I came here to find out where he is, and one of you is going to tell me."

Rosso took his eyes from Abby and looked at the other men one by one, a small smile inching across his face. "Can you believe the balls on this little girl?"

When his eyes met Franco's, they both chuckled. Mikey joined in and so did Monte from behind.

Abby couldn't help herself and started laughing, too, which sent Rosso over the edge to a full belly laugh, in turn causing the other men to laugh even harder.

She managed to compose herself and catch her breath. "That's funny, huh? I mean, really, what am I going to do?"

Looking at their laughing faces gave her a certain satisfaction for what was about to happen. She gave Rosso a dead serious stare, which caused his heart monitor to drop off for a moment.

In one swift motion, her left knee shot up, giving her the momentum to drive the heel of her foot into the side of Mikey's knee. She heard the joint pop as his leg twisted in an unnatural direction and he collapsed to the ground like a bridge with the support beams knocked out, screaming in agony.

She nailed Franco in the gut with her right elbow, and as he doubled over, she twisted her body and smashed the heel of her open palm into his nose, sending blood pouring from his face.

Spinning on her left foot, she swung around to kick Monte full force in the stomach, but he was too fast and jumped out of the way.

That's when Abby's plan suddenly fell apart in the most unusual way.

Monte aimed the .22, not at Abby, but at Franco doubled over on the ground, and sank two slugs into the back of his skull.

Rosso's heart monitor screamed, and so did he. "No! Franco!"

Abby froze. She couldn't understand what just happened. It was as though she were watching it on television and not actually there.

Mikey rolled over to see what happened, but before he could react, Monte took aim and put two holes in his forehead. Mikey collapsed, lifeless.

Monte walked over to Franco and rolled him over with his foot, confirming he was dead.

Abby finally found words in her throat. "What... why? Why are you helping me?"

He looked over and sneered at her. "I'm not. You're just last."

As he raised the gun toward her, she saw a shiny flash of light by Mikey's left hand about eight feet from where she stood. He fired the first shot as she dove through the air. A split second later, her hand wrapped around the familiar leather grip. She rolled on her shoulder, came to a crouched position, and fired her knife. It sliced through the short distance across the room and plunged into Monte's neck.

Choking and gurgling sounds escaped his mouth as his hands reached up and tenderly touched the handle attached to the steel blade embedded in his neck. He struggled and raised the .22 as Abby charged and collided with him full force, knocking him backward into the wall.

He dropped the .22 and wrapped his hands around her neck, using every last ounce of his strength to choke the life out of her. Abby thrashed, but his grip was strong. She couldn't break free.

Abby landed several punches to his midsection, but nothing loosened his grip. Then she remembered what he said earlier: *"You and me are gonna have fun with these later."*

Despite the blackness closing in from the sides of her vision, she smiled as she reached forward, found his belt buckle, the .45 tucked above it, flicked off the safety, and fired one massive slug right down his pants where it had been resting.

Monte released his grip immediately as a scream, or something trying to be one, found its way to his throat.

Abby took a step back as he fell to his knees, and she ripped her knife from his throat, causing blood to gush from his neck as he collapsed to the floor.

Abby's hands shook as she stood there holding her

knife, having freshly taken the life of a man she knew surely deserved it.

It took her another moment to realize how fast her heart was racing as she took her breath in gasps. She wanted to close her eyes, breath deeply, and calm herself, but she couldn't look away from the devastation in the room. As she surveyed the bodies, all silently laid out on the floor, she had forgotten there was anyone else in the room. She nearly jumped when she heard Rosso's weak voice from the bed.

"He must have known," Rosso said from behind her.

"What?" she turned, startled.

Rosso looked physically uncomfortable. He winced with pain, his breathing labored. "I put a hit on him. Not even thirty minutes ago…" He drifted off mid-sentence, looking at Franco. A tear escaped his eye.

"Franco," he continued. "Franco was supposed to take over. Monte over there, he wasn't so keen on it, so I instructed Mikey to take care of him." He gestured to the man whose leg was splayed in the wrong direction.

"Oh, Franco…" Another tear rolled down the old man's cheek as he patted his chest. Abby had heard the beeping of his heart monitor as background noise during the fighting and confusion, but it seemed to be in a fight with itself at the moment. His heart was speeding up, slowing down, and every few seconds there was a beep that seemed pretty out of sequence with the rest.

He looked to Abby. "He was like a son to me, Franco." He looked at the knife still in her hand. "It doesn't matter anymore. None of it."

She wiped the blade clean on a cloth at the end of the bed and deliberately slid the knife back into its sheath on her leg.

He shook his head, and Abby noticed a bead of sweat run down his temple. "I had a son once. He's gone. Franco is gone." He looked her in the eye. "If there is one man who can keep this family on its feet, it's Bryce, and I'll be damned if I'm going to sell him out to you."

"How is he going to do that?" she asked. "He's dead, remember?"

"He'll come back, and when he does, the men will listen. They'll listen to him. They'll respect him."

"There's really no one else?"

He leaned his head back into the pillows, wiping more sweat from his forehead, and nodded his head no.

"It's too bad about Nick."

The mention of his son's name brought Rosso upright, bringing a few extra beeps from his monitor. "What do you know about my son?"

"I know enough." Abby smiled, gently. She wasn't going to force the information she needed out of the old man. Not in his condition. He was unwell to begin with, and while she was no doctor, she knew that whatever the beeping pattern meant, it could not be good.

"He was a good boy, Nick." Rosso sighed.

"No, he was a good *man*," Abby said. "A good man who died before his time."

Rosso's eyes welled as he held his chest, shaking his head. He cursed the family who killed his son, almost under his breath. "Fucking Patrizios."

Abby shook her head. "Did you ever learn who pulled the trigger?"

"No. It was one of the Patrizio sons. It doesn't matter which one. They're all dead now thanks to Bryce." Rosso smiled at the thought.

She leaned close and took a cloth from the nightstand to dab the old man's forehead before she whispered in his ear, "I know who killed your son."

His eyes met hers, and he reached up, taking a firm grip on her arm.

She was surprised at the strength he still had. She knew she could easily get out of his grip, but played into it and let a little gasp escape her lips.

"How would you know who killed my son?"

"Bryce told me. He knew, too. He was there."

"What are you talking about? Who?! Who murdered my Nicholas?!" Rosso demanded, though his grip loosened a bit.

"If I told you, Bryce would kill me. Why do you think he wants me dead?" she smiled.

Abby watched Rosso's eyes as the realization set in. "No…"

She nodded her head yes and whispered, "Bryce murdered your son."

"No… no…" He shook his head in disbelief.

"Why do you think he's gone to such great lengths to kill me? What threat could I possibly pose to him and his power?"

Rosso just stared, waiting for answers.

"He took your son," Abby pressed forward. "He took him from you. Bryce was stealing from you, and Nick knew it, so Bryce killed him, then took his place at your table. That's the man you want to inherit your family?"

"No, it's impossible. He wouldn't…" The words were coming out, but she could see that he was thinking it through in his mind.

"He would, and he did," Abby said. "He came home—it must have been two in the morning—covered in blood. Nick's blood. He confessed the whole thing to me. Nick met him to talk. They went way out of town so no one would see them. Nick wanted to give him a chance to do the right thing, come clean with you, and start over. Bryce didn't see it that way and killed him. He killed him in cold blood."

Sweat poured down Rosso's head as he squinted at her and clutched his chest. "Why should I believe you?"

Abby shook her head. "You don't have to. But tell me this: Nick was a strong man; a smart man. How would he ever get himself into a situation like that? In the wrong part of town, no crew, didn't tell anyone where he was going... he was lured there. Lured there by a greedy man who murdered your only son and then took his place in your family."

Rosso was wrestling with the thought. It never made sense to him why they found Nick where they did, behind an abandoned school outside of town. "That son of a bitch." His heart monitor spiked into the one-sixties, chirping at full speed.

Abby started to panic. "He took my daughter, Mr. Rosso. He took her so I would come find her and he could kill me. Please, tell me where he is. I need to find Ava, and when I do, I swear on her life I will avenge your son's death."

Rosso clutched at his chest as the monitor beeped wildly in the background. "Shut that damned thing off!"

She hit a button with a slash through what looked like a speaker, and the device went mute. Abby held his hand as he struggled to breathe in short gasps. "Please, Mr. Rosso... please... I need to find my little girl."

They stared into each other's eyes from only inches away, thoughts racing through each of their minds.

"Please, Mr. Rosso." She blinked, a tear streaming down her cheek. "Please, I know you understand the love a parent has for their child. He took your son, and he has my little girl. Please."

He stared into her eyes silently, breathing in gasps, each shorter than the last, as she stared hopefully back into his.

"Upstate…" he finally said between gasps.

Abby was confused, "Upstate? Upstate what?"

"He's upstate… laundering money… the place…" His eyes widened and she felt his grip on her hand tighten.

Abby leaned closer. "Where? What place? What is it called?"

Rosso stared into her eyes, inches away, struggling to breathe. "Make that son of a bitch pay…"

His hand went slack, as his eyes were suddenly vacant. Abby looked at the monitor to see a flat line.

"No," she said, jumping on top of him on the bed, trying to pump his chest. "No! Where is he?"

She continued pumping and watching the monitor but saw nothing.

*What did he say? Laundering money upstate in a place…
DAMN! Come on!*

Abby was so engrossed in thought that she didn't hear the feet pounding down the hallway until the last second.

The door swung open as a man burst in, and Abby dove off Rosso toward Monte's body and came up aiming the .22 at the invader who had raised his own gun at her.

At the last second, Abby stopped short of pulling the trigger as a moment of clarity set in.

"Donny?"

10

"ABBY?"

She stood, reeling at the sight of him. His dark hair and eyes, his broad shoulders, his ready-to-fight-the-world stance. He had been her protector for so many years, and just the sight of him gave her a fleeting sense of security. She remembered the last time they saw each other, outside the conference room at the studio when he stood in for Bryce to sign away all of his rights before she went off to *Trial Island*. She remembered the tight embrace and the light kiss that he placed on her lips.

That kiss nearly broke the dam that held back their feelings for each other. Feelings that she pushed deep down to protect him from her maniac husband; feelings that he set aside so that he could be there to protect her. Then, after the kiss, he walked away as planned, out of her life forever. Until now.

Abby snapped out of their stunned silence first.

"Donny, what are you doing here?"

For his part, he was equally stunned. "What... what am *I* doing here? Abby, you're supposed to be dead... you *are* dead... how...?" His mouth hung open, speechless.

They stared at each other, until Donny noticed Monte at Abby's feet, the pool of blood spreading across the carpet. Next he noticed Mikey, Franco, and then Rosso. "Holy shit, Abby. Did you do this?"

"No. Well, yes. Some of it anyway. Not Rosso. He had a heart attack. Or those two," she said, indicating Franco and Mikey. "Just that piece of shit back there. It's too much to explain right now. How many others are with you?"

"No one, but there are four guys maybe five minutes behind me. They got a call a few minutes ago that the house was under attack. They're Monte's guys." Donny suddenly realized there were a lot of guards unaccounted for. "Where is everyone else?"

"Everyone else?"

"The other guys, Abby. Rosso had a dinner tonight for all the lieutenants."

"They're… um… indisposed."

Donny raised his eyebrows and pointed at her. "They're dead, too?"

She shook her head. "No, well, one other one I think. It all happened so fast. Most of them are just unconscious for now."

"Shit. What does that mean? You gotta tell me what the hell is going on. I mean, you're dead. Dead! I flew to Canada. I was *at* your funeral for Chrissakes. I…"

Abby suddenly pushed past him to look out a large picture window at the front yard. A car pulled up to the gate, waiting for it to open. She turned to Donny, "We don't have time to do this right now. Give me your phone, quick." She didn't wait for a response before ripping it from his belt. She quickly dialed a number and hit send as she looked out the window. The car had just driven through the gate when the water bottle bomb she had left out front exploded behind it. The driver slammed on the brakes as the men in the car struggled to figure out what had just happened.

"What the hell was that?" Donny stared out the window, taking in the fireball.

"A distraction. I've got to get out of here."

He looked into her soft brown eyes, the eyes he had fallen in love with so many years ago. "I'll help you, but you've gotta tell me what's going on."

She grabbed his hand and squeezed it, her heart fluttering. "There's no time now. I'll tell you everything, I swear, but we have to get out of here."

Donny thought a beat. "Alright, let's go down the back stairs."

They ran down the hall, where he burst through an unremarkable door that led down a narrow staircase and into the kitchen. Donny was taken aback by the destruction. The glass windows were completely shot out, and the cabinets were now shards of wood strewn throughout the room.

"Holy shit, Abby."

While he was distracted, she spied a phone on the corner of the counter. She took the receiver off the hook, quickly hit three numbers, and then tapped him on the shoulder. "Come on, back door. I've got a car about a half mile back through the woods."

As they went to ease out the back door to make a break for it, Max started barking.

"Fuckin' dog," Donny cursed.

Abby was surprised the dog was awake though he had been the first, and he didn't breath in the knock-out gas like the others. Still, she was worried the other men might start waking soon.

Suddenly, the front door flew open and one of the men called out. Both exits were blocked.

Donny thought a moment. "Do you trust me?"

She didn't have to give that much thought. Donny was one of the few men she had been able to trust in her adult life. Without him, she would have been dead long ago. He pulled the strings to get her a shot at *Trial Island*, he helped her smuggle Ava out of the country, and he helped her escape her life with Bryce. Had it not be for Donny coming to her aid one night when Ava was an infant, Bryce surely would have murdered them both.

"Of course I do."

"OK. Take off the knife and hide it." She gave him a

puzzled look, so he reached down, unhooked the sheath, and slid it into the back of her pants, pulling her shirt over the handle. "Just go with it, alright? I promise you'll be fine. Get on the ground."

Abby saw where he was going with this and complied.

When she was face down on the floor, Donny put his foot on her back and trained his gun on her. "Remember, just go with it, OK?"

Abby nodded, noticing he never flicked the safety off.

"Hey! In here!" he yelled toward the foyer.

Four men came ambling into the dimly lit library.

"What the fuck happened in here?" one of the men said, seeing the bodies on the floor.

Donny nodded toward Abby, under his foot. "She's an assassin. Came in shooting. I just got here. Bitch wasn't expected me."

One of the men ran over and kicked her in the ribs.

"Hey!" Donny shouted, holding up a hand. "Back off, there's enough bodies here. Rosso said to get rid of her, so give me a hand. Get something to tie her up with."

One of the men looked around and took a length of rope holding back a curtain, inspected it, and satisfied that it would do the trick, he put a knee into Abby's back and tied her hands behind her.

Donny and the man got her to her feet, and one of the

other men, a chubby little guy, let out a whistle. "Holy crap, she's hot, man." He looked at Donny. "Can I fuck her before we kill her?"

Rage boiled up in Donny's gut, hearing him speak of Abby that way, but he suppressed it.

Another man hit the first one in the chest. "Billy, what the hell is wrong with you."

"What? She's smokin'!"

"No shit. But wait until *after* we kill her. You see what she did here? That's a bad bitch. You don't want your dick anywhere near her if she's breathing."

The way he said it, so matter of fact, speaking from experience, sent chills down Abby's spine. She looked at Donny, who half rolled his eyes. *Don't worry about them.*

"Is Rosso OK?" one of them said.

"Yeah," Donny answered quickly. "I got here before she got to him…" he thought a moment. "Good thing I got there when I did. He's sleeping now. You know, the cancer, his heart… the old guy doesn't have long. Doesn't take much to wear him out."

They all nodded somberly at the mention of Rosso's decline.

Donny wanted to get them out of the house as quickly as possible before they had a chance to poke holes in his hastily thrown together story. Grabbing Abby by the arm he quickly lead them out the front door and to the car the other men had just arrived in. Donny pushed Abby into the back seat, and one of the other men took a seat next to her. He looked at the other three, "I don't think we'll all fit."

"No problem," one of the guys said. "Me and Billy will stay here. You go help Donny take care of this."

"What the hell?" Billy said. "I called it. I wanted to fuck her."

"Fine," the first one said. "You go. Jerry, get back here. We've got to clean up this mess."

Too bad for Billy, Abby thought. He and the driver were just going to get hurt.

The two men watched as the car drove away, and then walked into the grand home, past the bodies in the library and out to the patio where they were taken aback by the men laid out on the ground, blood smeared near a couple of them closest to the kitchen door.

"Son of a bitch," was all he could say.

"What the fuck do we do with all them?" Jerry said aloud.

"This is too many to bury out back."

"We can't just bury 'em. These guys got families. They need fuckin' funerals."

"I think we gotta talk to the old man."

"Donny said he's sleepin'."

Jerry rolled his eyes. "Well, let's just wake him the fuck up for a minute to find out what he wants to do with the dead bodies bleedin' all over his friggin' house."

As they walked upstairs, the other was thinking. Finally, he said, "Hey, I didn't see Monte. You think he's OK somewhere?"

"You know," Jerry said, "I didn't see Franco or Mikey neither."

They stood at Rosso's door, knocking, but got no answer.

"You open it."

"No, you."

"Fine, we'll open it together."

On the count of three, they opened the door and took in the macabre scene before them. Monte was laid out, surrounded by a giant pool of blood. Franco lay in a crumpled heap, a good portion of his skull missing. Mikey's legs were arranged in two entirely opposite directions. Worst of all, Rosso lay still on the bed, slack-jawed, his silent heart monitor showing a distinct green flat line.

Suddenly, the room lit up with blue and red strobes, and the two men ran to the window to see no less than a half-dozen police cars pouring through the front gate.

The two spoke in unison as they reached for their phones. "Oh, shit."

*   *   *

Donny, Abby, and their two mobster companions were about ten minutes from the house on a long, deserted, wooded road heading toward a landfill owned by one of Rosso's shell corporations, which happened to have the sanitation contract with the city.

Donny rode shotgun, Billy sat in the backseat behind Donny and next to Abby, who was behind the driver.

It was a precarious situation at best. Billy kept reaching over to stroke Abby's thigh, which she objected to, and Donny piped up and told him to keep his hands to himself. Then Billy's phone ring.

"Yeah?" Billy said, answering it.

He was silent for a few moments, listening, which made Donny nervous.

"What? Cops?" Billy nervously glanced forward at Donny for a split second.

Both Donny and Abby had the same thought at the same time.

"Alright, I'll talk to you later. Keep your fuckin' mouth shut, got it?" Billy hung up the phone and casually reached into his pocket, produced his gun, and pointed it at Donny. "What the fuck is goin' on?"

"What the hell, Billy!" Donny feigned surprise.

"Mike says Monte's dead, so's the old…"

That's as far as he got before Abby smashed the crown of her head into his left temple. The sudden impact struck Billy's brain against the side of his skull, knocking him out.

It happened so quickly that the driver was taken by complete surprise and fumbled for his gun.

In a move that Abby had mastered over the years, she looped her bound hands under her backside and feet, to be in front of her, and reached forward strangling the driver with the rope that bound her hands.

He forgot about the gun and the wheel and reached up, clawing at her arms trying to get himself free. Abby pushed her feet against the back of the seat, lifting herself up and applying all of her one-hundred-and-twenty-pound frame against his throat.

"Stop the car!" she screamed. "Stop the car!"

It was about thirty seconds of complete shock before Donny fully appreciated what was happening and jumped in to lend a literal hand. He grabbed onto the steering wheel and tried to keep the car from careening off into the trees. It didn't help that the driver was practically standing, his foot fully depressing the accelerator, as he tried to free himself from Abby's grasp.

"Stop the car!" Abby continued to scream.

"I can't. I've just got the wheel!" Donny shot back.

"Not you, the driver! Stop the fucking car!"

Billy came to in the backseat and took in the scene. It took a moment before he realized what was going on, but he couldn't find his gun. He reached forward, grabbing Donny around the neck. Abby didn't let this go on more than a second before she shifted herself and kicked him in the ribs with the hard heel of her right boot, breaking one rib instantly. Billy screamed and let go of Donny to grab his side.

Donny reached for the wheel again, but it was too late as the car finally jumped off the side of the road and crashed into a hundred-year-old maple. The driver had buckled in, but the airbag had exploded in his face, leaving him unconscious. Either that or it was the lack of oxygen from Abby's rope around his neck. Either way he appeared to still be breathing and would probably be fine.

Billy wasn't so lucky. He wasn't buckled and smashed into the front seat headfirst.

Donny shook his head to clear the cobwebs. "Abby, you OK?"

Her answer came in the form of a grunt.

"Hold on," he said as he stumbled from the car. Having whacked his knee on the glove box, he was limping a bit. He made his way to the rear of the car, where he helped Abby get out. He looked her up and down. "You alright?"

She nodded her head. "Yeah, I'm OK." She walked a few steps forward and looked in through the broken window on the driver's door. He wasn't moving. She placed her fingers on his artery to make sure there was a pulse. Satisfied that he would live, she looked into the backseat. "What about Billy-boy back there?"

Donny didn't even need to go back to look—he could hear him moaning. "He's hurt, that's for sure."

"Come on," Abby said. "We've got to get away from here."

Donny blinked, trying to clear his mind, and looked into her eyes. He was hard-pressed to catch up with what was going on. Abby had been dead for nearly a year, but now here she was in the flesh ordering him around. She was right about one thing: he helped her get away from Rosso's, and the men back at the house had obviously figured that out. "Alright, follow me."

They took off running down the road, staying close to the tree line so they could duck for cover if another car came along.

11

A HALF-MILE DOWN THE ROAD, Donny and Abby ducked into the trees, where he led them through a path and into a large, open, unlit area. The moon wasn't very bright, but he seemed to know the way. Abby followed him to a metal building, where he entered a code into the keypad. They entered, and Donny hit the lights, the flickering fluorescent bulbs lighting up a shabby office with faded green walls.

"Where are we?"

"The landfill." He looked around and found a large first aid kit tucked away under a bunch of junk and a half-dead potted plant on top of an aging, gray metal file cabinet. "Sit down," he said, indicating an old office chair.

Abby did sit, happily. She had been running on pure adrenaline for the past twenty-four hours, ever since she got the call Ava had been taken. It was starting to wear off, and she was hitting the wall.

She had various cuts and scrapes and a particularly nasty graze above her right eyebrow, probably from the car accident. It all happened pretty fast, but she seemed to remember hitting her face on the seat in front of her.

They sat silent while Donny cleaned her up with rubbing alcohol and gauze. There was so much to say, and so many questions, that neither knew where to start.

Donny finally broke the silence. "We shouldn't stay here long. This is where we were heading in the first place. The men back at the house know that. There could be some guys on their way here right now. The sooner we get out, the better."

Abby nodded her head. "I thought you were getting out of all this. After you helped me get away from Bryce, you said you were going to get out yourself."

"I thought you were dead," he said, looking at her. "It's kinda like seeing a ghost."

Looking into his eyes, she smiled—truly smiled—for the first time in months.

He finished up, her cuts and scrapes cleaned, and packed the first aid kit away. "So... what the hell is going on Abby? What happened back at the house?"

"I'm after Bryce. I figured Rosso would know where he is. So, I knocked on the door... loudly."

Donny shook his head, almost chuckling at her casualness. "I knew you changed on *Trial Island*. I could tell just watching you. I remember saying, 'I'm looking at Abby, but that's not Abby.' The way you carry yourself now... and you carry a gun? Where was this badass two years ago when I had to all but tie you up and throw you in a trunk to get you to leave Bryce?"

"I guess I found myself."

"You're damned right you found yourself. You just single-handedly took down the biggest crime family in the Midwest."

"He took Ava," she said. "That was all the motivation I needed."

"Bryce took her?"

"Yes. I'm sure of it. I've been trying to track him down for the last ten months, but haven't had any luck. The investigator is one of the best, but even he couldn't get anything. The family is locked up tight. But I knew Rosso would know, so I went straight to the source."

"I heard a rumor that he was still alive, but never saw him or anything. Just rumors. So what did Rosso say?"

"Not much," Abby said. "He was experiencing severe cardiac arrest at the time. The only thing I got was that Bryce is laundering money somewhere upstate."

"He just told you this?"

"He took some convincing," Abby conceded.

"You really are on a rampage, beating information out of a sick, old man. I guess I would be, too, if he put a hit on me."

"I didn't beat him. I had some information he wanted, so it was an exchange, so to speak. And he didn't put a hit on me. That was a cover story. It was Bryce who attacked us on my sister's lawn last year and," she made air quotes, "killed me."

Donny was still getting over his shock. "It was a pretty convincing story. You were about the only thing in the news for weeks. When it came out that you were a mob wife, the media spent most of the summer running 'Where's Abby' pieces. When you turned up dead on your sister's lawn at the hands of a mob hitman, everything just blew up."

"I know," Abby said. "I'm alive, remember? I watched it myself. Kind of surreal, actually." Abby shifted gears, uncomfortably glancing out the window, unable to see anything in the darkness beyond. "We should get out of here."

Donny looked at the clock. They had been there about fifteen minutes, and he figured they were essentially living on borrowed time at this point. "You're right, let's go."

Abby picked out a set of keys hanging by the door labeled for one of the pickup trucks parked on the side of the building, Donny shook his head. "No, that road we came down is the one way in and out of here, and this landfill is the only thing down here. If anyone comes looking for us, they'll be coming down that road."

"I guess we're on foot then," Abby said as she hit the lights.

As soon as she did, the unmistakable glow of headlights bouncing in the distance dimly illuminated the office through the front windows.

"Come on, through the back door." Donny grabbed her arm, and they raced out the back, careful to keep the building between themselves and the car coming into the complex as they made short work of the distance to the tree line.

Once they were in the trees, Abby pulled her night-vision monocular from her belt to look back toward the office building a few hundred yards away. All the lights were off, but she was able to see a couple of men walking around the building. One of them found the back door ajar and called another one over. Abby smiled for a moment as they bravely flung the door open and shot blindly into the space, hitting nothing but old office furniture.

"What's going on?" Donny asked even though the sound of gunfire made it clear.

"They're looking for us in the building," Abby said.

"They must have seen the lights on inside before we shut them off. It won't be long before they figure out we're not in there and come looking for us. We should go."

"You're right," Abby said, taking a last look at the men.

Just before she took the monocular from her eye, they must have figured out that the building was empty because someone inside hit the switch for the outdoor floodlights, lighting up the area around the building like Times Square.

"Son of a bitch," Abby cursed, ripping the monocular from her eye and rubbing it. The sudden burst of light had blinded her momentarily in the right eye.

"You OK?" Donny said, catching her as she stumbled a bit.

"Yeah, just glad these aren't binoculars, or I wouldn't be able to see through either eye right now." She blinked her eye purposefully. "I'll be fine."

"Good," he said, looking past her, "because they're searching the yard for us, so let's get the hell out of here."

Donny held onto Abby's hand to help guide her as they ran through the trees. It only took a couple of minutes for her to see straight again, but she was enjoying the closeness with Donny she hadn't felt with another person in a very long time. She held tightly onto his hand as they dashed toward safety.

*   *   *

As they came out the other side of the woods surrounding the landfill, Donny got his bearings and said they should go right. He knew of an auto repair business not far down the road. It was an old-school garage that patched tires, did oil changes, and got fifteen-year-old clunkers running again on the cheap. Nothing fancy.

As Donny suspected, it only took them three tries to find an older, beat-up, American-made pile of garbage with the key left under the mat. With that, the pair set off to get out of suburbia and back to the city where they could blend in and figure out their next move.

"How long is the ride?" Abby asked.

111

"During rush hour—close to an hour and a half. Right now, with no traffic and going the speed limit so we don't get pulled over in a hot car, probably forty minutes or so." He looked over at her. "You look beat. Why don't you close your eyes?"

"Thanks, I might," Abby said, watching him watch the road.

Donny stayed quiet for a little over five minutes, hoping she might sleep, but when it was clear she was still awake, he asked, "So what's next?"

"I've got to get my hands on a phone," Abby said. "Rosso's information doesn't do me much good, but I'm hoping it makes sense to the investigator looking for Bryce."

"Well, here." Donny fished the phone from his pocket.

"No, I can't risk the call getting traced back to you. I'll get a burner in the city."

Donny said nothing, but the puzzled look on his face told Abby he didn't understand.

"A disposable phone," Abby said. "J… um, my investigator, calls them that. The cheap, pre-paid ones you use and then *burn* them, usually by snapping the SIM card and throwing it in the garbage so that it can't be traced back to anyone. I'll buy a couple at some random convenience store once we're in the city."

Donny shook his head, amazed at the transformed

woman sitting next to him.

They rode in silence for a couple more minutes until Abby broke it. "Why didn't you get out?"

"I couldn't."

"That's a lie," Abby said. "We were in L.A. You had all your fake ID's, cash, and everything you needed to walk away. You were the last person I expected to run into at Rosso's place."

He sighed. "Alright. Well, I know I never said it, but you had to know how I felt about you."

He looked at her, and their eyes met.

"Of course I knew, but I also knew you'd be dead if either of us acted on it."

"I still cared about you. I still…"

"No," she said sharply. "We cannot. If you need to, pull the car over and let me out now, but I've got shit to get done Donny."

He almost chuckled. "You can't tell me you didn't feel the same way. You kissed me back after we signed the *Trial Island* papers."

She allowed herself a small smile. "It was just for appearances. You were pretending to be my husband. How would it have looked if I didn't give you a proper kiss goodbye?"

He smiled back. "Alright, that's bullshit." He thought

113

a minute. "Anyway, forget about it. I'm not sayin' I love you, or we need to pick up where we left off. You wanna know the truth? I'm kinda pissed off."

"Good," Abby said, trying to be cold.

"I mean, the hoops I went through to get you and Ava out, and now you're right back here? What the fuck!"

"I didn't want to come back here, and it's not exactly like we're in the same situation. I appreciate what you did. I really do."

Donny had a lot to say but wasn't about to give Abby the satisfaction of hearing it. He was pissed off, and rightfully so. Still, the conversation that continued in his head revealed more to him that he was willing to say aloud. *What I'm sayin' is that when you left, I lost you. I planned to get out, but how could I lose you and everything else in my life too? This is all I know. I could have left with you. I would have followed you anywhere in the world. But without you, what did I have? I dunno. It sounds stupid, but I just couldn't lose everything.*

"Go ahead and pretend you're upset," Abby said, interrupting his thoughts, "but you're helping me now, and I appreciate it. I owe you."

Donny nodded his head. "You know what? Call me a sucker for those beautiful brown eyes of yours, but I saw you, and there I was again, two years ago like not a day had passed. Of course I'm gonna help you. And what am I gonna lose? You killed Monte, my piece-of-shit boss. Rosso's dead. You think I wasn't ready for this to happen someday? I've got money stashed away, ID's, whatever. I can pick up and go whenever I need to. With the old man sick these last few months, the FBI is hot and heavy to move in the second he kicks the bucket, and I wasn't gonna stick around to see where the chips fall, if you know what I mean."

"Makes sense," Abby said, drifting off a little, watching the road.

After a few minutes, Donny chuckled and said, "Burner."

"What's that?" Abby asked, not quite hearing him.

"I just can't get over it. A few years back, Bryce beat you within an inch of your life, and you did nothing about it. Now you're some kind of commando, talking about burner phones, and taking out a dozen men like it's nothing. Is this just all *Trial Island*?"

"No," Abby sighed. "No, the island training was all about survival. Well, mostly about survival. They figure it's inevitable fights are going to break out, so they teach you a lot of self-defense. I was small and expected to get picked on, so I took it a step further and got some extra personal fight training."

"That was kind of obvious, watching the show. But where's the rest come from? Where did you learn to shoot a gun?"

Abby had gone back and forth in her head over the past couple hours on how much to trust Donny. She was skeptical of most people, but were it not for Donny getting her away from Bryce, she would have been dead by now. If there were anyone in the world she *should* trust, it would be him.

"This guy JJ," Abby said. "He's my investigator. I didn't just come here on a whim. While he's been looking for Bryce since he shot me and murdered Eric, I've also had him training me on all this stuff. He's ex-military, some sort of special ops," Abby said, pretending she didn't remember all the details. "I've been in rehab for my shoulder and leg, but on my own time I've done some personal rehab, learning to shoot guns and getting familiar with urban-combat stuff. Bryce went to great lengths to kill me. I intend to track him down and make sure he never gets that opportunity again."

Donny let out a whistle. "I've heard the phrase to beware the wrath of a woman scorned, but this is some next-level shit." He took his eyes off the road to smile at her. "Remind me not to get on your bad side."

Abby dozed off a bit as they drove, but her mind never truly shut off. She thought about the years of friendship she'd had with Donny. She remembered the first time she had really noticed him. It was the night Bryce snapped and tried to kill Ava as an infant. He beat the hell out of Abby as she wrapped herself around the baby to protect her. She always thought Bryce would have killed them both that night had Donny not burst into the room to tear him away.

From that day on, Donny always watched. He was a silent protector, always nearby if needed. Abby grew very fond of him, and while she had never admitted as much to him, she had dreamt of running off with him on many of the nights Bryce didn't come home.

Ava absolutely adored him; she always lit up when he was around. He was the only positive male role model she ever had in her life. Children are an excellent judge of character, and going by Ava's judgment, Donny was a keeper.

He made all of the arrangements to get Ava out of the country. It had been so long since she had thought about how much he had done for her over the years, all for the love of a woman he knew he couldn't have. The way he kissed her when they parted, there was no mistaking his feelings.

Abby opened her eyes and placed her hand gently on his shoulder. He looked at her and smiled. It was a comfortable smile as if they hadn't just gone the better part of two years without seeing each other. As if no time had passed at all. They were just friends on a road trip together.

She wanted to say *Thank you, thank you for everything,* but she didn't. No words were exchanged, but she knew that he knew.

They pulled off the highway and into a small plaza with an all-night diner next to a twenty-four hour convenience store. Abby got three phones at the store and activated them over some much-needed comfort food in the back corner of the diner. She stuffed two in her pocket and handed one to Donny. "This is how we'll communicate. I don't want a stupid thing like a phone call

117

to get us caught."

He nodded and smiled. "You're the boss."

"Don't placate me," she said seriously.

He grinned. He wasn't placating her—he meant it.

Abby excused herself to the parking lot to make a phone call. As she dialed the number from memory, she hoped he would be able to do something with the info she had.

JJ's groggy voice came from the other end of the line. "Yeah? Who's this?"

"I was able to get some information," she said excitedly.

"Abby, do you ever call at a normal hour?"

*   *   *

Donny watched Abby through the window. She was having an animated conversation with whoever was on the other end of the line. He couldn't believe she was back, yet he wasn't surprised either. Something inside always told him he would see her again.

Whether he wanted to admit it or not, there was truth to what he had been thinking earlier: he didn't get out when she did because he couldn't stand the thought of losing everything. It wasn't the mob life he was afraid of losing—it was her.

He had never been truly in with the family, even

though his dad had been part of the Rosso operation for years. Donny always felt like an outsider looking in. He tried going in another direction entirely, attending college to study film, but that was a career with a tough road ahead. He realized it early, and when he ran into a little financial trouble, he took some time off to work for his dad and make a little cash. One thing led to the next, and all these years later, he was still in the game.

He saw the life as a means to an end, but always felt like he could walk away at any point. At least until he met Abby. He was drawn to her and wasn't entirely sure why. Her looks would have been an obvious place to start, but he knew it was more than that. He felt a connection with her the first time he saw her, even though she didn't seem to notice him until that night he pulled Bryce off her.

Maybe it was because she was an outsider, too, caught up in this game and not sure what to do about it.

Now, she was a force to be reckoned with. He was proud that she had taken control of her life. No one would screw her over again.

He loathed Bryce more now than he ever had in the past. The bastard kidnaped a child—his own daughter—in order to kill her mother. He remembered that sweet little girl. The last time he saw her was at the airport when they put her on a plane to Canada so she could stay at Abby's sister's house. She wore a cute pink beret and her favorite navy blue dress. Abby was completely inconsolable after Ava left, and a short time later had just about completely cut him off. He couldn't blame her then or now. She had to protect herself emotionally and physically from everyone around her.

The thought of that adorable little girl, likely tied up somewhere with his monster of a former boss, enraged him. The guys back at the house had obviously pieced together what he had done as far as helping Abby. He had hidden his involvement in helping her get out before, but there was no doing that now. He couldn't go back.

*   *   *

"That's all you've got?" JJ asked.

"For now. Bryce is laundering money upstate. No info on where."

JJ thought about it. "Well, it's got to be upstate New York. I mean, I guess it could be somewhere else, but I don't know any other place that people refer to as upstate, do you?"

"That was my thought, too."

"Well, that narrows it down, but it doesn't give me too much. It's not like I was even looking in that direction. I've never had any indication before that he was in New York."

"Well, let's look at the money laundering, then. What do you have on that?"

JJ sighed. "There's a lot of money going through the family, Abby. I don't have a lead on all of it, especially as I've never had any indication that's where we should be looking." He thought a moment. "It does tell us where to look, though."

"Where's that?"

JJ was scrolling through the notes on his tablet on the other end. "Hold on a second… here it is. John Venzo. His name came up a bunch in the financials. He's got an accounting firm off Taylor Street, in Chicago, near the University of Illinois. Small place; looks like he's the only employee. A ton of cash goes through there, and all the businesses link back to Rosso in some way every time. I'm sure he's on the Feds' radar, too. It looks like he does the books for the family. He probably doesn't know where Bryce is, or even that he's out there somewhere, but if he's laundering, then the cash records are going to be there."

Abby was already planning in her head. "How tough do you think this will be to find?"

"Hard to say. I've got more stuff at the office, so let me go in and dig around. I'll call you back in an hour."

"You can't, I'm calling you on a burner. I don't want anyone tracing you to me, or what went down here tonight."

JJ was silent on the other end for a moment, knowing full well what Abby was capable of. "Who gave you this info about Bryce being upstate?"

"Rosso."

"Abby, how in the world did you…"

"Isn't a little mystery better than me just telling you? Watch the news in the morning if you really want to know what went down. You'll be proud, that's all I have to say."

"I can be out there first thing in the morning. It looks like I can catch an 8:30 flight, touching down at noon. Let me come out and give you a hand. These are dangerous guys. You could use the help."

"No, JJ. I've got no time to waste. Every minute that goes by is another minute Ava is with that lunatic, in God-knows-what condition. Besides, I've got someone helping me. I'm OK."

"You do? Who? Who is helping you?"

Abby looked at Donny through the window, sitting back at the table seemingly lost in thought himself. "An old friend. Don't worry, he's someone I can trust."

"Alright, well, be careful. Call me if you get stuck; we'll reassess."

"Will do. Thanks, JJ."

Abby went back inside and sat across from Donny, leaning over the table. "You know who this John Venzo guy is?"

Donny thought a second. "Yeah, he does the books. He's got a place in the old neighborhood. Why?"

"That's where we're going next."

12

HOURS LATER, in the middle of the night, Abby and Donny had seemingly gone through every piece of paper in the accountant's office. For all of their efforts, they had found nothing.

They had flipped through every folder in every file cabinet. Invoices and ledgers for an endless list of supply companies, restaurants, and construction businesses. Everything looked legitimate as far as their untrained eyes could tell, and nothing indicated a business in New York, upstate or otherwise.

"Do you think it would be on the computer?" Abby speculated out loud. They hadn't touched the computer yet; beyond waking it up to find it was—predictably—password protected.

"No," Donny said. "Nothing illegal ever makes it onto a computer with the family. Rosso never trusted them, and he's probably right about that. Venzo's got to have another set of books here. I mean, the feds could ransack this place just as easily as us, and they'd know what they're looking for. Anything that could be tied to laundering is not going to be easily accessible. This is just all the legit-looking stuff. It's not going to be on a computer. It's going to be handwritten—nothing that can be tracked or hacked."

"Well, where do we find it, then?"

Donny sighed. "Honestly, we could probably tear this place up from the floorboards and not find what we're looking for." He shook his head, looking around.

Abby checked her watch; it was three in the morning. The office would presumably open around eight, give or take. "You think he'll be here in the morning? With what happened last night?"

Donny thought about it. "That's a good question. Rosso is dead. Franco is dead. Mikey G. is dead. Even Monte is dead. Shit, they're all dead. The one that's got me worried is Jerry."

"Who's Jerry?"

"Monte's number two. He was in our crew. I guess he's in charge now. At least he'll try to take over what's left. I can guarantee two things: he'll be combing the city for you—us—and if he finds us, we'd better be ready. He's violent and reactionary. Doesn't really think things through, so I doubt his first order of business is going to be to call the accountant to fill him in on what went down. I'm thinking it's a safe bet that it'll be business as usual. At least first thing. Mob guys are worse than hairdressers when it comes to gossip, though, so it won't be noon before everyone knows what went down."

"That and they'll see it on the news," she said with a smile.

"I don't know about that. These mob guys are pretty

124

tight-lipped. I mean, yeah, there's four dead bodies, but I bet Rosso's the only one that will hit the news. They'll take care of the others themselves. It's not like the guys we left behind are going to call the police or something," he said with a chuckle.

"Well, maybe *they* didn't." Abby had a devilish smile about her.

Donny gave her a quizzical look. "What's that supposed to mean?"

"Before we left, I took a phone off the hook in the kitchen and dialed 9-1-1."

"You what?"

"Like you said, none of them would do it, and I did sort of gift wrap the whole place. Should be easy work for the detectives. Plus, it should keep them off our backs for a few days at least. Enough time to do what I've got to do and get outta here."

"Well, you're probably right—they'll see it on the news. Let's hope our guy doesn't watch the early broadcast before he comes in."

"What about the accountant? Do you know him?"

"No, but I know *of* him. Met him twice, but I don't know too much about him. He's sort of on the outskirts of the family. Keeps his nose and hands clean. He's got to. If he got pinched by the cops or the feds, that would be bad news for everyone. He's Rosso's distant nephew or something."

Abby walked over to the desk and took a gun out of the top drawer she had found there earlier. It was old school; a revolver, loaded. She emptied the bullets and put them in her pocket. She went back to Donny who was still fruitlessly flipping through some papers. "Here's what I'm thinking: we have a couple hours. Let's get some shuteye in the back room and have a little conversation with John in the morning."

The two of them spent the next thirty minutes going through the office, making sure that everything was put back exactly where they found it. There was a back room behind the main office with a microwave and a coffee pot on a small table pushed up against the wall, and a collection of old mismatched file boxes on the wall facing the door.

Abby curled into a ball on the floor next to the boxes. It had been more than twenty-four hours since she got the panicked call from her sister that Ava was missing, and she had been running high on adrenaline ever since. For the past hour, her body had been fighting her every effort at thought or movement, and she was ready to crash.

Donny took off his jacket and laid it over her to use as a blanket, then sat on the floor next to her, leaning against the boxes so he could watch the door, just in case.

"Thanks," Abby said. "Aren't you going to sleep?"

"I'm good. I can't anyway. I'll keep an eye out—you get some rest."

"Thanks again," Abby said, adjusting herself to put an

arm under her head for support as she lay on the floor.

"Here," he said, patting his leg. "You can use me for a pillow."

Abby looked up and thought about declining, but Donny's smile made her remember the comfort that one feels with a trusted friend. She laid her head on his thigh, enjoying a little cushion for her neck and the warmth of his skin that she felt through his jeans. Within seconds, she was asleep.

Donny rested his left hand on her shoulder and leaned his head back against the boxes, watching the door. In his right hand, he held his gun.

*   *   *

With her eyes still closed, Abby stretched out on the floor and inhaled the intoxicating aroma of a fresh brewed pot of coffee. She smiled, opening her eyes, almost forgetting where she was for just a moment. Donny sat on the floor next to her, also asleep.

Wait a second...

"Donny," she whispered harshly, shaking him awake.

He opened his eyes, rubbing the sand from them. "What time is it?"

Abby held her finger to her lips, giving him a silent *shhh.*

She listened but heard nothing other than the slow

drip of the coffee pot finishing its brewing cycle.

Donny realized what was happening and stood slowly, edging his way to the door and peeking through to see who was out there. He saw no one from his vantage point but couldn't see the entire room. He looked back at Abby and shook his head. "Nothing," he whispered.

Abby eased her way to the door, crouched low as she whispered, "I'll go low, you go high, on three."

Gripping her gun with her right hand, she used the fingers on her left to count down *3…2…1…*

They burst through the door at the same time, guns drawn, searching for a target and finding none.

Abby looked at the clock on the wall. It was five minutes to eight, and the blinds on the front windows were still drawn. She relaxed and turned back to the small room where they had come from, looking at the coffee pot. "Must be on a timer."

"Geez." Donny almost laughed. "That's a helluva way to wake up."

She smiled. "It'll get the blood flowing anyway."

With the coffee already made, they figured his little back room was probably the accountant's first stop when he got in. They poured some coffee for themselves and waited.

It was a few minutes after eight when they heard a key in the front door and the deadbolt turn. They put their coffees down, drew their guns, and eased behind the door so they would not be seen when he entered the room.

As they suspected, after opening the blinds and putting down his briefcase, John Venzo came waltzing into the back room for a cup of Joe.

*　　*　　*

Driving into the city, John was counting down the days he had left to make this damned commute. He had a nice little house just outside the city—a modest place, nice lawn, and a little back yard for his son to play in. Every morning he wondered if he would be coming back.

He wasn't worried about getting killed in a mob hit or anything like that. Rosso made sure that he was insulated from all of the more exciting parts of the family, and for that, John was thankful. Besides, since the Rossos had won their war with the Patrizios, there were no other powerful families to pose a threat. It was a nice situation to be in.

No, John's concern was with the feds. Specifically, how quickly could they relocate him and his family into witness protection once the old man died and he turned over all the evidence needed to lock up the remaining family? He felt no remorse for betraying the family. He hated the life; always looking over his shoulder, hiding money here and there, coming into the city every day.

Unbeknownst to him at the time, Rosso had given his mother money to pay for John's college education. When he got out, he wasn't given a choice: work for the family, or his mother had to pay back the loan in twenty-four hours. Eighty thousand dollars was more than she kept laying around, so working for the family it was.

He knew the feds had to be on to what his small but very profitable firm was doing for Rosso, and he left a few breadcrumbs here and there until they showed up at his front door about a month ago.

They knew Rosso was sick and were looking to shut down the entire operation. John was the key, and they ironically made him an offer he couldn't refuse. He and his family would be relocated to the Northwest, with every need taken care of. John would teach economics at a quiet state university to keep busy, and they would lead the life that he and his wife had been dreaming of for years.

As he entered the back room, he wondered if today might be the day. Last he heard, Rosso only had a few days left. His instructions were to keep everything running as quietly as ever after Rosso passed, and then report directly to Franco. Nothing else would change.

As he went to pour himself a mug from the ten cup coffee pot, he noticed it was only half full.

"What the…"

He heard a woman's voice behind him, cold as steel. "Turn around, and make it slow."

*　　*　　*

John turned, his arms instinctively raised. "Are you fuckin' kidding me?"

"No joke," Abby smiled. "I don't want to hurt you, but you need to help me. If you do, you'll be fine."

John put his hands down and turned to pick up his coffee. Taking a sip, he replied calmly, "Why don't you put the gun down and tell me what you want?"

Abby looked at Donny, a bit confused.

John laughed. "You think you scare me? You know who I am, right? This isn't the first time I've had a gun in my face, honey." He looked back and forth between his two captors, then over Donny's shoulder. "What's that?"

As the two instinctively looked behind Donny, John rushed toward the front room ahead of them, going for his gun. He fumbled with the drawer before finding his gun and whirling it around, stopping Abby and Donny dead in their tracks

"Put down the gun!" John yelled.

Abby lowered her gun to the floor and held up her hands.

Donny seemed surprised that she acquiesced so quickly but followed her lead and did the same.

John smiled at Donny. "You don't scare me. I know who you are, and Rosso is going to have you fuckin' drawn and quartered if I tell him you came here threatening me. I don't know what you're looking for, but I'm not telling you shit. Now why don't you and your little girlfriend get out of here before things end badly for you? If you're lucky, I won't tell Rosso about this."

Abby slowly moved forward. "I don't want to hurt you, but I need your help. Come on. Put the gun down and let's talk."

"Stop right there. Don't take another step."

She continued forward as she spoke. "You're not going to shoot me, John. Come on, put it down before someone gets hurt."

"I will shoot you. Don't take another step."

She shook her head and stepped forward again. John's hand slightly shaking, the gun aimed vaguely at her chest.

"Put it down, Jo…"

The click of the gun's hammer harmlessly hitting the bullet free chamber silenced the room. The accountant was stunned and pulled the trigger again and again.

"Looking for these?" Abby produced a handful of bullets from her pocket and let them spill from her hand onto the carpet.

John stared at the bullets, speechless.

Donny actually laughed out loud.

Abby moved so fast, neither man had a second to react. In one swift motion, she grabbed John's left hand, slammed it into the wall just to the side of his head, and drove the blade of her knife through his palm, nailing his hand to the drywall.

He screamed, eyes bulging at the sight of the large

blade pierced through his hand. Abby held her hand over his mouth to muffle his screams as she yelled in his face. "Do I have your attention? I asked you nicely to help me. Now shut up and listen."

John managed to stifle his screaming though the pain was still intense.

"I'm going to take my hand away," Abby said. "If you scream, the knife won't be going into your hand next time. Got it?"

John nodded.

She took her hand away, and he alternately gasped for air and glanced at his hand as blood starting trickling from the wound.

Abby took a step back and pointed her gun at him. "I didn't want it to go this way. Don't make this any harder than it needs to be."

"OK, alright," he said, catching his breath. "What do you want?"

Abby smiled and looked at Donny. "Now that's more like it, isn't it?"

Donny smiled back. *Wow,* was all he could think.

"Now," Abby said, shifting her weight from side to side. "It's pretty simple. There is a particular piece of shit named Bryce Haydenson laundering money for you. He kidnapped my daughter, so you're going to tell me where I can find him."

John shook his head. "You've got something mixed up there. Haydenson is dead, at least a year now."

"No, he's not. He's alive, he's laundering money for the family, and you're going to tell me where he is."

"I can't," John said. "You're wrong. I swear he's dead. And if he were alive, I'd have no idea where he would be. The money laundering goes through here, but I'm on a need-to-know. Rosso keeps me in the dark. Ask him yourself if you want."

"I did. He told me Bryce is alive, and he's upstate laundering money. It was the last thing he said before he died right in front of me. Now, I'll believe you that you don't know where he is, but you're going to tell me how to find him, or you're going to join Rosso."

She stared into his eyes and studied the pain and confusion on his face. He obviously hadn't heard, which was a good thing. *Is he gonna break?*

A photo on his desk caught her eye. It was John, with a woman too attractive for him, and a young boy. She turned back to him with a stare, "And then they're next. Got it?"

"Fine!" He spat the words out. "Fine. Christ, just get this thing out of my hand!" He had so much adrenaline pumping through his veins, he could hardly feel the pain— at least until Abby ripped the knife cleanly back out through the wound, drawing a yelp from him.

Donny had already located a first aid kit and tossed

some gauze pads and medical tape at him. "Why don't you clean that up before you get blood all over the place?" He leaned down toward Abby and whispered, "Nice job. You had me a little freaked out, though. When did you take the bullets out of the gun?"

She winked. "I'm full of surprises these days, huh?"

They allowed John a few seconds to sit down and dress his wound before getting back to business.

"So, how do we find him?" Abby asked.

"I don't know. I've got an idea. But it's all I've got, I swear."

"Let's hear it," Donny said.

"You said upstate, so I'm assuming you're talking about New York."

"That's the only upstate I know," Abby conceded.

John nodded. "The majority of the cash gets shuffled around here in the city. Into one business, out to another, lots of cash-heavy places. Bars, restaurants, you know, stuff like that. We don't do everything in town though. We've got a monthly drop that goes to Vegas. I know, cliché' right? But if you want to clean a ton of cash that's still the best place to do it. There's another out of town drop too, but I don't know where the money winds up. Every Monday at ten in the morning, two guys show up with New York tags on the car. I hand them an envelope with $9,900, and they disappear for another week."

"Any idea where they go?" Abby asked.

John shook his head. "No, I've never seen them around here. I always figured they were bound for NYC. They're the only contact I have with New York, I swear."

Abby was curious, "Why such a specific amount? $9,900?"

John opened his mouth, but Donny spoke up, "Any deposit a business makes over $10k the banks have to report to the feds. Laundering 101: don't move too much cash at once, or you'll get pinched. Right, John?"

He nodded. "We can only do so much in the city. That's why we have the Vegas drop. And New York."

"So we're looking for a business upstate." Abby was lost in thought for a moment, and then sighed, looking at Donny. "Where the hell do we start?"

Donny glanced at his watch. "In a little more than an hour it looks like."

Abby furrowed her brow.

"Today's Monday," he said. "If what he's sayin' is true, our two guys from New York will be here for the drop in about an hour and a half. We grab 'em and ask where they're going, or we can just follow 'em."

Abby tried to play it off that she knew that, but couldn't. She was exhausted and had completely forgotten what day of the week it was.

Donny smiled at her. "It's alright. You've got a lot on your mind."

"I guess we should get comfortable, then." Abby noticed John examining his newly bandaged hand, "You'll be OK. The knife went in pretty clean, I don't think I hit bone."

The three spent an awkward time together over the next hour. They considered tying John up, but that didn't make any sense given that he would have to be untied to make the hand-off to the New York guys. For the time being, he seemed cooperative, so they simply asked him to sit and stay quiet, and he obliged.

"Can I at least have my coffee?" John asked.

Abby granted him that, and the three occupied his office in silence until the shrill ring of the telephone made them jump. Abby looked at the old-school, desk-mounted phone. *That thing must be thirty years old,* she thought.

"I should answer it," John said.

Abby nodded. "Don't do anything stupid."

John lifted the receiver, and Donny leaned in close so he could hear both ends of the conversation.

"Hello?"

"Hey, John, it's Mark."

"Oh, hi. What's going on?"

Donny mouthed, *Who's Mark?*

John covered the receiver and whispered, "One of the guys coming for the drop."

"Listen, I dunno if you heard," Mark continued, "but I guess some shit went down at Rosso's last night. Did you hear?"

"No, no, I didn't. What happened?" John said, feigning surprise.

"I guess the old man is dead; some of the other guys, too. I dunno, I didn't get the whole thing, but the place got hit pretty hard."

"Holy shit! The feds?"

"I don't think so, but we don't wanna take no chances. We're not coming this morning."

Donny pulled away and looked at John, whispering harshly, *No, get him here! You get him here!*

Abby pulled her blade from its sheath and tapped the family photo on the desk. John got the message.

"Mark, um…" John thought for a second. "If something did go down, I've got to get this cash out of here. You can't skip the drop. If something did go down, Rosso's instructions are to go ahead with business as usual. The old man knew he didn't have long, so him being dead is no surprise to anyone."

"I know, but I'm not comfortable gettin' too close to things, ya know?"

"Listen, I haven't heard anything, and there's nothing going on here at the office. It's me, my coffee, and a bunch of numbers. The usual alright? I'll make some phone calls, but in the meantime, I've got to get the cash out of here. Swing by, grab the envelope, and hit the road. No one will ever know you were here. Same as always."

Mark was quiet on the other end. He knew his boss probably needed the weekly influx of cash.

"Mark…"

"Fine. We'll be by in thirty, but if we get pinched, I swear to God you're a fuckin' dead man. Got it?"

"Loud and clear." John smiled. He was used to being threatened. It seemed to have become a way of life in the past couple of hours anyway. "See you at ten." He hung up the phone and looked at Abby. "Happy?"

"Yes, very. You did fine," she assured him. "They usually park right out front?"

"Yeah, they pull up to the curb. They're not in here for more than five minutes."

Abby looked at Donny. "We should be down the street a bit. We'll pull out in traffic behind them and follow at a safe distance. Sound good?"

"You got it," Donny said. He looked at John. "We're going to need your car."

"Of course," John said, rolling his eyes. He opened his briefcase and tossed the keys to Donny.

Abby caught the lid as he tried to close it. She reached in and removed his wallet from a pocket in the briefcase. She flipped through it and found what she was looking for. Sliding his license from its slot, she read his address aloud. "Evanston, that's some nice real estate out there."

"It is," John conceded, swallowing uncomfortably.

Abby slid his license into her front pocket. "If you breathe a word to anyone about me being here—if you give these guys any kind of warning—I will hunt you down. You will make the handoff and go about your day as though absolutely nothing happened. Is that clear?"

John nodded.

"Good." Abby looked at her watch. "If they're coming at ten, we should go. It's going to take us a couple of minutes to get into position."

"Let's do it." Donny pointed at John. "You heard what the lady said, right? We're not screwing around."

"Don't worry," John assured them. "You don't want any trouble, and neither do I."

As Abby and Donny walked down the alleyway to retrieve John's car, she asked, "Do you really think we can trust him?"

"I think so. He knows we mean business, and he knows we've got his address. He'll play nice."

"I guess we don't have any choice, do we?"

"Nope." Donny unlocked the car and opened the passenger door for Abby. "Come on."

*   *   *

John sat behind his desk waiting for Mark to come through the door. He tried to act casual and sip his coffee, but the full weight of what was happening had started to settle on him and he was nervous. If Rosso was really dead, he had some phone calls to make. Specifically to the feds, and to his wife to tell her it was time.

For now, he had to concentrate on the task at hand.

Mark walked through the door, gut first as usual, his slicked-back hair almost dripping with product. He attracted attention wherever he was, mostly because his labored breathing made it appear as if he had just completed a marathon even though he had only walked the ten feet from the car to the front door.

"Hey, John."

"How are you, Mark?"

Mark looked around suspiciously. "Fine. Listen, I don't wanna be rude, but let's make this quick. I wanna get outta town, ya know?"

John walked over to a large cabinet and opened it to reveal an ancient safe. With a couple flicks of the wrist, he dialed the combination.

"What happened to your hand?"

John looked down. "It's stupid. I was trying to get the pit out of an avocado and slipped. Cut my hand wide open."

"That's what you get for eatin' fuckin' vegetables." Mark's glottal laugh seemed to squeeze itself out exclusively through the folds where his neck should have been.

John grabbed a medium-sized yellow envelope with exactly $9,900 in it and handed it to Mark, who slid it into his briefcase and nodded to John.

"Nice doin' business with ya, Johnny. Take it easy."

"The pleasure was mine," John said to his back as Mark waddled out the door.

When he was alone, John locked the door, emptied the rest of the cash from the safe into his briefcase, and slid out the back door where he walked a block over and hailed a cab.

"Where to?" the cabby asked.

"Evanston, as fast as you can get me there."

13

ABBY AND DONNY FOLLOWED the black, late-model Lincoln on I-90. They were a few hours outside of the city, traveling through a section of pavement in dire need of resurfacing. The suspension on the Lincoln in front of them was being subjected to an endurance test by the combined 650-pound weight of its passengers.

Had Eric been with her, he no doubt would have recognized the two men in the Lincoln as the ones who had tried—unsuccessfully—to kidnap him at the airport, though somehow they had become even larger.

After the first uneventful thirty minutes, Abby had mercifully fallen asleep, waking up a few hours later as refreshed as one could be in such a situation. Not entirely sure why, after stretching and cracking her neck, she reached over and playfully scratched the back of Donny's head.

He shined his warm smile, and a flash of Eric crossed her mind. Abby instantly felt guilty and pulled her hand away.

"Why are you helping me, Donny? Why are you still here?"

He shook his head. "I used to think you had low self-esteem, but maybe it's that you have no self-esteem."

"What's that supposed to mean?"

"Really, Abby? Don't you know why I'm here? Don't you know how special you are? It killed me to see you in the condition you were in toward the end with Bryce before we got you out. The only thing that hurt worse than that was saying goodbye to you, thinking I might never see you again. You were going off to *Trial Island,* the memories of the last ten years of your life—including me—to be wiped clean. Then, from there to disappear off the grid. When you really disappeared, despite my own feelings, I was happy for you. But when you turned up dead, the day the news broke… man… I've never felt so low in my life."

Abby watched as he went quiet and shook his head.

"I felt like it was my fault, you know? Like I should have been there for you. I felt so fucking helpless. And now?" He gestured to her sitting next to him. "The second I saw you at Rosso's all those feelings just came rushing back. So, to ask me why I'm helping you?" He quietly shook his head again, thinking a moment before his tone took a harsh change. "I didn't think. I just acted. It was what I was compelled to do. So here we are."

They sat quiet, letting his words hang in the air. Abby couldn't tell if he was angry with her or the situation. Either way, it hurt. She didn't want to pull him in, to hurt him, to put him in danger like she did Eric. She thought about asking him to pull over. She could get out and go on by herself, but as she mulled that over, she realized, for better or worse, they were tied to each other now because the men back at the house knew he had helped her.

There was so much more that Donny wanted to say. Behind his gruff façade, the conversation continued in his head. *To lose you AND the rest of my life at the same time—I would have gone crazy, so I stayed here. I thought about leaving a million times the week after you left, but where would I go? Montana, was it? I don't know anyone there, and I wasn't ready to start over. Part of me thought you might come back someday, or wished you would.*

Abby broke his interior monologue before long. "I'm sorry. I didn't mean to drag you into this. I had no idea you were even still around."

"Don't be. I made the decision to stay and to get involved."

"It's a lot. Trust me, I get it. *Trial Island* was our plan, though. I'm sorry you had to go through what you did, but you know that's not entirely my fault. Don't be mad at me for what we planned together."

"Sorry, I know," Donny said. "It's just… I know it was the right thing to do, I just didn't realize how hard it was going to be for me. Sorry, I should have said something before."

"No, no, I get it, and I needed to hear it. I honestly have no idea what you ever saw in me. I'm not the same Abby you knew a few years back."

"No? Are you sure about that?"

She chuckled. "Oh, I'm sure. Have you not been paying attention these past couple hours?"

"Sure, some things have changed. Physically, mentally, you're stronger; a fighter. Focused. Hell, that's probably an understatement. But you know, inside I think you're the same. We are who we are. Different traits might come out, but at our core, we're the people we've always been. That's my take on it anyway."

They were quiet a moment before Donny continued.

"You said you have no idea what I ever saw in you?"

"Yeah, I mean… what is it, honestly? There must be something to me I'm not seeing. You put your life on the line to get Ava and me out a couple years back, and you're doing it again. And Eric…" She stifled a tear at the thought.

Donny could see she was having some difficulty. "I didn't know him, Abby. Just what I saw on TV or read about him, but he seemed like a good guy. He saw something in you, too."

Abby shook her head. "He died for me. It was supposed to be me Bryce hit with the car. He pushed me out of the way at the last second."

"They didn't say that in the news."

"That's what happened, though. I should have been laying there dead on the lawn, not him."

Abby's heart wrenched at the thought of Eric, lying there, unable to move, willing to sacrifice himself for her. Then she heard Robert's voice. *Eric would not want you to spend your life in mourning. He chose for you to continue living, so if you want to honor his memory, that's what you have to do!*

She breathed deeply.

Donny went on. "He saw something in you Abby, same as me. Like I said, I didn't know him and I can't pretend to, but I can see why he felt that way about you." He glanced at her in the passenger seat, and their eyes met for a moment before he turned back to the road as the conversation continued in his head. *Those damned beautiful brown eyes get me every time. Something about the way you look at me makes me feel like I'm the only guy in the world.*

They rode in silence while Abby pondered the future beyond the next day. She and Donny couldn't possibly pick up where they left off. She wasn't even sure where they left off. They spent years hiding their feelings, not only from the outside world but each other. They both knew how they felt, but never acknowledged it for fear of putting the other in danger.

Was she ready to move on with her life? She had only been with Eric for a year, but had given herself to him so fully it felt like it had been a lifetime. It had also been the better part of a year since he had died, and that seemed like a lifetime, too. *Should I move on?* Robert was right—she had to keep living. That's what Eric would want. She knew the answer in her heart but wasn't ready to admit it aloud yet.

She couldn't deny she had feelings for Donny. So many times over her years with Bryce she had dreamt of running away with him. She looked at him, really looking at him, for the first time in a while. It wasn't just that he was attractive; though he filled out the standard-issue mob suit better than just about any other man she had met. His black sport coat hid arms and shoulders that would rival most professional quarterbacks. His dark eyes held an intensity that was intimidating, but when he let you in, she remembered a softness to them that made her weak in the knees. It had been two days since his face had seen a razor, but the stubble only served to make him look more rugged.

She had to admit it was a sexy look.

Beyond his appearance, though, he had been her rock through years of hard times and had put it all on the line to save her and Ava. Now here he was again, no questions asked, by her side, ready to save her daughter again.

Donny was truly a man. Bryce, Rosso, the whole lot of them, were boys. Boys who intimidated innocent people with guns and torture. Donny was a man who did what was right despite the consequences. She didn't know how he had made it so long in the organization. Despite his tough-guy exterior, he had a big heart. He may have gone back to the mob life before, but he couldn't now. Not that he wanted to. And not that there was much to go back to. Abby had seen to that.

She reached over and ran her hand down the length of his arm before finding his hand and giving it a squeeze. A silent *thank you* passed between them. He looked down at their hands, then back at the road. A barely detectable smirk crossed his lips just for a moment, but she saw it and gave him a little smile herself.

14

THE RIDE HAD BEEN uneventful to this point, but they were in the country now and it was getting harder and harder to stay unnoticed. It was late afternoon, and they had gone from the highway to an altogether deserted country road.

Donny stayed as far back as he could while managing to keep the Lincoln in sight, but there were only a couple of cars on the road aside from them at the moment. When they planned to follow Bryce's men back to him, they hadn't counted on being so exposed. They had been traveling this way for quite a while before deciding that the men in the Lincoln would have to be completely inept to not realize that they were being followed by the mid-level luxury car with Illinois tags.

Abby checked her .45 and .22, making sure she had spare magazines at the ready. Her knife, as always, was securely sheathed to her thigh. She still had a single flash-bang grenade on her belt; however, that would do them no good in the daylight and out in the open. She had no more quarter-sized explosive discs from Ace, and her canister had been lost in the shuffle somewhere at Rosso's though she still had her small Taser and a few zip ties.

She didn't intend to go with guns blazing, but these

were dangerous men and she wanted to be ready for whatever might come her way when they got made.

"When they pull over," Donny said, assuming that they have to at some point, "I'm going to continue on by and let them get behind us. Hopefully, I can find a spot to pull off the road and out of sight. When they go by us again, we'll start the tail again."

"You've done this before?" Abby asked.

"Once or twice," Donny said.

They didn't have to wait long. Minutes later, the Lincoln slowly pulled off to the side of the road and onto the shoulder.

As they were about to drive by Donny said, "You should duck, just in case they start shooting as we pass."

Abby gave him an "Are you serious?" look, and then said, "Not a chance. I want to get a good look at these guys."

"Just look straight ahead," Donny said. "Glance at them if you want, but we don't want them making you."

Abby did as she was instructed, confident that she wouldn't be recognized anyway. She glanced over at the stopped car, hand on her .45 with the safety off just in case. Fortunately, no one fired, and Abby and Donny continued by.

Had she continued to look at the driver and been able to read lips, she would have picked up on him saying,

"Holy shit, do you know who that was?"

Donny continued forward and around a bend in the road a couple hundred feet. Looking in the rearview mirror, he saw one of the men get out of the passenger side just before the Lincoln disappeared behind thick trees on the side of the road. "I'm going to pull over, but I don't think they're coming."

"Why not?"

"I just saw one of them get out of the car," he said as he pulled to the side of the road.

Abby jumped out. "Give me a couple minutes to head back and check it out."

"Are you nuts?"

"Just do it, OK? If I don't come back in five, come looking for me."

With that, Abby ran to the tree line, leaving Donny shaking his head in the car, watching her run away.

She followed the tree line until she reached the black Lincoln around the corner. Crouching low, she ducked into the trees and made her way slowly forward to get a closer look at the parked car.

The two men were both outside the vehicle, with driver leaning on the trunk with his forearms, pushing down the rear shocks to an impressive degree. He appeared to be watching the road ahead, waiting for someone to appear. The small gun in his meaty hand confirmed that they had indeed noticed they were being followed.

The other man stood on the grass next to the passenger side of the vehicle, holding up his phone and walking around staring at the screen, probably looking for service. As he started punching at the screen with his thumbs, Abby stepped forward to place herself near the edge of the trees, hoping to hear anything that might get said. When she did, she unintentionally rustled a patch of dry leaves that had probably been sitting there since last year, causing both men to look her way immediately.

"There she is!" cried the fat one behind the car. He raised his gun and fired in her direction, doing nothing but tearing bark from the trees around her.

The one with the phone stuffed it into his pocket and took out his gun, opening fire a second later.

Abby dropped to the ground, raised her weapon, and fired six quick rounds at the men. As the slugs crashed into the glass and sheet metal, it made a lot of noise but did no damage to her targets.

As the men dove for cover, Abby realized that all of the accuracy she had honed over the past several months was done with targets that didn't shoot back. The adrenaline rush she felt trying to dodge bullets while shooting was unlike anything she had felt before.

Just a short distance away, she heard the squeal of tires as Donny came speeding to her aid.

She didn't see him coming, but her targets did and turned their attention to Donny. The fat man behind the Lincoln repositioned himself more toward Abby's side of the car and started shooting at Donny as soon as the car came into sight.

Donny swerved as two bullets cracked his windshield and struck the passenger seat where Abby had been sitting just minutes before.

Abby took advantage of the distraction, raised her .45, stared carefully down the sight, and dropped the beast standing behind the car like a Costco-sized sack of potatoes with a single round to the side of his knee. His head smacked into the corner of the bumper on his way to the ground, and he didn't move from where he landed.

Donny sped toward the parked car, window down, gun drawn and firing. He hit the man with the phone with three rounds to the chest, sending him rolling down the hill toward Abby. By the time he came to rest, he was dead.

Donny's car slid to a halt on the gravelly shoulder behind the Lincoln, and he jumped out, running toward Abby. "Are you OK?"

"Yeah, I'm fine." She looked up and down the road, not seeing any cars coming. "Quick, search the car. See if we can figure out where they were going."

"Right."

Donny ran toward the car and began going through

the contents of the glove box, suddenly hearing moaning from behind him. He looked back to see Abby club the man on the ground with the butt of her gun.

"Holy shit, Abby! Didn't you kill him? I thought you shot him!"

A few seconds later, his hands and feet were zip-tied. "I shot him in the knee. Come help me drag him to the side of the car."

With a colossal effort, the two dragged him to the side of the car so that no one driving by could see him. They spent the next several minutes looking through the vehicle.

Abby backed out, frustrated. "Eventually someone is going to come along and see this. We've got to get out of here."

Donny was still in the car. "Nothing but a ton of empty take-out bags."

She walked over to the car and picked up one of the many discarded bags from the floor. She read the name of the restaurant aloud, "Buena Sera, Sunny Point, NY…" She peered at the floor in the back seat. "There have got to be twenty bags back there."

"Well, they're some big guys. I guess they must spend a lot of time there."

They looked at each other and had the same thought at the same time. A restaurant—one of the best places to launder money according to the accountant.

"Come on," Abby said running to their car.

Donny jumped in and they took off, kicking up gravel as they sped away.

The fat man who had rolled down the hill was quite dead thanks to Donny, though his phone wasn't. When it finally found a weak signal, it sent a terse message to Bryce:

BAD CELL SERVICE, CAN'T CALL. ABBY IS ALIVE AND FOLLOWING US. WHAT SHOULD WE DO?

15

BRYCE SNEERED as he read the message on his phone.

"Well, looks like Mommy is coming to get you after all," he announced to the empty room.

He was in his office at the back of Buena Sera, a restaurant Rosso bought as a place for Bryce to lay low and launder a little cash for the outfit. He didn't buy it outright, of course. That would have tipped off the feds. But it was his money that found its way through various accounts until it wound up in the pocket of one "Hunter Bryson", Bryce's new identity. Thus was born the finest Italian cuisine in Sunny Point, New York.

Out front stood a deck with outdoor seating for fifteen tables, which overlooked Lake Erie in the distance, a little less than half a mile down a gradually sloping avenue. Inside was a comfortable waiting area by the hostess stand, with a plush Oriental rug and several rich leather sofas. Off to the side sat a handsome dark wood bar, with half a dozen tables for diners to enjoy drinks and appetizers while they waited for their table.

Through the columned archway, guests found a finely decorated dining room with seating for another twenty tables. The dining room was unmistakably Italian while avoiding the tackiness that so often accompanied such a place.

The brick opening into the gourmet kitchen allowed guests to hear the chatter of the Italian-born chefs calling back and forth to one another, adding an additional layer of authenticity. Italian arias played quietly through the sound system in the ceiling in lieu of the Sinatra tunes that usually found their way into the background of so many Italian restaurants.

This was not a restaurant that anyone would venture to guess was tied directly to the mob. If guests didn't know better, they would think they were sitting in Tuscany.

Bryce loved running the place. It was an unbelievable gig. Business was great, and that gave him a certain sense of pride, but it didn't matter in the grand scheme of things. With the regular influx of cash from Chicago, the place would meet its bills and obligations regardless.

He had been a terrible student, especially with math, which gave him pause when Rosso brought up laundering. However, it was such an easy gig that his problems with numbers didn't matter. Each week a large batch of receipts were forged to explain the money coming in. The cash went to the bank, where it was then redistributed to his vendors for products never received. The vendors, of course, were also owned by companies tied to the family, and the money continued along until it came out clean a few more stops down the road, placed into purely legitimate business ventures the family had interests in.

Directly under Bryce's back office, in a small and secluded room in the basement, Ava slept for the first time in days. She sat upright, tied to a wooden chair, mouth gagged and duct-taped. After being awake for several days, however, her body had to shut down and recharge.

There was only one way into the room: the bookcase behind Bryce's desk was anchored to the wall on the left by a hinge, and had a small caster under the right so it swung out like a door, revealing a small, spiral staircase just large enough to walk down. The staircase had been a forgettable and inconvenient way to access the basement and the food storage room below, but was a major selling point when Bryce walked the property the first time. It could be his safe room, or a place to keep his enemies.

After purchasing the property, Bryce walled off the corner of the basement entrance to the staircase, creating a narrow room that ran the length of the restaurant. It took up so little space and was so well integrated that not even someone familiar with the basement would realize it was there.

This is where he kept most of his weapons, his second set of books, and anything that linked back to his old life. This also currently included Ava, whom he snuck down there in the middle of the night when the restaurant was empty.

She was a scrappy one. Abby had obviously seen to it that Ava enrolled in some type of karate training. If there hadn't been three men against one little girl, she might have gotten away. Bryce believed Ava not only inherited her mother's diminutive stature, but also her spirit.

With his finances taken care of, Bryce had plenty of

time to dwell on the past. He had originally faked his death to draw Abby out. She knew his darkest secret—that he murdered Rosso's son, Nick. Now, he had to make sure she never told anyone. Even now with Rosso at death's door, his disloyalty to the family would not play well with the new regime.

His plan had worked. He drew her out and murdered her and that good ol' boy Eric. He stayed in hiding after that because the government still listed him as dead, and he saw no reason that that should keep him from enjoying a good life. No need to pop up on anyone's radar again.

A few months ago, however, he caught wind of an investigator out of Boston trying to get information on him. He had come to town trying to work the local snitches, saying he had reason to believe Bryce was alive. This did not sit well when word got back to Rosso, who demanded to know why anyone would be insinuating such things. Bryce assured Rosso there was nothing to worry about, but he knew better.

Two people outside the family knew Bryce was alive. One of them was tied up in his basement; the other was Abby. If someone were asking about him, then that someone was either Abby or someone on her behalf.

But Abby was dead. He had shot her himself. He saw the headlines the next day about her assassination at the hands of a mob hitman. He even attended her funeral, albeit sitting in the back in disguise.

The only thing he could figure was that billionaire daddy stand-in Robert somehow helped her manipulate the media. He decided there was one surefire way to find out if Abby was dead. First, kidnap Ava, done handily by a couple of his thugs in the middle of the night. Second, get the word to one of the snitches that he was alive and well up at Lake Erie, which was done this morning.

On the way to pick up the weekly drop from the accountant in the city, his guys stopped by a local coffee shop in the old neighborhood frequented by one of the snitches asking about Bryce. His men bellied their sizeable guts up to the counter a couple seats over from the snitch, and over some steak, eggs, and greasy hash browns, had an animated conversation that sounded more like old ladies gossiping than a couple of mobsters.

"Did you hear about Haydenson?"

"Who?"

"Bryce Haydenson. You know, the one that masterminded the bank robbery last year that got all those guys killed."

"Oh, yeah, yeah, I remember him. The feds buried his ass, too."

"That's the thing. They did, but I just heard from my buddy Ralphie that he's alive!"

"What?"

"Yeah. Word is Rosso's got him stashed in New York, living under the name Hunter Bryson."

"What the fuck kinda name is Hunter?"

"Tell me about it."

What Bryce hadn't foreseen was that the snitch would be ballsy enough to chat with his guys.

"Hey, I heard you guys talkin' about Rosso."

The two fat men turned to look at the wiry snitch. "Yeah, what of it?"

"I don't recognize you guys. Are you... ya know... in?"

"What the fuck is it to you?"

The snitch held his hands up, "Jeez, buddy, relax. I was just wonderin' if you heard."

"What's that?"

"The house got hit last night. Everyone's talkin' about it."

This got the attention of the obese thugs, enough that one of them actually stopped cramming sausages down his throat for a split second. "What are you talking about, got hit?"

The snitch leaned in, greedy for the attention, and whispered. "Got *hit* hit. Bloodbath. Word is even Rosso was taken out. One of the security guys, I forget his name, he was left half for dead and rung up one of Monte's guys for help. By the time Monte's crew got there, it was over. I heard cops were crawling all over the place."

The second man wiped bacon grease from the corner

of his mouth before using his toast to soak up the gristle from the steak. "You serious? How many guys got hit?"

"I dunno." The snitch thought a minute. "I heard they were having some sort of meetin', so coulda been a bunch of guys."

The man grunted then shoved the last of his greased toast into his face before throwing down a twenty and mumbling. "Thanks" through his bread-stuffed piehole.

His twin in corpulence gave up on his fork and used his hand to shovel the last of his eggs down his gullet. He then followed his portly associate out the front door, where they called Bryce to deliver the news.

He told them to check in with the moneyman to see if they're still on. In the meantime, he'd get in touch with one of his people. Two people in the family knew about him: Rosso and Monte. That circle expanded to three a couple weeks ago when Rosso told Franco. Calls to all three went straight to voicemail, which gave him pause.

Now with the text from his man saying Abby was following them, Bryce had the crazy thought that maybe Abby had something to do with the Rosso rumor? He dismissed the idea as absurd. What purpose would it serve?

Bryce was thrilled that she had showed up on the radar so quickly, though. He sent a message back to his man.

LET HER FOLLOW YOU. DON'T LET ON THAT YOU KNOW. LET ME KNOW WHEN YOU'RE CLOSE.

*   *   *

"I can't believe you actually called at a normal hour," JJ said, smiling through the receiver.

"Ha ha," Abby said dryly.

"Seriously. I don't remember the last time we spoke when the sun was up."

"Are you done?"

"I am, and I'm actually really glad you called. I've got some info for you."

"And I've got some for you, too," she said. "You first."

"One of my sources dropped a dime this morning. He heard that Bryce is alive and that Rosso has got him stashed in New York living under the name Hunter Bryson. I did some digging and found one guy who appeared out of nowhere a few months after Bryce faked his death. He's running an Italian restaurant a little more than an hour south of Buffalo named…"

"Buena Sera," Abby said.

"Yeah. How did you know?"

"I've been doing some digging of my own," Abby said coyly.

"Yeah, I saw the news this morning. It wasn't much, but they said there were reports of a raid on Rosso's estate. Total bloodbath was what they said. Looks like you and that old friend of yours did some serious damage. You're lucky you didn't get yourself killed just walking into a place like that."

She scoffed. "I didn't just walk in. You taught me better than that. I had a plan. And it was just me. I met up with my friend after." She looked at Donny, whose eyes were glued to the road.

"Well, the odds are in your favor again. I'm going to head to the airport. I can catch a flight from Boston to Buffalo and be there in three or four hours."

Abby looked at the speedometer. Donny kept his speed at a steady 65 mph. The last thing they wanted to do was get pulled over for a speeding violation with a carload of weapons and not a genuine ID between them. She did some quick math in her head. "That puts you a few hours late to the party. We're on our way there now. Should be there within the hour."

He sighed on the other end of the line. "I suppose I can't talk you into waiting until I get there?"

"Not a chance. But do you have anything helpful you can give me now?"

"You got something to write with? I'll give you the home address I dug up."

As Abby wrote the address, she almost chuckled. "What are the chances one of your sources finally comes through with some info today?"

"You know it's not a coincidence."

"Of course I know that. He snatched Ava and left some breadcrumbs to lead me to him. He's setting me up."

"That's why I'd like you to wait for me. Let me get out there. You're skilled, but having an extra pair of eyes and some firepower can only help you get Ava back and keep you alive."

"I can't sit on my hands knowing that my little girl is with that maniac."

"I understand. Just know he's waiting for you. He'll be ready."

"That's where you're wrong. He can't be ready. He thinks he knows what's coming. He doesn't."

"Be safe." JJ clicked off the line, knowing what Abby said was true. Still, he worried about her. Anyone can get lucky, and it would be just plain stupid to walk into a trap she knows Bryce has set. Stubborn as she was, there would be no talking her out of doing exactly that if she thought it would get Ava back.

16

AGENT EDDIE VINES WAS finishing a late lunch when his phone lit up on the table in front of him. He recognized the number as Randy, his primary source inside the Rosso compound. He had been a huge acquisition for Vines. Randy was on Rosso's security detail and spent his days watching the video feeds at the estate. He knew the details of every move Rosso was making.

Eddie punched the phone with a thick finger. "Randy, to what do I owe the pleasure of hearing from my favorite scumbag?"

"Hmmph, Roos…"

Eddie pulled the phone away from his ear to see that he had a clear and secure connection. "What the hell? I can't understand you. Say again?"

Slowly a slurred voice came from the other end of the line, "Rooossso… iss… deead."

Eddie's eyes lit up as he bolted upright in his seat. "Randy, say that again, I can hardly understand you. It sounds like you've got marbles in your mouth."

After a pained few seconds, Randy quietly replied, "Rosso is dead, and my jaw fucking hurts."

Eddie's mind began racing. *Rosso is dead.* This was a phone call he had waited on for years, and for the past few weeks sat on pins and needles expecting it any moment. His plan, years in the making, was about to swing into action. He stood on the precipice of greatness. He had several informants and snitches lined up. When factions loyal to Monte and Franco started fighting, he would take the family down like dominoes as one turned on the next.

"This is great. This is better than great. What's the word on Monte and Franco? How fast is this going to get ugly? I've got agents, warrants, and subpoenas ready to go."

Silence.

"Randy, talk to me."

"They're both dead."

"What are you talking about? Who is both dead?" Eddie's mind was racing ahead, trying to make the connection. *Shit, if Rosso and Franco are both dead, Monte is going to wrap the family up tight, and I'll never get any cooperation. Shit. Shit. Shit.*

"Monte and Franco. They're dead."

"What? I thought you said Rosso was dead."

"I did. So are Monte and Franco."

"What the fuck are you talking about? You're speakin' nonsense here. And what the fuck is wrong with your voice?"

He sighed and spoke slowly, in pain. "Last night, Rosso had a meeting with all the captains."

"You're supposed to let me know when this shit goes down."

"It was last-minute, and I'm lettin' you know now, OK? You gonna let me talk?"

Vines was silent, trying to quiet his mind from playing through a million different scenarios. He needed to concentrate on what Randy was saying.

"OK," Randy said, "so Rosso's giving them his final instructions. Work everything out; keep the good things goin', right? So everyone's having coffee or whatever, and next thing you know, we get fuckin' attacked."

"By who? Another family?"

"One girl. One fuckin' girl. You'd think there was twenty of her, though. It was crazy. Fuckin' explosions, guns blazin'. Kicked the shit outta me. Cracked my jaw with her boot or something, I dunno. Knocked me out, I guess. I wake up and the place is swarming with cops slapping cuffs on everyone. Kept me in the tank overnight, but let me go this mornin'. Told me not to go far. They'd need me for questioning."

"What about the girl? Did they get her, too?"

"No. I been diggin' a little. Monte's guys got here about ten minutes before the cops. A few of them grabbed her and were taking her down to off her, ya know, but they found the car wrecked on the side of the road. Two of the guys were still in the wreck, but one of the guys and the chick were gone."

Agent Vines was in a state of shock. He was hearing everything Randy was saying, but it just wasn't sinking in. "This doesn't change anything, Randy. The dominoes will fall. You stay put, and I'll get you out when the time is right."

"What are you talkin' about? What dominoes? They're all dead. The cops already got the two surviving captains, shot in the ass or something, I dunno. Who are you putting away? A bunch of low-level guys like me for some petty shit? Screw that."

Vines let that sink in a moment. Randy was right. With Rosso, Franco, and Monte dead, who was he putting away? He could claim jurisdiction and take the remaining captains, but for what? They were small potatoes compared to the ones who were dead. Millions in laundered money, racketeering charges, his dream of shutting down the family—that all came from the top down and someone cut off the head.

"Who, Randy? You said it was one girl? Who was she?"

"You remember Bryce Haydenson?"

"Yeah, piece of shit," Eddie cursed, remembering the bank job. His superiors silenced his conviction that Bryce was still alive and out there.

"Couple of the guys said it was his wife or somethin', I

dunno, I didn't get it. I thought she got killed."

"Yeah, she died last year, killed by a mob guy. They said it was a hit."

"Yeah, yeah, I remember that. I never did hear nothin' about that hit."

"No one did, Randy. You think you're my only guy on the inside? I've got half a dozen of you, and not one of you worthless pricks ever heard shit about anyone putting a hit out on that little bitch."

"Hey, no need for name callin', Eddie."

Eddie seethed. "Fuck you."

"Fuck you!" Randy shot back. "I've been feeding you info for over a year now. You better make good and get me the fuck out of here."

Eddie tried his best not to let his rage boil over. "You keep your ears open and your mouth shut. Call me with anything you get, you understand?"

"Fine." Randy ended the call.

Vines' blood was boiling. It never made sense that he couldn't get any info on the supposed hit on her. That would have been huge if he had broken that case. Hell, he would have retired. He had six good informants and not one of them ever got a whiff of anything. If the order came direct from Rosso, it would have been over their heads, but that was so unlikely. Why would he give a shit about her?

ESCAPE
Dead End

But Bryce was another story. What if he were alive? What if he was trying to keep her quiet about something, and that's why she disappeared in the first place? What if he tried to have her killed, or Rosso did, and this is how she got her revenge?

None of it made sense. Eddie's mind was swirling in a thousand different directions, and he had to make it stop. Taking down the Rossos was going to be his crowning achievement; his ticket to a better life. Some pint-sized bitch just came in and flushed that all down the drain.

He rubbed his temples and closed his eyes. *What do I know for sure? I know some chick laid waste to the Rosso place and killed everyone at the top. I know that the guys left behind are saying it was this Abby girl. What I don't know is her motivation, but it has to be tied to Bryce.*

Agent Eddie Vines opened his eyes and looked ahead, focused. He had to follow his hunch that Bryce was alive and find him.

If I find him, I'll find the girl.

Maybe he wouldn't be the man who took down the Rossos, but he could still be a huge part of this story. Finding Abby would put him in the national spotlight even faster.

Agent Vines grabbed his gun and badge from the top drawer of his desk and took off running.

*   *   *

For the past hour or so, since they had taken care of

Bryce's thugs on the side of the highway, Donny had watched Abby nervously play with the handle of her knife while she stared blankly out the window.

"Ava must be getting big," Donny said, breaking the long silence.

"She is." Abby continued to stare ahead.

After glancing her way several times with no reaction, he continued. "What's going on?"

Abby turned to look at him blankly.

"Up here," Donny tapped his temple. "What's going on in there, Abby?"

"Thinking, that's all."

Abby didn't seem to be eager for conversation, but Donny had grown tired of the silence. More importantly, he had been thinking about what Abby had said; that he didn't know who she really was and that concerned him. He thought he knew what made her tick, but how much had she changed since they parted ways two years ago?

"Me, too," Donny said. "I've got a lot going on upstairs, you know?"

"Oh, yeah? Like what?"

"Oh, you know. The usual. What's on my grocery list, should I get an oil change, oh... and the houseful of dead bodies we left behind, not to mention the injured men we left strewn on the side of the road. Is that what you're thinking about?"

Abby smiled a bit. "Are you asking if I feel bad?"

"Do you? I mean, taking someone's life, that's not an everyday thing. Not for me anyway. I mean, I have before, but I'm not proud of it. That fat guy behind the car was my first in a hell of a long time."

"I suppose I do, but Monte deserved what he got. He was scum. He did all sorts of reprehensible things to innocent people… to me." She cringed, but quickly shook off the thought. "I'm sure he's probably got family or someone who will miss him. Maybe I feel bad for causing them some grief. It's not how I drew it up, but he's dead. Do I feel bad that he's done murdering, kidnapping, and intimidating innocent people? Hell no."

"Fair enough," Donny conceded.

They rode silently for a bit longer before Donny spoke again. "Water always finds its level."

Abby looked at him for a beat. "What's that?"

"It's an expression I heard once. I don't really know what it's supposed to mean. I guess sometimes there's way too much water, the seas are rough, or the riverbanks are overflowing. Sometimes there's not enough and you've got a drought and a whole bunch of dead crops. But water always finds its level. It always gets back to normal."

"I'm not sure that makes sense."

"Maybe it doesn't, but that's the sense I made out of it

anyway. My point is, where is your level?"

"What do you mean?"

"Your level. Your normal. What are you trying to get back to? What's a normal life for you? I mean, life sucked for quite a while with Bryce. From what I gather, it sucked for a few years before that, too, and since we've parted ways, it hasn't been all rainbows and puppies either. So what's your normal? Your end game? What are you getting back to?"

Abby just stared for a while, her light brown eyes glassing over before she let out a long sigh. "Well, shit, Donny, you sure do know how to sweet talk a girl."

"I'm sorry. I'm not trying to kick you when you're down. I'm just trying to figure out what's making you tick? I'm putting it all on the line for you, and you're saying I hardly know you anymore, so fill me in."

Abby nodded. "Well... you're right. What's normal? Things have sucked for a while I guess. Since my parents died, I got involved with Rick, the drugs, stripping, Bryce... I guess that's a decade I'd rather forget."

Donny smiled. "You did forget it, remember? We had this same conversation before, right before you went on the island."

Abby agreed. She would have given anything to forget all of the hurt, and Donny had found a way. *Trial Island* was predicated on the fact that no one knew they were on a television show. Abby still had the implant that allowed them to wipe clean the ten years between the time the show was announced and when she was on it, though when they deactivated it, all of the memories and hurt came back.

Donny asked, "You told me—swore to me—that you would not have your memory restored, and that you would live out the rest of your life having forgotten all the pain. What happened?"

"I tried, but I couldn't. If Bryce hadn't shown up and tried to kill me as soon as I got off the island, I probably could have, or at least would have had a better shot. Even after I got away and was living in peace, I always found myself wondering about him. Who was he and why would he do something like that? Trust me, I was living an amazing life after the island. Eric and I had a little villa on the beach on some remote island you've never heard of. It was such a simple and beautiful life. But Bryce was always in the back of my mind.

"When I heard that he died, instead of feeling like I was finally safe, I got a feeling that I could finally go back. It's hard to explain, but it was like I knew Ava was out there, like she was calling to me. When Bryce faked his death, he did it to draw me out. I knew his deepest secret, one that would ruin him, and he had to make sure I would never talk. It worked, as you know. I figured I'd finally be safe with him thinking he had killed me, but obviously he didn't buy it, and well... here I am."

"So what's the plan? You and Ava ride off into the sunset?"

"Something like that. But I've got to end this first, that's for sure. No more games; no more playing dead; no more looking over my shoulder."

"I believe you. I'm just a little worried about your state of mind. Killing your husband, the father of your child… do you wonder what that will do to you?"

Abby laughed. "It can't be any worse than what him being alive does to me. No fucking way. I'm the judge and jury on this one. I've got no moral issue with that. Either Bryce or I will be dead before sunrise tomorrow. God willing, it's him, and Ava and I will disappear for good this time."

Donny shook his head, "I believe you, Abby, I really do."

17

EDDIE VINES FOUND himself walking down a darkened alleyway between two old brick buildings in what Rosso's men would have lovingly referred to as the old neighborhood. Both trash and homeless people littered the corners of the alley. Despite being a sunny afternoon, the alley remained cool and dark, given that the sun's rays only penetrated it for an hour or so a day when it was directly overhead.

As he strode toward a black door at the end of the shaft, he thought about his predicament. He needed information. He needed to find Bryce. Unfortunately, Randy knew nothing more. He was forced to go after some even lower-level guys in hopes of getting some usable information. He didn't expect anyone outside Rosso's inner circle to know where Bryce was, but he had to start somewhere.

Vines turned the knob and gave the door a push, but it stuck about six inches in. He pushed a little more and finally moved it enough to let him enter the dark hallway. When he got to the other side, he saw a woman lying down, or more likely passed out, behind the door.

For a moment, he thought about checking for a pulse, then decided he was just plain tired and didn't give a shit, so he made his way up the creaky stairs. There was a bit more light when he reached the hallway, as the sun shone in as best it could through the dirt and grime caked on the window at the far end. Several other bodies, either passed out or sleeping, littered the passage as he made his way down to door 26.

He tested the knob. Finding it locked, he pounded on the door with his closed fist.

Nothing.

He pounded again. "Lucky, I know you're in there. Come out."

A skittish voice came from behind the door. "Who is it?"

"It's Vines. Now open the fuckin' door before I break it down."

Silence.

"Lucky?"

"What do you want?" the voice came again.

Vines raised his voice. "I want you to open the door, or so help me I'll break it down, and then you're next."

He smiled as he heard the deadbolt latch click and the door cracked open to reveal the gaunt face of the most nervous little man Vines had ever met.

"Can I come in? I just wanna talk."

Lucky tried to look up and down the hall through the

crack in the door. "You alone?"

"I'm alone."

"OK, come on in." He closed the door, and Vines heard him slide the chain from its lock, then reopen it. "Just for a minute, OK?"

As Vines walked in, he took in the unmistakable smell of crack cocaine. It was a delightful bouquet that he would describe as the perfect blend of rancid cat pee, burnt plastic, and spicy Indian food. It wasn't fresh, so he figured Lucky probably hadn't hit it since that morning, but the smell lingered.

Lucky watched, nervously chewing on the ends of his fingers, as Vines strode around the apartment. Trash filled the corners of the sparse room. A dilapidated coffee table and an old, ripped couch that doubled as Lucky's bed filled the space in the middle. Ashtrays were strewn about, each overflowing with cigarette butts.

"Nice place you've got here," Vines said with a smile.

Lucky wasn't "in" the family, but he knew people. He was a dealer, or rather a distributor that other dealers reported to. He reported to Monte's crew and was compensated well enough, or would have been if he hadn't been so into his own product. He smoked almost every dollar he made for the family, and often wound up owing Monte money at the end for extra product. But he was a connection to a certain class of people that Monte was selling to, so the relationship worked.

Fortunately for Vines, Lucky had no other way to make extra bank when he needed to, so in stepped the Bureau, and he was kept as an informant. Since then, Vines had kept him clean enough to be useful, but not so much as to arouse suspicion.

"I need to find someone Lucky."

"Who's that?" His eyes fluttered nervously around the room, unable to focus on Vines or any one thing really.

"A guy you probably haven't seen in a while. You used to work with him. His name is Bryce. He was Monte's boss awhile back."

"Bryce, Bryce, Bryce…" Lucky looked around the room as if checking to see if Bryce was there with them. "Nope, nope, no Bryce."

"Think hard," Vines said, stepping closer. "Tall guy, blue eyes, blond hair… real mean sonofabitch."

Lucky silently mouthed "Bryce" a few more times before his eyes finally focused on Vines. "Yeah, yeah, I remember him. Robbed a bank. The feds shot his ass, don't you know that? He's dead. That's how Monte got his spot."

"That's the story anyway," Vines said, looking around. He walked over to a pile of unopened mail and flipped through it while Lucky watched, eyes darting around the room again. "You hear about what went down last night?"

Lucky's eyes stopped, and he stared straight at Vines. "So you did?"

"That's some messed up shit, Vines," Lucky said, shaking his head.

"Who pulled the hit? You know? You hear?"

Lucky shook his head. "No, I ain't heard nothing."

Vines studied his informant thoughtfully as he slowly walked up to him. "I believe you. You wouldn't know. That's OK, though. I know."

"You do?"

"Well, I got some good information, and I'm putting the pieces together. There's one piece that I really need, though, and you're going to help me get it." As Vines stared down Lucky from just a foot away, he watched his informant uncomfortably glance around the room.

"I ain't heard nothin', Vines. I told you."

"Sure, not about last night, but I'm thinking about your old boss, Bryce."

"I told you he's dead. Feds got him."

Vines advanced on Lucky as the snitch backed away. "I'm going to level with you, Lucky. I'm going to tell you something that not many people know because I need your help and dammit, you're going to help me."

Lucky backed himself to a wall. He had no choice but to stand there as Vines continued.

"I've got a guy inside Rosso's compound…"

"Then ask him. He'd know more than me."

"Shut your mouth and listen up. I did ask him, and he says he knows who pulled the hit. The problem is, if I'm going to get my hands on this person, I need to find Bryce. Does that make sense to you?"

Lucky shook his head. "No, it don't make no sense. Bryce is dead, man. A couple years now at least."

Vines punched the wall just to the side of Lucky's head, "He's not! He's not dead! I was at the bank myself, and he was not there, so stop telling me he's dead."

"OK, OK, he ain't dead, but I don't know where to find him, man, I swear it."

"I wouldn't think that you would know. Not some low-level, drug-dealing prick like you. But he was tight with Monte, and you're in with his crew."

Vines violently shoved his hand into Lucky's pocket and came out with a beat-up cell phone, "Make some calls and get me a meeting."

Lucky stared at the phone. "I can't, man, I can't."

"Oh, you can and you will, you piece of shit." Vines slapped him hard across the face.

Lucky withdrew like a scared dog. "I'm serious, man, I can't. My guy, my contact, some fat prick named Billy, got it last night, too. He's messed up real bad. In the hospital and everything. I got nothing else, man."

Vines was incensed, his blood boiling. He had to find Bryce in order to find Abby, and Lucky's stubbornness was standing in his way. "Now you're feeding me bullshit, and you know how much I hate bullshit."

"Come on, man," Lucky begged, but to no avail.

Vines grabbed him by the shirt and slammed his back into the wall. "Stop lying to me! There were eight guys taken in last night, five more dead, and not one of them was a fat prick named Billy. Now make the call and set up a meeting."

"I can't, I swear…"

Vines backhanded the snitch. "Stop saying that and set it up!"

"I swear, man, he wasn't at the house. They found him in the back seat of a car down by the landfill. Car was wrecked. Him and another guy were totally messed up. I swear, man. Call the cops—they'll tell you!"

Vines stared hard into Lucky's eyes.

Shit… he's telling the truth.

He cocked his fist, ready to deck the skinny bastard. He just felt like he needed to hit something. Lucky flinched and turned his head, opening one eye when the impact never came.

"Who else do you know? Bryce is out there, and I've got to find him."

"I really don't know, man. I swear I don't. I thought he was dead. You say he's still alive, and I believe you, but I ain't never heard that before."

Vines let go and threw up his hands, cursing under his breath. He needed to get into the family, and Lucky was the best shot he had. He paced the room, willing himself to think of alternatives as Lucky nervously watched.

Suddenly, Vines spun around to face him. "The money. Who do you make your drops to?"

"They always went to Billy, man. He handled everything. I didn't know anyone else."

Dammit... Vines continued pacing, his mind racing to make a connection. *Money, money, money...* There was something he was forgetting.

"Did you ever interact with anyone else besides Billy?"

"Never, man. He always did the delivery Monday afternoon, then picked up the cash Sunday night. He'd get pissed if I didn't have the cash for him Sundays. Said they were running a business and he had to deposit shit on time, something like that."

That's when it hit Vines. The money! The money would lead him to Bryce.

Vines mumbled a "Thanks" to Lucky and flew out the door.

If Bryce is alive, he's still paying into the family. Follow the money, and I'll find Bryce at the end of the rainbow.

*   *   *

"Where would you go?" Donny asked, thankful the long car ride allowed him to get reacquainted with Abby.

She looked at him for a long time, an internal debate raging about whether to tell him the truth. *Can I trust him? Should I trust him?* He had willingly jumped to her aid back at Rosso's and hadn't left her side since. She would be dead without him today. Those two thugs on the side of the road would have killed her.

Of course, I can trust him.

But is it good for him if I trust him? He was a wildcard she hadn't planned on, and he could be taken out just for helping her. Her conflicted feelings led to a long silence that made Donny uncomfortable.

"Abby?"

Coming out of her trance she looked at him. "Yeah?"

He laughed. "Did you hear me? I asked where would you go?"

She sighed. "Someplace far, far away from here. Someplace quiet and simple. Someplace where no one knows who I am. Someplace so far away no one would come looking for me."

"Rosso's dead, Abby. The whole organization is falling apart after the damage you did last night. Once Bryce is out of the picture, who do you have to hide from?"

"If only it were that simple. I'm one of the most recognizable people in the Northern Hemisphere, but I want nothing to do with it. I want a quiet life. I think about growing up in my parent's quiet neighborhood in their little house, and that's all I want for Ava. You asked earlier what I was trying to get back to. I guess that's it. That's my normal. That's what I want. To live a quiet and peaceful life with my little girl. I know a place where I can do that, and I intend to get back there."

Donny smiled. "That sounds great. It sounds like what everyone wants. You know, after all of this," he waved around with a free hand, "I'm going to be in the market for a new place to call home myself. I can't go back to my life, not now, not after what I've done. I'm not saying 'Take me with you', or anything, but someday, maybe you'll have room for an old friend."

"Maybe, Donny. Maybe." Abby continued staring out the front window, her mind trying to push all of these complicated thoughts to the side so that she could concentrate on the only thing that mattered: finding Bryce and ending him.

*   *   *

After fruitlessly pounding on the front door for a good ten minutes, Vines broke into the rear door of Venzo's Accounting Firm, CPA, only to find the office completely abandoned. The smell of burnt coffee lingered in the air, but the accountant was nowhere to be found.

Vines called the Bureau to find out that Venzo had contacted his handlers a few hours ago and was at home waiting for further instructions. Vines quickly routed himself to the Venzo household and found himself talking to Mrs. Venzo through a closed front door.

"How do I know you are who you say you are?" she asked.

"If you'll open the door, you can see my badge, ma'am. I assure you, I'm a federal agent, and I urgently need to speak with your husband."

"I'm not opening the door. I'm calling the police."

Vines didn't care about the authorities, but getting the local cops involved was going to delay things, and he was in no mood for delays.

"No need to do that, ma'am. I'm going to slide my badge and ID through the mail slot, OK?"

Absent a response, Vines did just that. A tug from the other side confirmed that she had grabbed his identification and was looking it over, probably with Venzo standing right next to her.

That was confirmed a moment later when a man's voice spoke up from the other side of the door. "What's this about? You're not the agent who's supposed to debrief me."

"No, I am not. John, I'm here about what happened last night. I'm trying to put together the pieces. Time is crucial, and if you'll let me in we can discuss it further. Call your handler if you want to. They'll confirm why I'm here."

After ten minutes of sitting on a rocking chair on the front porch waiting for Venzo to do just that, the door opened and the accountant appeared. "Sorry about that," he said, extending his hand. "Come on in."

Vines looked around the home, his eyes settling on several boxes and a half-dozen suitcases sitting in the small foyer. "You're not wasting any time, huh?"

"No," John said with a smile. "We're ready to move on. I don't know how quickly these things work, but we're hoping to get on with the whole witness protection thing sooner rather than later. A new start, a new life, you know?"

"Good for you," Vines clapped him on the shoulder. "Listen, Mr. Venzo…"

"John is fine. Please call me John."

"Thanks, John. Now listen, I'm trying to follow up on a lead about what happened last night, and I need your help."

John looked confused. "My help? I wasn't there. I'm not sure how much help I can be."

"I know you weren't there, but I spoke with someone who was…"

"Wait. Who?"

Vines smiled. "That's going to remain my secret. No offense, John, but I'm not here to brief you on what went down last night. It doesn't really concern you. What does concern you is helping us out right now. Can you do that for me John? Can you help me out?"

John nodded.

"Good. So my contact ID'd the assassin, but I need your help tracking her down."

Her. John swallowed hard and looked down. *So it's true. The little bitch at the office pulled the hit.*

"I'm not sure what I can do for you. I don't know anything," John said, still looking at the floor.

Vines studied him. His body language said it all. John knew something, and Vines was going to get it out of him. "What happened to your hand, John?"

He looked up. "Oh, this? I sliced it trying to get the pit out of an avocado, stupid thing."

"Looks fresh," Vines said. "Happen this morning?"

"Yeah."

"If you don't mind me saying so, John, you don't look like the kind of guy who has an avocado for breakfast. You seem more of a bagel guy like me." Vines patted his own his spare tire, nodding at John's.

"You know, trying to start eating healthier." John chuckled awkwardly.

"Uh huh." Vines stared at him for an uncomfortable moment before continuing. "So this woman, she's not really tied to the family, but she did have ties with a Bryce

Haydenson. Does that name ring a bell?"

John raised a brow. "I haven't heard that name in a while." Of course, he'd just heard it that morning, but why tell the FBI. They wouldn't kill him for talking. "Didn't he get killed a year or two ago?"

Vines chuckled a bit under his breath. "It would seem that way. At least that's what everyone seems to think. See, the thing is, John, I'm not convinced he's dead. In fact, I'm pretty convinced that he's alive, and if I can find him, I can find the hitter from last night."

"Well, good luck with that, but I can't help you. If there's nothing else?" John indicated the door.

Vines didn't budge. "I'm glad we could play nice for a bit, but it's time to cut the bullshit." Vines grabbed John's hand and pressed hard on the wound, causing him to let out a painful yelp.

His wife came running from the kitchen and gasped when she saw Vines with her husband's hand in his grip. "What are you doing?"

Without taking his eyes from John, he pointed at the couch and commanded her to sit down.

"I will not," she said, advancing on him. "Let go of his hand! You're hurting him!"

Vines squeezed John's hand even harder, causing his knees to buckle. He then pulled out his gun out with his other hand, pointing it at Venzo's wife. "Sit. Down. Please."

Terrified, she backed away and sat on the couch.

Satisfied, Vines turned his attention back to John. "Are you going to stop bullshitting me?"

John nodded his head. "Yes. Please, don't hurt her."

When Vines released his hand, John gasped and rubbed it for a bit, wincing in immense pain.

Studying the bandaged hand, Vines spoke. "How did that really happen?"

John looked at his wife, who had the same question on her face also. He sighed, "This woman came to my office this morning. Freakin' nailed me to the wall with her knife. Said she'd kill my family if I ever told anyone she was there. I figure, what the hell now, though, right? We're going into protection. It's not like she'll be able to find us."

Vines stared at him. "So she was there? Abby? In the flesh?"

John hesitated for a moment and swallowed hard before conceding. "Yeah, her and some guy... Danny... Johnny... Mikey... I can't remember his name. Everyone's got a nickname that ends with a fucking Y. I've met him once or twice. He was helping her. They were going to look for Haydenson and persuaded some information out of me."

Vines was practically giddy. "That's the best thing I've heard today, John. Where do I find that piece of shit?"

John sighed and brought Vines into his home office,

where he unlocked a large safe hidden behind a painting. As John started opening it, Vines stopped him.

"Hold up." Vines physically moved John to the side and opened the safe himself. Quickly looking over the contents, and satisfied there wasn't a gun or other weapon John would turn on him, he gestured to the accountant. "Go ahead."

After scanning through a couple dozen composition books, he produced one labeled *Buena Sera*. "This will be the property of the federal government soon enough."

Vines flipped open book. On the first page, in neat handwriting, was an address in Sunny Point, New York. "What's this?"

"It's a restaurant. Italian place. It's Haydenson's cover. That's where you'll find him."

Vines ripped the phone from his belt and punched in the address. It looked to be about an hour or so southwest of Buffalo, along Lake Erie. He could be there in a couple of hours if he flew to Buffalo and drove from there. "What time did you see Abby this morning?"

"They were there when I got in at eight."

"And what time did they leave?"

"I'm not sure." John stood there, unsure how much to reveal about the bag men and the regular pick-up. He decided not to reveal anything more than necessary. "I think a few minutes after ten."

Vines did some quick math in his head, "Shit, they'll probably be there within the hour." His mind checked through his options. "OK, John, thank you for this. Listen, sorry about the hand. Do me a favor—let's not bring up this little conversation with your handler, alright?"

He didn't wait for an answer as he hurried to the door, quickly offering another apology to John's wife before running to the car. As he drove to the airport, he dialed his director at the field office, who was never terribly happy to hear from him.

"Eddie, to what do I owe the pleasure? Are you retiring a couple weeks early? Please tell me it's good news."

"Damn right it's good news. I just got a hot lead on Haydenson. He's in Sunny Point, New York, about an hour outside Buffalo. We need to get a team there ASAP."

"Haydenson? Really? Eddie, we've been down this road. I know you don't want to let it go, but I'm not spending any more resources following your hunches to dig up dead mobsters."

"He's not dead, Jim, and you know it."

"He is as far as the Bureau is concerned. We buried this, and it's going to stay that way."

"But I can link the hitter at Rosso's back to Haydenson. She's on her way there right now."

Jim stopped on the other side of the line. "You've got a lead on the hitter? Who?"

"You remember Haydenson's wife, she was on that show *Trial Island*?"

"Are you fucking kidding me? She's dead, too! Remember, the mob hit you couldn't get a fucking lead on to save your life? What the hell is wrong with you? I know you're trying to make one last play before retiring, so I'm sorry the Rosso thing fell apart. But I'm glad the local cops made the collar instead of us. Less fucking headaches. Seriously, get ahold of yourself, Vines. You're chasing ghosts here. Stop wasting your time, and stop wasting mine."

The line went dead.

Damn it!

He continued toward the airport, fully taking advantage of the flagrant disregard for traffic laws his government plates afforded him. He had to come up with a plan. *Who do I know in the Buffalo office?* He crossed out a few names of agents he had pissed off over the years before settling on a young kid he'd trained for a while before he was transferred upstate. Matt Fredrickson was young, impressionable, and in awe of Agent Vines' stories. He dispatched Matt to the restaurant, no questions asked, to keep an eye on things. Matt's partner would pick up Vines at the airport.

"Why doesn't Director Hastings get more guys on this?" Matt asked.

"We've got to move fast, so keep this close to the vest," Vines said. "Don't even tell your director. Just grab your gear and get on the road, OK?"

"I'm on my way. Be safe, Agent Vines."

18

BRYCE HAD MESSAGED his man a couple of times over the past few hours, with no response. He had been mulling over the fat man's message ever since.

BAD CELL SERVICE, CAN'T CALL. ABBY IS ALIVE AND FOLLOWING US. WHAT SHOULD WE DO?

Bryce ordered them to let her follow them to the house, then forgot about it for a while. They were still hours away, giving him plenty of time to prepare for Abby's arrival. He loaded a plastic body bag, cinderblocks, and chains onto his boat at the back dock. He placed his pistol in the small of his back and checked on several backup weapons around the house.

Once he had time to sit and think, he found himself wondering what led Abby to follow his men. He didn't believe in coincidences. Sure, his location had been leaked to the snitch that morning, so he expected Abby to come his way soon, but it seemed far too coincidental that she wound up behind his guys on their way back from Chicago an hour later.

He knew the snitch was working for an investigator who had been sniffing around, no doubt reporting back to Abby. She must have been hiding right under everyone's noses in the city. The snitch must have called the investigator, who relayed the information to Abby, who showed up to follow them. Certainly a remarkable flow of information, but it was the only thing that made sense. But did it?

The only information revealed to the snitch was that Bryce was alive, and what his alias was. The snitch didn't know that the fat men were connected directly to Bryce, did he? Could the investigator really have linked all of the information together so quickly that Abby wound up behind his men on their way back? He shook his head. Too many unanswered questions. But none of that mattered. What mattered was that she was walking right into the trap that he had set.

Bryce checked his phone again—still no response. Curiosity was getting the best of him, and he would like at least a little heads up as to exactly when they would be arriving. He didn't want the fat bastards leading her to the restaurant and complicating things, as that was usually their first stop when they got back. He figured they should be back within a half hour, but like a kid at Christmas, he couldn't stand the anticipation.

He hit the call icon on his phone again and listened to it ring several times, and then someone finally picked up for the first time that afternoon.

"This is Detective Nacimiento. Who is this?"

What!?

Bryce immediately disconnected the call, pulled out the battery and smashed the SIM card. He never used a regular cell phone, and never used the house phone for anything but legitimate business calls, so the call couldn't be traced back to him, but still his heart was pumping.

What the fuck happened?

He thought about calling Chicago. He didn't get an answer that morning on calls to Monte or Rosso, and was starting to worry that there might be some credence to what the snitch told his men about trouble at the compound. If that was the case, he didn't need another burner number popping up there and the two getting connected. He had stayed in hiding for as long as he had by laying low and not making any noise, so he would continue to do just that.

But if the police have the fat guy's phone, where is Abby?

Was she involved with the police? Was she leading them to him?

His mind started turning. Had this been Chicago a few years ago, he would have laughed at Abby for going to the police. He owned half the force and her cries would have been inconsequential, no matter the crime. But this wasn't Chicago. Times had changed.

Bryce was mainly a legitimate businessman now. Sure, he had a couple of cops that were regulars at the restaurant and could take care of a parking ticket if he needed it, but no one was going to look the other way on kidnapping.

Stupid, stupid, stupid! He cursed himself. He assumed Abby would be coming for him on her own, not bringing a squad of feds or New York's finest. His hubris had gotten the better of him, thinking he could predict her moves.

He grabbed his coat and checked that the safety was on his piece before he grabbed his keys to head for the door. There was nothing to hide here, but he had to do something about Ava in the basement of the restaurant. She was well-hidden, but he wasn't going to take the chance she could be found. He never intended to kill her, but now had little choice. He enjoyed his life here and wasn't about to lose everything—even for his daughter.

As he grabbed the door handle, he froze as the house phone rang.

He walked over to a receiver in the hallway and stared at it for a moment, weighing his options. No one outside of his business partners, and maybe the local pizza delivery place, had his landline number.

Cautiously he picked it up. "Hello?"

* * *

Donny pulled the car into the parking lot at Buena Sera right around dusk as the outdoor lights came on. Apparently it was a popular place, judging by the parking lot. He found a spot away from the building near the entrance to the lot.

Abby and Donny took it in. "Nice place, huh?"

"Sure looks like it."

Abby remembered some advice JJ gave her months ago: *If you know you're going into a fight, don't meet the enemy on their terms if you can help it. Get them into the open, on your terms.* Obviously Bryce wanted her to come to his home, so she came to his restaurant. She wasn't going to meet him on his terms.

Donny looked to her. "So what's the plan?"

She smiled. "I'm going to walk in there and ask for him. If he's not there, I'll have a seat and wait. Simple enough, right?"

"Abby, you can't be serious. What if he's got guys watching the place? What about all the people eating? What if you get recognized?"

"I don't care anymore. I'm here to kill Bryce and get my daughter back. I can't do that hiding from my own shadow." She opened the door and stepped out.

He quickly unbuckled himself to follow.

"No, you stay here," she commanded more than told. "Watch the parking lot. You've got my number, call me when you see him. I'll handle this."

With that, she shut the door and strode toward the entrance with purpose. Donny thought maybe Abby was right: he didn't know her anymore.

*   *   *

Vines used his position to procure a seat on a commercial flight that was stopping in Buffalo. After the captain announced that they were on their final descent for this leg of their journey, Vines called his man on the ground for a status.

"Hi, Matt, where are you?"

"I'm about a half hour from the destination, sir, and my partner Agent Brogan is waiting at the airport for you."

"Very good. What do we have for intel?"

"I got what I could, sir, which isn't much. It's an upscale family dining spot. Should be busy enough tonight given the timeframe. According to the aerial shots, there's a large parking lot and a fair distance from neighboring buildings. A street view shows a main entrance in front and one on the side. Judging from a set of stairs in the back that show up on the aerial shot, there has to be at least one in the back, too. When I arrive, I'll do a quick sweep of the perimeter to get my bearings, then I'll hold near the entrance while I wait for you."

"Good, yes, and be sure to wait for me if either of the targets show up. If they go on the move from there, follow them and call me, but do not engage. Understood?" Vines didn't see Matt as the trigger-happy type, but he didn't want to find out the hard way.

"Absolutely, sir. Anything else?"

"You haven't told anyone what's going down, have you, son?"

"No, sir, per your orders."

"Good, let's keep it that way. One other thing: the tactical team that's on standby tonight, how are they? Is it a solid team?"

"They're a good crew, sir. Hell, they're all good crews. As usual, they're at headquarters and ready to go at a moment's notice. Why?"

"Just wanted to know. I'll see you soon. Call me when you arrive."

After Vines disconnected the call, he sat back in thought. He intended to snag Bryce and Abby himself, with his young partner's help. He hoped to have no use for the tactical team, but the thought had crossed his mind that if things went really wrong, he might have to call in for backup. It was good to know they were on standby less than thirty minutes away by chopper. They would be a last resort, though, and one he would not exercise unless he had an eye on the targets and could confirm with absolute certainty that he would not be bringing any embarrassment to his name or the Bureau. He needed to confirm this was Bryce Haydenson, or his big score before retirement could ruin his reputation for good.

19

IN THE WAITING AREA at Buena Sera, the hostess, Marie, gave the petite yet tough-looking woman on the other side of the hostess stand a look up and down and decided to proceed delicately. For such a diminutive woman, there was something about her that gave Marie pause. She wasn't sure if it was the way she was holding herself or the glint in her eyes, but something gave her the feeling that she was wound up pretty tight.

The hostess breathed slowly and repeated herself. "I'm sorry, miss, but the owner is not here, and I'm really not sure what time he'll be in tonight if at all."

Abby looked around the crowded restaurant at the patrons enjoying their dinners. There was no one among them that looked like Bryce. She took a step to the side so that she could see through the open wall into the kitchen.

"Miss, really, I'm sorry, but..."

Abby held up a finger to cut off the hostess as she scanned the kitchen. No Bryce in there either. She walked back to the hostess stand and slid her sunglasses off, leaning closer to the young girl.

Marie looked at Abby. She recognized her face but

203

was having a hard time placing it.

"Take a good look," Abby said. "Do you know who I am? Maybe picture Eric standing next to me?"

A beat, then the hostesses covered her mouth with the palm of her hand. "Oh, my God, I knew I recognized you! You're…"

"Yep, I am. But please keep it down."

Marie leaned in closer, examining Abby's face. "But you're supposed to be dead? It was on the news and everything."

"Well, I'm not, am I?"

Marie just shook her head.

"Now, could you call your boss and tell him who is here waiting for him."

Marie smiled, "What could you possibly want with Hunter? Do you know him or something?"

Abby smiled back. "You could say that, sweetie. Yeah, I know him. And I want to see him."

Marie just gazed, a bit starstruck, as she held up her phone. "Do you mind if I get a pic with you?"

"Nothing personal, but I'd rather not. You know, I've sort of been lying low for a while? Remember? You thought I was dead two minutes ago?"

"Oh my God though, no one is going to believe this!"

"Sweetie," Abby leaned closer and motioned Marie to do the same. "I'd appreciate it if the only person you told about me was your boss, Hunter. Could you give him a call do you think?"

"Oh, yeah, sorry. Um… OK… I'll call him. Wow. I can't believe he never said anything about knowing you!"

Abby flashed a smile. "Thank you. I'll be right over there," Abby gestured toward the bar. She slid her sunglasses back on and walked through the bar area to a small, round table facing the door, watching everyone who walked in.

*   *   *

"Hi, Mr. Bryson?"

Bryce breathed a sigh of relief at hearing the voice of the hostess at Buena Sera.

"Hi, Marie. What's up?"

He listened intently for a moment.

"Just say that again to make sure I'm hearing you right. Who did you say is there?"

Bryce smiled as Marie confirmed the name.

"And she's alone?"

"I didn't see anyone else come in with her. She just walked in and asked for you."

"Are there any cops with her, or out in the parking

lot?"

"No, she's alone." Marie walked to the large window next to the door, "I don't see anyone in the parking lot either. Is everything OK? Why would there be police?"

"Don't worry about it Marie, but call me if any show up. I'm on my way."

*   *   *

Looking back at Marie, Abby saw her on the phone, presumably with Bryce. *This is a really nice place,* Abby thought. She had a hard time believing Bryce was behind the day-to-day operation of something so nice.

The walls were a mix of dark wood and a beige stucco-type treatment that had a very authentic Italian look. The sconces on the walls were dimmed to barely illuminate the space, as most of the lighting came from small oil lamps in the center of each table. The Italian arias playing overhead added to the relaxed and amorous atmosphere.

Very romantic. Eric would have loved this place.

And for a moment, her eyes welled up, making it difficult to continue her surveillance. Still, she managed to spy Marie looking out the large window while talking on her earpiece.

He's carved out a nice little life for himself. Why bother with me anymore? I'm dead, or at least that's what he's supposed to think, right? She knew why he wouldn't let sleeping dogs lie, of course. It was his secret. *If only he knew I already told Rosso that he killed the don's beloved son.*

Bryce was a sociopath, and she doubted that would make a difference. Aside from her knowledge of his secret, she had both shamed and disobeyed him. Bryce would never accept such treatment from anyone, but a woman who promised to honor and obey him before God? That person had to die. One way or another, he wanted her dead, and she doubted Rosso's demise would have any impact on that.

Marie walked over to the table. "Hi, Miss... Abby. I just spoke with Hunter. He'll be here soon."

Abby nodded without looking up. That title, "Miss Abby", rang in her ears. She thought of little Ben back on their island. *Probably not so little anymore.* Her eyes got a little glassy as she thought, *I wonder if I'll see him again.*

*   *   *

Bryce hung up the phone and let it sink in. Abby at the restaurant. Alone. No cops.

They could be waiting down the street, though.

He would like to have his guys sweep the area to figure out if it was a trap, but his guys were nowhere to be found. Whether dead or in jail didn't matter—they were unable to help him now.

Like Abby, he'd have to go it alone.

As he drove to the restaurant, he planned how the scene would go down. He would do a sweep up and down the street himself, checking the neighboring parking lots for anything suspicious—namely cops waiting to move in.

If everything were clear, he would park behind the restaurant and enter through the back door.

Thinking more as he drove, he slowly convinced himself that it wasn't a trap of any kind by the police. He was positive he figured out Abby's plan.

"Of course," he muttered to himself.

Why would she be at the restaurant? To get me away from the house. She lures me to the restaurant while some lackey of hers ransacks the house looking for Ava.

Bryce chuckled a bit. He didn't know who would be helping her. *Maybe her sister. Maybe that investigator.* But as far as the law was concerned, Hunter Bryson was an upstanding and honorable citizen. A pillar of the community. He also lived in a nice home with a top-of-the-line alarm system. Whoever tried to break in looking for Ava would set off the alarm and have the cops there within five minutes. With nothing to find or substantiate whatever crazy claims the burglar might make, the cops would have no reason to look at Bryce as anything but a victim.

I just have to take care of Abby quietly. That would be simple enough. He would have Marie show her to his office where he would be waiting. He didn't intend to fool around with anything fancy. Just a bullet between her eyes from a silenced pistol the second she walked through the door.

He planned to bag her and stash her down in the basement with Ava. He'd tell Marie that everything was all set, and Abby left out the back door. He assumed he would then get a call from the police that his home had been broken into. He certainly couldn't arrive home with a body in the trunk, so he'd go home first to deal with the police and come back in the middle of the night to retrieve Abby's body, and Ava's, as well, disposing of them at the bottom of the lake.

Part of him felt a little badly that he was going to kill his daughter. She really didn't have to die. She didn't know anything damaging per se. It was a shit deal, but he reasoned that she kind of had a shit deal since the day she was born.

Man, it's gonna be a busy night.

*   *   *

Ava gave up trying to scream at least a day ago. The duct tape over her mouth turned any sound she tried to make into muffled noise. She couldn't hear much outside the dark room she was in, but there was enough movement and noises from overhead that she could tell there were lots of people here. This pained her even more, but what could she do?

Her wrists were raw and her shoulders ached from trying to wriggle out of the plastic zip ties that bound her hands behind her back. With her hands secured to the seatback as well as each other, her shoulders had been stretched in the same backward position for two days now. They had been fine at first, but they had ached ever since she fell asleep with her head slumped forward for a few hours overnight.

Her young eyes were more than well adjusted to the darkened room, so she was at least familiar with her surroundings. There were two half windows high up, which told her she was in a basement. They were both boarded up to keep the light out, or she figured more likely to keep anyone from peering in. Through the cracks, however, some light seeped through in the afternoon when it seemed the sun shone on them directly.

She figured there must also be some type of outdoor lighting, as artificial light dimly illuminated the cracks after the sun had gone down.

There was a small, spiral staircase in the far corner, which appeared to be the only way in or out of this place. There was a small desk, a file cabinet, and piles of boxes that bore no labels but swelled at the seams.

The lone light bulb overhead never came on, but she recognized her captor's voice. She was also smart enough to know why her father had kidnaped her. He was trying to get to her mom, *and what better way than to use me as bait?*

Ava had given up crying yesterday, as well. It certainly didn't seem to get her anywhere. Her father was as cold and cruel as her mother had said. She was exhausted, dehydrated, bound by her hands and feet to an old metal chair, with the stale smell of her own urine soaking her from the waist down hanging in the air.

She missed her Aunt Sarah. She had grown so close to her over the past couple years. She missed their home and the smell of the blankets on the couch. She wished she were there now.

210

ESCAPE
Dead End

She was sure her father's plan would work. Her mom would come for her, but then what? Her hopelessness was so overwhelming that Ava wanted to cry but had no more tears left.

The duct tape around her mouth had really started irritating her skin a few hours ago, and she had rubbed her face on her shoulder off and on for the past couple hours in hopes of relieving the itch. She did so again, then stopped and stared into the darkness at the realization of what she had just felt. There was just the slightest tug as she had pulled her face away from her shoulder. The smallest bit of tape on the corner had ever so briefly stuck to the cotton nightshirt that she was still wearing from when they snatched her out of bed.

Ava stretched her neck to rub her face on her shoulder again, and felt the same tug.

She did this again, but this time when she felt the tug, she pressed her cheek as hard as she could to her shoulder and worked her face back and forth. She took a breath, and with a renewed sense of hope, tried to rub the duct tape off her face while stuck in this awkward position.

*   *   *

Unaware that her daughter was struggling to free herself just a few feet below, Abby anxiously sat at the small table flexing her hands open and closed into fists. The delicate light flickering from the small oil lamp in the center of the table reminded her of the many candlelit nights she had spent with Eric in their villa.

Of course, this only caused the knot in her stomach to tighten.

She glanced at her phone, eagerly awaiting a message from Donny in the parking lot. He would give her a heads up when Bryce pull in.

She was wound up like a tension-driven machine, but all she could do was wait and pray that the tautness she felt from head to toe didn't cause her to collapse in on herself. She needed her wits about her if she was going to go up against a killer like Bryce Haydenson or whatever he called himself today.

20

ABBY JUMPED in her seat when the throwaway phone in her pocket vibrated. Her hand had a slight tremor as she read the message from Donny:

HE'S HERE. DROVE AROUND THE BACK. I'LL WATCH THE FRONT A FEW MINUTES. MAKE SURE THERE'S NO ONE ELSE. I'LL BE IN AFTER THAT.

Abby watched the small hallway behind the hostess that led back to the kitchen. She tried to act cool but was a ball of rage inside. Knowing that he was in the building, it took every fiber in her being not to run back there and snap his neck. She forced herself to wait at least a few minutes to see what his next move was.

The hostess touched a finger to her earpiece, presumably to answer a call. She spoke in a hushed tone, looked at Abby, and then signaled her to come over.

"Yes?" Abby asked as she walked up.

"Mr. Bryson is here. He'll meet you in his office. It's just down the hall, behind the kitchen." Marie indicated an area just behind her.

Abby smiled, but she wasn't about to meet Bryce on

213

his terms. Who knew what he had waiting for her back there? No, she would meet him in public first. "Is he still on the line?"

Marie nodded.

Abby briefly opened, then closed, the front of her thigh-length leather jacket. It wasn't open more than half a second, but that's all the time Marie needed to see the large gun holstered to Abby's side and the seven inches of steel strapped to her leg.

She indicated for Marie to lean close as she quietly said, "Now you tell that piece of shit to get out here, or I'm going to start killing his employees. He's got thirty seconds. And Marie, you seem like a nice girl, but you have no idea what you're standing in the middle of. I swear, if you call the police, I'll slice your throat before you finish dialing 9-1-1."

The hostess tried to gulp but coughed instead. Her lip quivered as she whispered, "Mr. Bryson, did you hear that? I think she's serious."

Abby smiled sweetly and indicated an older man making cocktails behind the bar, "Marie, I'm going to start with him. Thirty seconds. The clock is ticking."

She walked away and stood toward the end of the bar, watching Marie speak frantically into the earpiece. Abby didn't intend to kill what seemed like a lovely gentleman, but she was banking on the emotional young hostess to get her boss out here.

Abby pretended to look at a watch and mouthed a countdown to Marie. "10... 9... 8... 7... 6... 5..." She reached into her coat.

A look of horror came over the hostess's face as she spoke harshly into the phone. "Hunter, get out here right now!"

"4... 3... 2..." Abby slowly started opening her coat.

"No! Stop! He's coming!"

The patrons in the dining room and the bar looked up, startled by the yelling. The restaurant fell silent but for a soprano in the overhead speakers singing a beautiful aria, and the rapid footsteps of a man's dress shoes clicking on the tile floor in the small hallway behind the hostess station.

All eyes were on Bryce as he entered the room. He looked around, smiling for a moment, trying to find Abby.

Cloaked in black, combined with the dim lighting on the bar side, he didn't see her until Marie pointed in her direction. Meanwhile, several patrons greeted him, which he returned with smiles and handshakes, before turning toward Abby's direction and waving her over, never losing his smile.

Apparently, he intended to play it cool. This was his restaurant, after all. The last thing he wanted was a public scene. The murmur of conversation nearly returned to normal, until Abby's voice rose above the others and broke the din.

Her voice came out as more of a scream than she intended, the pent-up rage finding its way through her throat. "WHERE THE FUCK IS OUR DAUGHTER?"

Silence again, save for the soprano overhead powering through her aria.

Bryce scanned the room, offering a comforting smile to his patrons, "Please, go back to your dinners. I'm so sorry." To Abby, his eyes turned cold, even if his outward demeanor remained as relaxed as ever. "Can we talk in back?"

She took a step in his direction. Despite her small stature, her determination was obvious, her eyes bright with rage. "Last time I'm going to ask nice. Where is Ava?"

His face was trying to be kind, but she could see the vitriol in his eyes. He lowered his voice. "Can we please talk in the back?"

Abby's eyes quickly flitted around the room. She saw several phones out, with one particularly ballsy young man pointing his in her direction from across the bar, likely taking video of the exchange.

Might as well give them a show.

With startlingly fast hands, Abby snatched the oil candle off the table in front of her, spun, and hurled it across the room at Bryce with every ounce of strength she had. It missed him and smashed into the wall just behind him, exploding in a shower of glass and flames as she screamed across the room, "Tell me where she is!"

Suddenly the restaurant was a burst of activity as diners screamed and jumped from their tables.

Abby grabbed candle after candle from the tables, pitching them at Bryce, feeding the growing flames with each smashed lamp as she screamed at the top of her lungs.

By this time, all the diners had leapt from their seats and charged toward the door as the flames quickly climbed the walls, spreading across the ceiling and scorching the floors in spots where the oil had pooled.

Abby saw Bryce among those trying to escape. Jumping onto a table, she launched herself into the crowd, wrapping her arms around his head and using her momentum to fling him to the ground.

None of the patrons seemed concerned for the fallen restaurateur as they continued to pour out the door.

*   *   *

Ava was having a hard time processing what was happening in the restaurant above. She could hear the chaos but could not understand the cause. She had worked off at least an inch of the duct tape, but there was at least that much to go, and she was disoriented from exhaustion and dehydration. So disoriented, in fact, that she swore she heard her mother's voice yelling overhead. There was so much noise it was hard to tell. A moment ago it was relatively quiet, but now it sounded as though there was a stampede happening.

There it is again… Mommy?

The young girl thrashed about in the chair. It wasn't a question any longer—she was sure she heard her mother yelling overhead. Tears streamed down her cheeks as she rocked back and forth, trying to figure out a way to stand with her arms and legs tied down.

Suddenly, the chair tipped, and unable to right herself, both Ava and the chair toppled and crashed to the floor. At this angle, she could no longer maneuver her cheek toward her shoulder. Her face simply rested on the floor. For a split second, she felt defeat, until she tried to pick up her head and felt the tacky side of the tape sticking to the floor ever so slightly.

With renewed hope, she feverishly went to work dragging her face against the smooth concrete floor, slowly but surely peeling the tape back.

*　　*　　*

Abby used her momentum and leverage to flip Bryce like a ragdoll, sending him crashing to the floor on his back less than three feet from the bar. He lay motionless for a second with the wind knocked from his lungs. Abby seized the moment and drove her boot into his ribs, feeling at least one crack upon impact.

Bryce gasped and grabbed his side.

Abby produced her .22 from the small of her back and pointed it at his head, "Where is she Bryce? Tell me, and I'll make this quick."

He looked up, confused, until a smile spread across his face. "Fuck you, Abby."

Abby studied his features in the glowing light of the blaze. She had almost been oblivious to the room around her becoming engulfed in flames, the roar of the fire growing in her ears. Flames trickled down the wall from the ceiling behind the bar, like water. It was almost beautiful.

She cocked the gun and took aim a little lower. "I can shoot a flea off a cat's tail from a hundred yards, Bryce, and it's pointed right at your dick. Last chance."

In a shockingly fast move, Bryce leaped from the floor and smacked the gun from Abby's hand before she could get off a shot. She countered without hesitation, landing two hard jabs to his rib cage where she had just cracked a rib moments ago. The man collapsed to his knees under the pain.

While he was helpless on his knees, Abby grabbed the back of his head and drove her knee into his face, sending him reeling onto his back. She jumped on top of him, again driving her knee into his rib cage.

She could hear JJ's voice in her head: *Find your enemy's weakness and exploit it.*

He screamed as he bucked her off of him and grabbed a brass pole on the side of the bar to help him stand up. Seizing the opportunity Abby kneed him in the ribs again, and as he fell to his knees once more, she grabbed a damp, thin towel that had been sitting on the bar and secured it around his wrists, tying him to the brass pole.

Smoke continued to fill the room as the crackling fire consumed the wooden bar. Her lungs began to burn as she pressed into his broken rib, "Tell me where she is Bryce!"

He managed to stop groaning long enough to shout, "Stop it! Stop!"

She did.

The fire danced in his eyes as he turned to her. There was no kindness, no remorse, not the slightest hint of humanity in the way his gaze pierced her, though it was his smile that sent a chill from the base of her skull, down her spine, and into her toes.

"She's gonna die, Abby. Burning. You made sure of that."

Panic washed over Abby as her head spun on a swivel looking around the room. "What? She's here?"

Bryce let out a deep, evil, hearty laugh. "You dumb, fucking bitch!"

With Abby distracted, he freed his hands, and as she looked around the room trying to figure a way out, he leapt up and grabbed her by the neck, lifting her off the ground, choking the life out of her.

Abby had learned so much about hand-to-hand combat over the past few years, but none of her training came to mind at this very moment. Instead, schoolyard instincts took over, and she slammed the toe of her leather boot straight into his crotch.

He dropped her as he yelped like a wounded dog. Abby sprung from the ground, grabbed a chair, and smashed it on the back of his head. She looked down at his motionless body as the flames crept closer. "Burn in hell, you piece of shit."

She scanned the room. The path to the front door was still clear though the dining room and hallway leading to the kitchen were almost wholly in flames.

At that second, her ears picked out a distant sound only a mother could hear. Through the roar of the fire, from down the hallway, she heard the faintest of screams.

Ava.

21

DONNY HAD BEEN CAUGHT completely by surprise. One moment he was getting ready to step out of the car and go into the restaurant, satisfied Bryce didn't have any backup in the parking lot, and the next moment a flood of patrons began running out. He hadn't heard a gunshot but assumed that someone must have opened fire. *Why else would everyone run out?*

He jumped from the car and ran across the parking lot toward the restaurant, having to slow his pace as he navigated through the large crowd gathering in front of, and continuing to exit, the restaurant.

A beefy older man in the crowd grabbed him as he neared the front door. "Where ya goin', young fella? There's a fire in there."

"A fire? My... um... my girlfriend is in there."

"Don't worry. Everyone's coming out. She's probably out here somewhere."

"Thanks," Donny brushed him off and started scanning the crowd. *A fire?*

His eyes darted from face to face without seeing Abby. As the last of the patrons filed out and the doors closed behind them, he realized he didn't see Bryce either. *It's probably a distraction. He's taking her out the back!*

Donny pushed his way through the crowd and raced to the back of the restaurant where Bryce had gone in. As he ran down the side of the building, he saw smoke starting to filter through the windows and roof. Once around back, he found the kitchen staff, and a fair amount of the wait staff, milling around and on their phones.

No Abby, no Bryce, and he didn't know if he could trust any of Bryce's employees.

Donny ran to the back door, but a couple of men in aprons stopped him.

"Sir, you can't go in there. The place is burning up."

He shoved one of the men aside and swung the door open. A ball of flame leapt from the doorway and knocked him off his feet. The intense heat singed his hair and left minor burns on his cheek.

One of the other men rushed to help him up and drag him away from the door. "Are you crazy man?"

"My girlfriend is in there!"

"She's probably out front."

"I didn't see her out front." Donny got to his feet and brushed himself off. He looked through the open door at the kitchen completely engulfed in flames, trying to figure if he could run through them.

The cook held his arm. "You're gonna kill yourself running in there. Don't do it."

The sound of fire engines rang faintly in the distance.

"They'll be here in a few minutes. Let's go out front. Come on."

Though the employees all started moving around the building toward the front, Donny didn't walk with the group. He ran ahead to scan the crowd in front again.

No Abby, no Bryce. She had to be inside.

The crowd was well away from the door now. With no one in his way, he made a break for it. No one was going to stop him.

He heard a few people yell as he ripped open the front door and ran in, but it closed behind him. No one followed him.

"Abby?" He did his best to quickly take in the surroundings. There was a small hallway straight in front of him behind the hostess station leading back to the kitchen. To his left, at a large dining room. To his right, there was a good-sized bar. Sections of ceiling had fallen in the hallway and dining room, and the smoke immediately burned his eyes.

"Abby! Where are you?"

Hunched over, he searched the floor, expecting her to

have collapsed from smoke inhalation. It wasn't long before he saw a foot in the bar area. He ran over and knelt down next to the body. He didn't have to flip him over to know who it was, but he did anyway.

He's totally out.

Donny leaned his ear to Bryce's face and felt him exhale. *Still breathing, but who gives a shit. Where's Abby?*

He quickly looked around the rest of the bar and saw no one.

Turning back to Bryce, he slapped him hard across the face. *Come on!*

"Bryce! Wake up!" He slapped him again, sharp, right on the cheek. "Wake up!"

His eyes fluttered open, only to reveal confusion.

Donny leaned in, shouting, "Where's Abby? Where is she, Bryce?"

A section of ceiling behind Donny crashed to the ground, sending up a spectacular cloud of sparks and ash.

Bryce smiled and closed his eyes again.

Fuck it. Let him choke on it.

Donny crawled along the floor to avoid the smoke. There was no one else in the bar, and he was guessing she wasn't in the dining room either.

He looked down the hallway, engulfed in flames.

There was a wide opening on the left that clearly went to the kitchen. But straight ahead stood a wooden door, slightly ajar. *That's got to be his office.*

Donny saw a slim path through the flames toward the right, and quickly crawled along, though he barely made it a third of the way before half a wall and a large section of ceiling collapsed at the end of the hallway, sealing off the office door and sending a wave of smoke and ash toward him.

"Abby! Abby!"

The smoke stung his eyes and lungs as he coughed, gasping, unable to catch his breath through the thick smoke.

"Abby!"

As his eyes closed, his last thought was that he hoped she had somehow made it out.

*　　*　　*

Abby stood in what she assumed was Bryce's office.

I swear I heard her. He said she was going to burn; she's got to be here somewhere.

"Ava! Ava! Can you hear me?"

She heard the faint scream again but couldn't tell where it was coming from. It sounded as though she was close, but not in this room. *How is that possible?*

Abby looked around the room and saw another door,

a closet. She ripped it open to find a few old coats and boxes of files piled on the floor.

"Ava! Where are you? Keep yelling!"

She heard it again, louder, right in front of her. The screaming seemed to be coming from behind the bookcase. It took her just a second to realize that Bryce had built a secret room and she grabbed onto the edge of the bookcase and started to pull with all her might. There was just the slightest bit of give, but it budged.

Ava heard her try and intensified her yelling.

"Mom! Mommy! I'm down here!"

Abby flung the books from the shelf to reveal a handle and a deadbolt hidden behind them.

She quickly looked around the office, eyes settling on the desk in the center. She ripped open the top drawer to find a key ring. As she ran back to the bookcase, she thought she heard a man's voice yelling outside the office door.

Is that Donny?

She didn't see him as she looked back toward the open door, but she did see flames licking their way up the doorjamb. She couldn't waste any more time. She tried the keys one after the other. Finally, the fifth key turned the lock. As she swung the bookcase on its hinge, there was a crash in the hallway and the office door blew wide open to reveal a pile of collapsed wall and ceiling blocking the only way out.

Flames shot through the open door and immediately climbed the walls and ceiling of the office. Abby ran down the cramped spiral staircase and burst into tears as she saw Ava lying on the floor, tied to a chair and screaming.

"Ava, honey, it's OK. I'm here! Mommy's here!"

She righted the chair and held her daughter's face in her hands, taking her in.

"Are you OK, honey?"

Ava couldn't speak through the sobs, and the glow at the top of the staircase told Abby she didn't have a moment to waste.

She ripped her knife from its sheath and quickly cut Ava's hands and feet free.

The little girl fell forward and collapsed into her mother's arms, sobbing.

Abby's heart raced as she stroked her daughter's long brown hair. "It's OK sweetie, it's OK." She pulled away and looked her in the eyes. "We've got to get out of here, honey. Can you pull it together?"

Ava nodded, holding back the tears.

Abby looked around, panicked. "How do we get out of here?"

Ava pointed to the spiral staircase as flames licked the edges of the doorway, having completely engulfed the bookcase. "That's the only way. Oh, my God, Mom, I don't want to die. I don't want to die!"

Abby grabbed her daughter by the shoulders. "I'm not going to let that happen. We'll find another way."

She scanned the room—no other doors, but there were two boarded up basement windows at the ceiling of the room.

"Look around. Find something we can use to bust those open. Come on!"

Mother and daughter started going through the desk drawers and stacked boxes. It wasn't long before Ava held up a hammer and yelled, "Here, here!"

Abby grabbed it and began pounding on the boards. They dented but didn't break.

She pounded harder and harder until her hand was numb from repeated blows, but all she managed to do was put a bunch of dents in the thick old boards.

Ava screamed as pieces of the floor above began to drop from the ceiling. One flaming piece of debris hit her on the shoulder.

Abby quickly patted her down to make sure she wasn't going to catch fire, then took off her leather jacket and slung it over her daughter's shoulders and held her tight. Abby couldn't believe it had come to this. All the years of protecting her little girl—all the years of running, all the training—and for what? To die in a basement in a fire that she caused?

They closed their eyes as the smoke began building up and stinging them.

"I love you, Ava. I'm sorry, I'm so sorry... for everything." Her mother squeezed her tightly.

"It's OK, Mommy, I love you, too. We'll be OK," she said, trying to be brave.

Abby shook her head. She knew they wouldn't be. Ava was still of the age that if she said it, she believed it to be true, but Abby knew better. The only two exits were blocked, and the fire was growing.

It won't be long now.

She hoped that Ava would at least pass out from the smoke before she felt the sting of the flames on her skin.

Tears streamed down Abby's face, flowing like a river.

Ava felt her cheek becoming wet from her mother's tears and found the strength to comfort her.

"We'll be OK, Mommy, we'll be OK." Ava squeezed Abby as hard as she could. Abby gasped just a bit as the handle of her .45 pressed into her ribs.

A split second later her eyes shot open, and she pushed Ava away.

Abby ripped the gun from its holster and checked the magazine. It was full, and she had two more full magazines on her belt. She looked around the room and pointed to the far corner. "Ava, go over there, quick!"

The little girl did as she was told without hesitation.

Abby raised the gun, and from just a few feet away, fired eight successive shots, emptying the magazine into the boards of the window. Slamming a fresh magazine into the gun she repeated the exercise. Shards of wood flew around the room as the thick slugs tore into the boards, sending shrapnel flying into the smoke-filled room.

She grabbed the old metal chair Ava had been tied to and slammed it repeatedly into the shattered boards. With the third strike, they gave way and Abby felt a rush of air from the outside, which also fed the flames, giving the fire a renewed vigor.

"Come on, come on!" she shouted as Ava ran toward her.

She shoved the child through the window, and then jumped onto the chair to climb out herself. Looking around, they found themselves in the back of the restaurant, the blaring fire engines right on top of them. They were pulling into the parking lot right out front.

"Are you OK?" she asked Ava.

The little girl nodded. "Yes, I think so."

"Good. We've got to run now, alright?"

Grabbing her daughter's hand, the two made a sprint for the woods behind the restaurant where they disappeared, just as a fire truck pulled around back.

*　　*　　*

231

As Donny's eyes opened, he found himself on a gurney in the parking lot, a safe distance from the burning restaurant.

It took a moment to realize that he was looking at Bryce, sitting up on another gurney ten feet away and speaking with a fireman.

He sat up a little, trying to hear what the fireman was saying.

"So a bunch of people are saying that some woman threw candles at you, and that's what started the fire?"

Bryce nodded his head. "They were the little glass lamps with the oil and the wick." He shrugged.

The fireman continued. "No one saw her exit the building, but you're saying she's not in there?"

"No," Bryce shook his head. "She ran out the back, through the kitchen. I saw her. Must have ran off that way."

Donny tried to sit up. He knew full well that Abby wouldn't have left without Ava, nor would she have left Bryce alive. *What if she's still in there?*

"No, you don't, sir," a heavyset woman behind him put her hand on his shoulder and eased him back onto the gurney.

Donny grabbed at his mask, ripping it off to speak, but started choking immediately.

The woman put the mask back on. "There you go. Rest a few more minutes, OK, honey?"

He glanced at Bryce and they locked eyes. No doubt Bryce knew Donny didn't just happen to be there, and would kill him with his bare hands right now if there weren't so many witnesses around.

The fireman continued speaking with Bryce. "That makes sense about the oil candles. This thing got out of hand really fast. It's an old building, and she was literally pouring fuel on the fire. It's gone, you know." He shook his head.

Donny looked around trying to figure out what the fireman was talking about. The hoses weren't pointed at the building, which was simply a thirty-foot tall bonfire by now. They were pointed at the wooded areas around the building. Other firemen directed cars away from the building. The restaurant was too far gone to save, and they were going to let it burn to the ground. Their only concern now was keeping the fire from spreading to the nearby trees and reaching the homes beyond.

Donny looked at Bryce and saw what he could only describe as a twinkle in his eyes. Abby had to be in there, and he was letting her burn.

That son of a bitch!

Donny forcibly sat up and ripped the mask off, but couldn't catch his breath to speak. The fireman looked over as Donny waved for him to come over.

"Are you OK, sir?" the fireman asked.

Donny shook his head no. He tried to speak, but only coughed, unable to catch his breath.

The fireman looked back at Bryce. "Who is this guy?"

"I dunno," Bryce lied. "I assume he was here for dinner like everyone else."

Donny managed to shake his head no while he gathered his breath to speak. *I'll tell them the truth. They'll go in after Abby, and get the cops here to take care of this piece of shit.*

Just as he opened his mouth to speak, he felt the throwaway phone in his pocket vibrate. Only one person in the world had that number. Donny looked at the fireman, the heavyset paramedic, and Bryce, all waiting for him to speak. He gasped and coughed a few more times, then meekly managed to say, "I was here... for take-out."

*   *   *

Matt had left Buffalo minutes after speaking to Agent Vines, but found himself stopped on the street across from Buena Sera, unable to enter the parking lot being blocked off by a line of firemen. Apparently he had already missed something important, but he wasn't sure what. His badge would have gained him entry, but Agent Vines said to lay low on this for now, so he thought better of it.

He parked and walked into the parking lot from the side, going up to a large group of onlookers. "What's going on here?" he asked to anyone listening.

The beefy man who had stopped Donny from running into the building earlier spoke up. "Some crazy woman was screaming at the owner and chuckin' candles at him. Place went up like tinder. She was yellin' something about their daughter. Must be an old girlfriend or something."

Matt nodded his head. He spoke with a couple others and got the same story. He also gleaned that the fire department intended to let the place burn, as everyone had gotten out and it was too far gone to save.

He called Vines to fill him in.

On the other side, Vines was quiet, processing the news.

"You get a good look at him?" Vines asked.

"Yes, sir. I compared him to the photos you messaged me. Different haircut, different glasses, but it's definitely the same guy. You found your man."

"Good, good."

"You want me to take him into custody?"

Vines thought about it. Bryce was going to be a huge get, the biggest of his career. He intended to redeem himself just in time for his retirement with this story. But Bryce *and* Abby would be an even bigger story if he could get both of them. Technically, he didn't have enough evidence for a warrant on Abby, but just bringing her in for questioning would be enough of a story.

"No, let him walk, but don't lose him. Abby's out

there somewhere, and she's not gonna be far away. Once she shows up, we'll grab both of them, OK?"

"Yes, sir. Tail him, don't lose him. Got it."

"Call me if anything happens. I'll be there in less than an hour."

22

THE PARAMEDICS INSISTED on transporting Donny and Bryce to the hospital to be treated for smoke inhalation. Bryce successfully argued against such measures and signed a waiver. He had been up speaking and walking around for quite a while.

Donny, on the other hand, barely had his breath and could not argue his way out of a trip to the hospital. He found himself in the back of an ambulance bound for Mount Saint Charles hospital twenty minutes away and one town over.

After the ambulance pulled away, Bryce turned to see his restaurant's roof entirely collapse under its own weight. The fire had obliterated the support structure below.

The fire department now insisted on clearing the parking lot entirely and made quick work of moving the rest of the onlookers out.

The chief came up to Bryce, who stood and watched the blaze.

"We're trying to get everyone out of here, sir. You can keep an eye on things from the street if you want."

Bryce shook his head without taking his eyes from the

fire. "No. I can't bear to watch this. I'm going to head out."

"We'll be here until the structure is gone and it's just smoldering. It'll make the demo easier for you. We'll douse it then, probably another couple hours at most the way this thing is raging. There's supposed to be a big storm coming tonight—a few inches of rain at least—so we're not too worried. Just want to make sure it's out before we call it a night."

Bryce looked at his watch. "Late night for you guys, huh?"

The fireman shook his head. "Naw. We'll tape off the scene. Probably be out of here sometime between midnight and one. Not too bad."

Bryce nodded. "That's good. You don't need me for anything else then?"

"Not tonight, sir. From the interviews we've done, the cause seems pretty straightforward, but the investigator will want to interview you in the morning anyway. Your insurance company is going to want that report, if nothing else."

"Thanks. I'll be home. He can reach me there."

Bryce handed the fireman his card, got in his car, and set off for home.

As he drove, he thought about Donny showing up with Abby. *How long have they been in it together?* He wished he could have jumped across the gurney and choked the life out of him right there in the restaurant parking lot. No matter. He'd hunt Donny down and take care of him in good time. His first order of business was to take care of the two bodies in the wreckage of Buena Sera before any insurance investigators or demo crews showed up.

He glanced at the clock in the car to see that it was just after 9:00. The fireman had said they would be there for another few hours, so he began working on a plan. He'd grab some power tools and his truck before returning to the restaurant. He wasn't sure exactly what unburying the bodies would entail, but was optimistic that if there was any heavy debris to move, like beams or chunks of concrete, he could lash a rope around it and pull it off with his truck.

He knew what corner they would be in. As he had lain there on the floor of the bar, dizzy and unable to stand, he heard Ava screaming, too. He saw Abby run back to the office and knew she would find her. She was a smart woman—that much he had learned. She never came back out, and when the support wall in the hallway and the ceiling collapsed to block the only exit from his windowless office, he smiled and decided he could die happy, knowing that those two bitches would burn, too.

When the firemen dragged him out, it was just icing on the cake.

Thinking ahead to disposing of the bodies, he realized that he didn't really have to alter his original plan that much. He would need another bag, another length of chain, and a few more cinderblocks, but those were all items he kept stocked in his garage for just such occasions.

With his background, and living on one of the Great Lakes, he figured he would never regret keeping these things around. He had buried more than one body out at sea in his relatively short time in the area and was fine with adding two more to the total.

He smiled as he pulled into his driveway. *Abby and Ava will be at the bottom of the lake by sunrise.*

His secret would be forever buried with his dead ex-wife.

*   *   *

Donny had spent the past forty-five minutes on a gurney in the hallway of Mount Saint Charles Emergency Room. It was a busy enough night, and with the exception of a nurse who took his vitals when he arrived, no one had looked his way.

He spent the twenty-minute ride over, and the first half of his time here, with an oxygen mask strapped to his face. Wondering if anyone was paying attention, he slid it off about ten minutes ago, and no one gave him a second glance. He had been wondering how his breathing would be without it, and determined that it was good enough.

His right pocket started vibrating again, and he immediately answered the call.

"Abby?"

"Oh, thank God you're OK!"

"Yeah, I'm fine. They took me to the hospital, but I'll

be all right. Where did you go?"

"Long story. We got out the back and ran through the woods. I couldn't just walk around the front of the restaurant."

"We? So you got Ava?"

"Yeah, she was in the restaurant. I'll fill you in later. Can you meet us?"

"Of course. Where?"

"Remember the truck stop right before the exit where we got off?"

"Yeah, sure. You're there?"

"Yeah. We came out of the woods by the highway and I recognized the sign, so we went this way. Ava's a little shaken up, but she's tough, she's OK. We cleaned up in the ladies room and are going to have a bite to eat. How fast can you get here?"

Donny thought. The car they had stolen from the accountant was back at the restaurant parking lot, but he could certainly procure another one in the parking lot of the hospital one way or another. "Twenty-five, maybe thirty minutes, tops. So what's the plan? Go back to your sister's across the border? Or do you have another place? Either way, I'll get you where you need to go."

"It's not over, Donny."

"What are you talking about? You got Ava back."

241

"I did, and now I'm going to end this. He survived the fire. According to the news, they pulled two men from the blaze. One of them was your dumb ass, and there was only one other person in the place."

"Yeah, Bryce lived. I saw him. So we're going after him?"

"Yeah. I'm going to end this once and for all, OK?"

"OK. I'll be right there."

Stuffing the phone into his pocket, Donny ditched the mask and the oxygen sensor on his finger and walked out of the front door without anyone even raising an eyebrow.

*　　*　　*

In a quiet booth at the rear of the truck-stop diner, Abby slid the phone into her pocket and smiled across the table at Ava.

"You OK?"

The girl nodded her head, staring at her plate of food without looking up.

"Hey," Abby said, putting a finger under Ava's chin to lift her head. When their eyes met, Abby melted. Her daughter had her soft brown eyes, but they were glassed over as she struggled not to cry.

"Come here." Abby stood, gesturing for her daughter to stand up for a hug. Ava practically leaped from her seat into Abby's open arms, where Abby stroked her long brown hair while the little girl sobbed into her mother's shoulder.

"It's OK baby, it's OK. It's over now."

Ava wiped the tears from her eyes and looked at her mother, "No, it's not. We have to go to the police or something. He should be in jail!"

"Shhh, keep your voice down. Let's sit. We need to talk."

"What do we need to talk about? He tried to kill me; he tried to kill you. Why isn't he in jail?"

"Can we sit, honey? Come on." Abby gestured to the booth.

Ava looked at the seat across the booth from her mother and had a thought. "Can I just sit on your lap?"

"Sure." Abby smiled as her little girl snuggled in. "Ava, sweetie, we need to have a talk."

"OK, what about?"

"About your... I can't even call him your father." Abby sighed, "About Bryce. This is a grown-up talk, but I think you can handle it. Can you?"

Ava nodded her head gently, staying serious to show her mother she was ready.

Abby took a deep breath. "Ava, honey, we can't go to the police."

"Why not? Auntie Sarah always said that if I got in trouble I need to find a police officer. They stop the bad guys. They'll help us."

Abby nodded her head. "Well, that's good advice. If you're lost, a police officer can help you find your way home. If you're hurt, they can get you to the hospital. But they can't help us with this."

"Why not?"

Abby thought a minute. "Honey, have you ever known a mean dog?"

She nodded her head, "Yeah, a couple houses down from Auntie Sarah, there's a really mean dog. His name is Bear. He's scary; always barking. When they let him out, sometimes he chases and bites at the kids. He's the worst."

"OK, and what do the owners do so the dog doesn't chase the kids or bite them?"

"I don't know. They usually have him on a chain in the backyard or put him in the house so he can't get to anyone. Why?"

"Well, think about it this way. They chain him up or keep him in the house, but every time Bear gets out he goes chasing and scaring the kids again, right?"

Ava nodded her head.

"Well, honey, if we call the police, they'll bring Bryce to jail, but he won't be there forever. It could be a few days, a few weeks, a few years, but eventually he'll get out again."

Ava nodded her head but didn't really understand. "But why?"

"Because that's how the system works sometimes. While your… while Bryce waits for a judge to send him to jail, he'll be free, and we can't let that happen. We have to do something about it or he'll hurt us." As Ava pondered her mother's words, Abby continued. "Honey, if that mean dog down the street keeps chasing kids and scaring them every time it gets out, what do you think the owners should do?"

The girl didn't need to think about it. "Get rid of it. That's what all the kids keep saying. Get rid of Bear so we don't have to be scared of him anymore."

Abby nodded her head. "Do you understand what I'm talking about now?"

Ava thought a moment, but eventually shook her head no. "Sorry, I don't know, Momma."

"Honey, Bryce is like a mean dog. If we call the police, they'll take him away, but he'll get out again. He always does, and then we have to be scared again."

"So we have to get rid of him, like the dog?"

Abby nodded. "Exactly. Then we don't have to be scared anymore. He can't hurt us anymore."

"How?"

"You let me worry about that, OK, honey?"

"OK," Ava wrapped her arms around her mother and buried her face in her neck. "I love you, Momma."

"I love you, too. But now you need to eat something, OK?"

Abby reached across the table to slide Ava's plate of burger and fries from the other side, and the two ate in silence, huddled next to each in the protective corner of the diner. Both had been deprived of food for so long that they were past being hungry, to the point that they hadn't even felt hungry when they sat down. However, once they started, they devoured their dinners in a matter of minutes.

The little girl leaned against her mother. "Momma, have you ever not been hungry at all, and then once you ate something, you're suddenly starving?"

"Yup!" Abby smiled. "That's what dessert is for!"

She flagged down the lone, aging waitress, and five minutes later mother and daughter were gorging on warm apple pie a la mode.

Satisfied, Abby leaned back. "There's nothing better than diner pie with my little girl."

Ava planted a big kiss right on Abby's lips and spoke to her staring into her eyes from just a few inches away, as only children can do. "There's nothing better than diner pie with my little momma!"

The two laughed though Abby quickly held her

daughter close so she wouldn't see the tears that had sprung from her eyes. She was overcome with joy, but she also felt a hole in her heart where all of the memories with her little girl should be.

She had missed so much over the past two years and didn't want to miss another minute, but knew they had to part ways again, hopefully only briefly. Abby knew that if she could succeed in getting rid of Bryce, they could lead normal lives from now on. The possibility that she could fail, and never see Ava again, was in the back of her mind, though she refused to acknowledge it.

A deep voice from just behind them said, "Well, isn't that just the sweetest thing ever?"

Ava opened her eyes to look up and scream, "Donny! Oh, my God!"

In an instant, she jumped from Abby's arms and gave Donny a big hug.

He smiled. "How ya doin', kid?"

It had been more than two years, but Ava fondly remembered Donny. He was a good man, Abby had told her when they were living under the same roof with Bryce. *He saved our lives*, her mother said. Ava didn't remember that, but certainly had many happy memories playing games in the living room with Donny during his visits. She also remembered feeling safe when he was around though she couldn't explain why.

"Momma, it's Donny!" Ava beamed.

"I know," Abby smiled, finishing drying her eyes with the napkin before embracing him, too.

He held on for a little longer than necessary and whispered in her ear, "I was scared I'd lost you again."

Abby shook her head, forcing her eyes to remain dry as she pulled away. She shook her head and whispered with a smile, "Nope, not again."

Ava was bouncing up and down with excitement. "Donny, what are you doing here?"

"Trying to keep your mom out of trouble."

"Who, me?" Abby deadpanned.

"Are you hungry?" Ava asked. "We just totally stuffed our faces!"

"I'm good, but thanks," Donny said. He stared at Ava until she smiled back at him.

"What?" she asked shyly.

He shook his head. "I'm just so happy to see you, that's all." He turned to look across the diner, more than anything to keep the little girl from seeing his eyes misting up.

Ava followed his gaze and her eyes settled on a very old machine with glass sides near the door of the diner, filled with stuffed animals, "What's that you're looking at?"

"You see that claw at the top?" Donny pointed. "There's a joystick that lets you use the claw to pick up the stuffed animals. If you can pick one up, you win it."

"Cool!" She looked to Abby. "Can I try?"

"Go ahead."

Ava was off running toward the machine before Abby said the word "Go".

"Wait," Donny reached into his pocket and gave Ava a handful of bills. "You'll need these."

The two sat and watched Ava play. After a moment, Abby leaned over and asked in a whisper, "You said you saw him?"

"Yeah, I was sitting right next to him. Wanted to choke him right there, but we were both being treated by the paramedics. They brought me to the hospital, but they let him go. Probably back at his house. We'll find him."

Abby mulled that over.

"What's the plan with Ava?" Donny wondered. He was completely on board with Abby's plan to get rid of Bryce for good, he just wasn't sure if having Ava in tow when they did it was a great idea.

"You're going to have to take her."

Donny did a double-take. "What's that?"

"You heard me. You have to take her while I finish things with Bryce."

"What? No! I can't let you go after him alone."

249

"Well, it seems pretty fucked up to bring her along for the ride to go kill her father, and I can't exactly leave my daughter alone, can I?"

"No, but there's got to be another way. What would you do if I wasn't here?"

"Improvise, which is what I'm doing now."

Donny didn't have a response—he simply grimaced, and Abby could tell his wheels were turning.

"Donny, there's no one else I can trust."

"What about your sister? She's what, six hours away? Let's get her into the mix so you and I can go after him together."

Abby shook her head. "Right now, he thinks I died in the fire. He's probably going back tonight with every intention of retrieving my body and burying me before anyone finds it. We can't even wait until morning. He'll know I'm alive and come after me again. Right now, I have surprise on my side, and I don't want to lose that advantage."

Sitting next to each other in the booth, he placed his hand on hers. "What if that's not enough?"

"What?"

"The element of surprise. What if it's not enough? What if the worst happens, and I'm not there to help you?"

She shook her head. "That's not going to happen."

"Don't underestimate him, Abby. The worst repeatedly happens when Bryce is around."

She sighed. "I programmed speed dial number three on that phone I gave you. If the worst should happen—which it won't—then call that number."

"Who is it?"

"Someone who will take care of things. See to it that Ava is safe. Sarah, too. Just tell him who you are and what happened."

Donny nervously tapped his fingers on the table. "I don't want you going in against him alone. We can park the car somewhere isolated and leave Ava there."

"For how long? Long enough for one of Bryce's thugs to find her? And what if the worst does happen? What if both you and I end up dead? Ava will be stranded there, completely alone. What happens to her then?"

Ava had run out of money without procuring anything from the claw machine and made her way back to the table as Donny let out a defeated sigh.

"What's going on?" Ava could tell the adults were having a serious discussion and wanted in on it.

Abby explained that she was going after Bryce, and that Ava would stay with Donny, who would protect her.

"What are you going to do, Momma?"

"I'm going to make sure he leaves us alone, for good."

"How?"

Abby shook her head, "You let me worry about that."

"Mom. I'm not stupid. You have a gun. You're going to kill him, aren't you?"

"Shhh… keep your voice down."

"Well, you are, aren't you? How else are you going to make him leave us alone forever?"

Abby stared at Ava before finally answering with a quiet, "Yes."

Ava's face turned pale. "What if… you know… what if something happens to you?"

"It won't, sweetie, I'll be fine. It's going to be fast, and I'll meet up with you real quick."

Ava looked at Donny. "What do you think?"

He was surprised at her frank tone. Abby knew what he thought, but he also felt like he needed to be strong for Ava's sake. "I think your mom is right. She'll be back with us before the sun comes up, right?" He looked toward Abby and smiled.

"Right," Abby agreed.

The three were quiet for a few minutes, each digesting the gravity of the conversation until Ava broke the silence.

"Momma, remember you said how Bryce tried to kill me when I was a baby?"

Abby nodded her head, remembering that night many years ago. Had Donny not busted into the room to tear him away, he probably would have killed both of them.

"And Momma, remember when he tried to strangle me when I told him to stop hitting you, and we hide in my room?"

Abby remembered that day, too. He picked up the little girl by her neck until Abby fought him off and locked herself away with Ava. She nodded.

"I remember how he used to hit you all the time, Momma. I used to cry in my room when I heard you fighting. I remember when he shot you in front of Auntie Sarah's house after he shot Eric. Remember?"

Abby's eyes spilled a few tears over the memories as she nodded her head. "Yes, Ava, honey. I remember all of those things."

Ava's eyes met Abby's with a cold look beyond her years. "Then make sure he's dead this time so he can't hurt us ever again."

Abby smiled. *That's my girl.*

The three of them checked into a small motel behind the truck stop. Abby double-checked her weapons before kissing Ava goodbye. "You be good, OK? I'll be back soon."

Ava nodded her head.

Abby turned to Donny and pulled him close enough to whisper in his ear, "You still have your gun, right?"

Donny shook his head no. "It must have fallen out in the fire."

Abby discreetly slid her .45 from its holster and into his hand. "Just in case."

He nodded.

"Wait no longer than sunrise, OK? If I'm not back, assume the worst. Get out of town and call the number I gave you. Swear it."

He just stared back into her eyes, motionless.

"Swear it, Donny."

He gave just the slightest nod of his head.

"OK," Abby said. "I'll be back."

"Wait!" Ava called out as her mother turned to leave. "Don't forget to kiss Donny goodbye, too!"

Abby shook her head and smiled before placing a soft kiss on his cheek and whispering, "Thank you," as she slipped out the door. Donny locked the knob, then slid the deadbolt in place, still kicking himself that he wasn't with her when she needed him most.

23

BRYCE POURED himself a straight vodka over ice and grabbed a bag of pretzels from the cabinet to snack on as he looked out the back kitchen window toward Lake Erie just beyond.

The boat had a full tank of gas, a couple of lengths of chain and padlocks, and two thick body bags. The key was in the ignition, ready to go. He had dumped bodies out there before. He would go out about twenty miles in the dark to dump them in one of the deeper parts of the lake. Figuring it would take him at least a couple hours to get the bodies from the wreckage of Buena Sera, he was hoping to be back in from the water before sunrise, but he wasn't too concerned if he wasn't. Anyone who saw him would just assume he was out for some early morning fishing.

He checked the time to see that it was just after midnight. He figured he should wait about an hour before heading back to the restaurant. By then the firemen should be cleared out, and he could start searching for the bodies in the wreckage.

Bodies in the wreckage... Bryce was practically giddy with excitement that Abby was finally dead. He would drive to Chicago tomorrow to report the news personally to Rosso and maybe ask about coming back to the city. With Abby out of the way and the restaurant gone, he didn't have much reason to stay here.

He was still a little off-put that his men had been picked up by the police and he hadn't been able to get in touch with Monte and Rosso. He was feeling a little spooked about it. *Maybe the city isn't the direction to go?* He put that thought from his head, though. He needed to get some answers, and that was the obvious place to start.

*   *   *

Abby drove by Bryce's house to get her bearings. It was a nice place built with lots of stone and wood, almost to look like a rustic cabin, but it was at least a four-bedroom home in the neighborhood of 2500 square feet. In the dark, it was hard to tell, but the front appeared nicely landscaped. It was set back from the road, probably on an acre and a half or so, and bordered on each side by a wooded area to separate it from the neighboring lots.

She continued down the street past a black sedan on the side of the road. Abby had passed a newly constructed home with a for sale sign about a quarter mile back, and intended to circle around, park the car there, and return on foot.

*   *   *

Leaning back in his seat, Vines watched the driver from a distance. She was staring at Bryce's house as she drove by. Before she looked ahead again, he bent down to conceal himself.

Was that just Abby?

It had to be. So she's not dead. Matt had briefed him on what he was able to gather from restaurant employees and customers. A woman fitting Abby's description came in and set the place ablaze, but no one saw her come out. Bryce told the fire chief that he saw her go out the back door, but no one else did, and the police had turned up nothing.

Vines had coupled that information with his men having watched Bryce make at least four trips to his boat carrying cinderblocks. He assumed Abby was actually dead in the restaurant and Bryce was going to be doing a burial at sea for her later tonight. Vines intended to let Bryce bring the body back before making a move, catching him red-handed.

That would just be the tip of the iceberg. They'd get him on money laundering, racketeering, the whole nine yards. And with so many of Rosso's family dead, they didn't even have to offer him a deal. There were almost no names for him to give up.

With Abby alive, it appeared there would be no body to recover, but having her in the flesh would do just fine, too. She had obviously gone to the restaurant with the intention of killing him, so it was safe to assume she was here at Bryce's home for the same purpose.

He checked in with his two men, Matt, and Jeff, on

their earpieces. "Abby's alive. Repeat, Abby's alive. I just saw her drive by."

"Copy that." Came Matt's voice. "Awaiting further instruction."

Vines mulled things over. She was here to kill Bryce, though she's the one that Vines would prefer to see dead. Having laid waste to the Rosso compound, and thus his plans for glory, he had a special hate for this woman he had never met.

Maybe we can kill two birds with one stone.

"Hold your positions. No one moves. Let's see how this plays out," he instructed.

Vines planned to take Bryce down one way or another tonight. If they let him kill Abby first, that would satisfy Vines' need for revenge. A clear-cut murder charge would stick better than the laundering and racketeering, too. More than anything, Vines thought about the headlines that the story would generate, and he would be right in the middle of it.

He checked back in. "Boys, Abby is no doubt here to kill Bryce. Unless you live under a rock, I'm sure you know why."

"Should we move in?" Matt's voice sounded eager for action. He and his partner had been holding their positions in the wooded areas bordering Bryce's home for the past hour. One in front, one in the back.

"No, we're not moving in yet."

"Why not, sir? Based on what you've said, we have enough to take both of them in."

But if we snatch them now, the bitch doesn't wind up dead, son.

Vines thought a moment. He wanted to choose his words carefully. "If we move in now, we only get Haydenson. Wait for Abby to make a move. What we have here are two people who faked their deaths and are capable of going on the run. Let's get them both tonight so we don't spend months chasing them again. Now hold your positions and let's watch this play out. As soon as one of you has eyes on her, call it in, and we'll converge. I don't know which direction she'll be coming from, but she'll probably be on foot. Is that clear?"

"As a bell, sir."

Vines realized the two ex-lovers wouldn't wait more than a second to start shooting. While either one dead would make for great headlines and a great ending to his career, Bryce was the bigger legal fish, and he would prefer to see to it that he lived through the night. Sure, Abby was a star, but after what she did at the Rosso compound, she would probably be hailed as a hero. A bigger hero than Vines, and his name and notoriety would be lost in the story.

No, I have to make sure Bryce lives through this so I can hang him out to dry for Abby's murder. I'll be the man who brought her killer to justice.

*   *   *

Abby emerged from the wooded area on the left side of Bryce's home about a hundred feet from the back deck overlooking the lake.

It must be a spectacular view at sunrise, she thought.

She stayed right at the edge of the tree line, where she was sure she wouldn't be seen on this dark night. The full moon had shone bright thirty minutes ago when she drove by, but clouds obscured it now. She slid her night vision monocular from her belt to get a better lay of the land.

There was a good-sized wooden deck off the back of the house, and it appeared there was a hot tub at the base. Otherwise, the yard was mostly a green lawn running down to the lake, with the exception of a few decorative trees here and there. At the lake, the green expanse of the lawn abruptly ended at a short stone wall. A small set of stairs went over the wall to a dock where a boat sat uncovered.

Putting the monocular down, she looked into the well-lit kitchen where Bryce was snacking on something and tossing back the end of a drink.

Abby smiled.

Enjoy your last meal.

*　　*　　*

Matt's voice broke the silent communication channel, startling Vines. "Sir, I've got her."

"Where?" Vines held his hand to his earpiece as if it

would help him hear better.

"She's on the west side of the property, at the edge of the woods, about one hundred feet from the main house."

"Good," Vines said as he emerged from his car. "Where exactly are you?"

"East side. The target is clear across the property, probably three hundred feet from my position," Matt whispered. "I'm halfway between the main house and the water, about ten feet from the tree line."

"Alright, I'll be there in just a minute. Hold your position."

Jeff was on the west side like Abby, but was watching the front yard. Vines intended to leave him in front for now. He didn't need another officer complicating things. "Jeff, get back to the car and keep an eye on the front of the house."

"Sir?"

"You heard me. Move!"

Vines jogged to the wooded area and carefully made his way through the trees as quickly and silently as he could. When he was close enough, he pulled a small set of night-vision binoculars from his interior pocket and made a full sweep of the back yard.

There she is.

Abby would have been impossible to pick out with the

naked eye, barely five feet tall and dressed in black from head to toe at the edge of the trees.

Vines looked to his right and saw Matt about thirty feet away, eyes on Abby. A shadow moved across the light that was spilling onto the deck through the sliding doors off the kitchen. Vines looked over the binoculars into the well-lit room to see Bryce checking his watch, looking impatient.

Looking back to Abby, he saw that she was standing about ten feet out into the yard just behind a short, decorative tree. It appeared as though she was going to go for the house, and Bryce didn't appear to have any clue she was back there. Vines didn't want her to surprise Bryce. If she got the drop on him, the wrong person would end up dead.

"She's on the move sir," Matt whispered.

"I see that. I'm on your nine o'clock, about thirty feet."

They both saw her pull a gun from the small of her back and check the magazine.

"I don't think this is a friendly visit, Agent Vines. What's the call, sir?"

"Hold your position."

Vines looked around at his feet for something he could use. She had already dispatched every other prize Vines could have hung above his mantel—he wasn't about to let her take the most valuable one of all. Had he not had the baggage of two other officers with him, he would have just taken her out himself, but there was no way around that now.

*   *   *

Abby surveyed the area between the tree and the back of the house. About one hundred feet of open lawn. She would have to cross this significant expanse to get to the back of the house. Once there, she would have a clear shot at Bryce through the sliding glass door. She intended to use three bullets to take him out: one to break the glass, the second to hit Bryce, and the third for insurance. With the full moon still behind the clouds and the bright lights in the kitchen, the interior glass would act as a mirror and he would never see her.

She thought it was a shame that she wouldn't be able to look him in the eyes as she pulled the trigger. She wanted the satisfaction of seeing the life drain from his body. She wanted him to know who brought death to his door.

Maybe if I aim for the chest he'll live long enough to see me step through the shattered door and put another bullet in his head. I promised Ava I'd make sure he's dead, and this time, I will.

That cold thought chilled her.

She pulled her .22 from the small of her back and checked the magazine and the chamber one last time.

Abby said a silent prayer to steel herself, and then set off at a sprint toward the back of the house.

She only made it about halfway when she was stopped dead in her tracks by a loud crash as the glass of the rear sliding door shattered in front of her.

Abby froze.

*   *   *

What the fuck?

Bryce grabbed his gun and hit the switch next to the sliding doors, flooding the back yard with light. In a second, he saw Abby standing in the middle of the lawn, no more than fifty feet from the back of the house.

The shock wore off instantaneously as he ran toward her, gun raised.

*   *   *

Abby had been in this same situation many times before. Charge and fight, or turn and run? It wasn't even a decision. Her feet pounded the lawn as she raced toward Bryce, firing her .22.

She cursed herself for not having much experience hitting a moving target that shoots back. She hit the ground and rolled as he fired in her direction. He didn't appear to be aiming as much as trying to buy time, and he leaped behind the hot tub for a moment.

Abby stood.

"Get out here and fight like a man, you piece of shit!"

Nothing.

She emptied her magazine into the hot tub, sending wood trim and water everywhere.

As her weapon clicked, Bryce jumped from his hidden position and fired a few rounds at Abby as she dove behind the stairs.

"You think you're tough?" he yelled at her. "You come to my house and think you can take me?" His own weapon clicked as he fired his last bullet.

The thick clouds parted to reveal the bright full moon as Abby stepped from behind the stairs and glared at him. "I do."

He chuckled, a bit uncomfortably.

"You think that's funny?"

She sprinted toward him, quickly closing the distance as she ripped her knife from its sheath and went for blood.

24

"STAND DOWN!" Vines said harshly as he grabbed Matt by the back of his shirt and pulled him back.

"But sir!"

Jeff's voice came over their earpieces. "Did I hear shots fired?"

"Yes," Vines replied. "We're fine. Hold positions."

"I think I should call this in, sir."

"Like hell you will!"

After a moment of silence, the voice came again, "Matt, what do you think?"

Vines stared hard into his apprentice's eyes and shook his head, almost pleading. "We got this. I need this one, Matt. Come on."

Matt nodded. "We're OK. Stand down."

*   *   *

Bryce had begun to charge at Abby, but froze as she lunged through the air, knife raised to slash at his neck. He ducked, raising his forearm to shield himself from the blow. The seven-inch steel blade sliced through his coat and skin like a hot knife through butter, and he screamed as he twisted away and held tight to his arm as Abby rolled away.

She circled him just out of reach, holding the knife at arm's length, letting the full moon glint off the blade, keeping her prey's eyes on the steel instead of her face.

She lunged just an inch or two, and he quickly juked left. To an observer, it might have looked like she was toying with him, but she was testing him. Again she lunged, and again he juked left.

Good.

Abby charged forward. When Bryce went left, she hit the ground and used his own momentum to sweep his feet out from under him with her legs. He hit the ground with a thud, and Abby jumped on his back. Grabbing a fistful of his hair, she raised his head up off the ground as she brought her knife to his throat.

She leaned forward, clenching her fist tightly, tearing a fistful of hair from his scalp. As he groaned, she seethed, "Any last words?"

He mumbled something, incoherently.

"What? Speak up!"

Just clearly enough, he mumbled again, "I'm sorry."

The words shocked Abby like a hit from a Taser. "What?"

267

"I'm sorry," he said a bit more clearly.

In her shock, Abby eased her grip ever so slightly, just for a second. Bryce used this to his advantage, he grabbed her knife hand and pushed it away from his throat as he bucked her off and flipped her onto her back.

"I'm sorry I didn't kill you the first time," he spat as he punched her square in the face just as she began to sit up.

It's like getting hit with a sledgehammer, maybe worse, she thought as she fell and smacked the back of her head on the ground. As he went to land a kick to her midsection, Abby caught his foot, quickly twisting it and pulling him toward her in the direction of his kick, throwing him off-balance and sending him tumbling.

She sprang up as he hit the ground and quickly searched the area around her feet for her knife. *Where did it fall?*

The glint of steel flashed in the corner of her eye just in time for her to leave her feet and jump over his hand as the blade slashed toward her mid-thigh. She wasn't fast enough, and the blade sliced open her pants and blood trickled down her leg.

She felt nothing as she landed. Her adrenaline was pumping too hard for pain to phase her. She used his off-balance position on the ground to kick him in the jaw, knocking him to the ground again. Their fight had taken them nearly the length of the yard, and the knife flew from his hand and landed on the edge of the dock twenty feet away. She jumped on his back, wrapping her arm around his neck in a chokehold and squeezing tightly.

He tried to shake her off, but Abby was a woman possessed. She held fast as he thrashed about, trying fruitlessly to loosen her grip. As he sunk to his knees, choking for air, Abby's heart raced. *Just another minute, and he'll black out.* She was surprised he was already on his knees, but he had probably been breathing hard to begin with.

At the last second, as his hand came up to the side of her head, she saw the snub-nosed barrel of a tiny revolver he had pulled from his ankle holster. She jerked her head to the side as the gun fired three rounds right next to her ear, missing her, but leaving her eardrum ringing.

Off balance, she fell to the side and hit the ground with a thud.

"Get up," Bryce commanded.

Abby turned and looked up, the small revolver pointed at her only a few feet away. "Fuck you."

Bryce aimed the gun a bit lower, "Stand. Up."

"Fuck. You."

He squeezed the trigger and the white-hot, searing pain of flesh being torn by lead flashed through her body as the bullet ripped through her boot.

Abby screamed in pain as he grabbed her by the arm and stood her up, thrusting her forward.

269

"Get on the boat!" he said. "Walk!"

She stood with her back to him, staring at the steps of the dock just a few feet away, the boat and the endless expanse of water shimmering in the moonlight just beyond. She took a step forward, testing her foot. It hurt, but to her surprise, she could grit her teeth and bear weight on it just fine.

I've been through worse.

"Get on the boat," he said again from behind her.

"No."

Bryce sighed. "What do you think is going to happen here, Abby? Get on the fuckin' boat."

"No," she said, staring out at the water, calming her breath. "If you want to shoot me, you're going to have to shoot me in the back like the coward you are."

*   *   *

"I don't think I can do this, sir," Matt whispered to Vines. "I can't sit back and watch that monster kill an unarmed woman."

Vines grabbed him by the collar and turned to get in front of his face. "Listen to me, and listen good. The Rosso case that I spent the last decade of my life on is over. That unarmed woman singlehandedly destroyed everything I worked for. I have nothing else. Bryce is it. Do you know how embarrassed I was after the bank heist? Do you know what it's like to be forced into retirement by a director who wasn't even born when I joined the Bureau? Bryce is the last one standing in this family, and a murder rap puts him away for life. I'm the hero who found him and took him down. That's how this is going to go down, got it?"

"I got it. She ruined your case, you want her dead. But this is wrong."

Vines shook his head. "Talk to me in thirty-five years when your life has gone to shit. Tell me what you think then."

Matt nodded his head thoughtfully, looking over Vines' shoulder at the shoreline in the distance. "What the…?"

As two more shots sounded, Vines turned and gasped, "What the fuck just happened?"

Both men turned toward the fight out in the middle of the lawn, but couldn't put their eyes on Bryce and Abby for a good twenty seconds.

Finally Matt saw they were down near the dock, but couldn't make out what was going on. "Look, there."

He raised his night-vision goggles to figure it out, not believing what he saw. "Oh, shit."

*　　*　　*

Moments before the gunshots, Bryce took a step toward Abby, "So you got out of the fire. How about Ava, our little sweetie? Did she get out?"

Abby offered no reaction.

"I bet she did. Don't worry, I'll find her. I'll take care of her, too, but you're first. Now get on the boat or I'll shoot you where you stand and put you on it myself." He pressed the snubbed-nose gun into her back.

When the gun touched her back, it set Abby off like a spring-loaded trap. She reached up and back, grabbing the back of his head and swinging herself behind him, locking her forearm across his throat. As she hung there, feet dangling about a foot above the ground, she squeezed his neck with every fiber in her body.

In shock, Bryce raised the gun to shoot her. She thrashed him back and forth until the two remaining shots fired harmlessly into the air. Abby then applied every ounce of strength she had left against his neck. His fists pounded uselessly on her arms, but she would not let go for anything.

As he wavered and stumbled, she knew his vision would soon go as black as the water in front of them. He teetered forward toward the dock, trying to pry himself from her grip. Weakening, he stopped fighting and fell forward, crashing to the dock as Abby jumped up, watching him, waiting for him to move.

Nothing.

Wait… is that?

The faint sound of sirens called in the distance. No doubt the gunfire had raised the ire of the neighbors. Even though the nearby houses could not be seen, they no doubt heard the shots fired.

Abby quickly collected her knife and rolled the unconscious Bryce next to the boat. She could not roll him in, as the edge of the boat was about eighteen inches above dock level. She leaned him against the side, jumped into the boat herself, grabbed him under the arms and heaved with everything she had, flopping him into the boat, his body crashing to the deck.

The sirens were louder, maybe even on the street by now. She quickly released the tie line on the front of the boat and ran to the back. As she unraveled the back line, she heard three men yelling as they charged down the lawn in the moonlight, bright flashlights bouncing as they ran.

She could hear them shouting.

"Stop! FBI!"

She turned toward the steering wheel and saw the key in the ignition. The men were making short work of the distance, guns drawn as the oldest of the three arrived at the shoreline.

"Stop, Abby! You're under arrest!"

How does he know my name?

"Who are you?"

"I'm Agent Vines. I know what you did at Rosso's. Now get off the boat and surrender, and we'll go easy on you. They were scum."

273

Abby stared at the three of them. They had their guns and flashlights trained on her, but Agent Vines was closest.

"I know the man at your feet is Bryce Haydenson," Vines continued, "and trust me, he'll pay for his crimes, too."

Abby let that sink in. *He'll pay for his crimes too?* Where were the authorities ten years ago when she was getting regular beatings from the heap of garbage currently at her feet? Where were they when she went to bed every night fearing for her life? They were on the family payroll. On the take, with their hands in their pockets. Where were they when Ava was taken from her bedroom just a few days ago? Where were they when Ava was trapped inside a burning building about to die?

No, I haven't come this far to turn him over to the police.

Abby turned her body and hit the deck, grabbing the key and twisting it in the ignition. She jumped as shots were fired in her direction. As the engine caught, she pegged the throttle all the way forward and launched the boat away from the dock while staying low. Glancing back, she could see the flashing of red and blue strobes lighting up the neighborhood in front of the house.

She could also see the three agents, or at least their flashlights, bouncing along the shoreline as they raced toward a neighboring dock where a sleek fishing boat bobbed in the waves Abby created.

25

BRYCE'S NEIGHBORS were not as cavalier about their boat keys, but FBI agents pounding on their door in the middle of the night quickly convinced them to turn them over.

The three agents piled into the boat and took off from the dock, telling the local officers to stay behind in case Abby returned. Vines turned to Jeff, who had been watching the front. "Did you call for back up? I specifically told you not to. We can take her ourselves!"

"No, sir, I did not," he said, looking back at the strobe lights flooding the neighborhood. "I'm guessing the neighbors did that once they heard shots being fired."

Vines stared at him a moment before turning back to the water and reprimanding him, "Don't be a smart-ass."

"She's just about ten o'clock, sir," Matt called out from the front of the boat, pointing to the left.

Vines squinted. *There she is.* He picked out Abby's boat in the bright moonlight and adjusted course to put her right in his sights before feeding full power to the engine and closing in.

He estimated her to be at least half a mile, if not more,

ahead. Being the only boat on the calm water, however, made her easy to pick out. He could already tell they were gaining on her, albeit incrementally, but they would catch her. Their boat was bigger and faster.

"We're going to catch her," he announced. "It'll be about ten minutes before we overtake her boat. I want you boys to be ready to board the moment I pull up alongside. Got it?"

"Sir," Matt said, "don't you think we should coordinate with local law enforcement? I'm sure they've got at least one boat in the water, if not more."

"No, this is my collar boys. This is the big one, and I'm not sharing the spotlight, got it?"

The two junior agents nodded, but also glanced at each other, unsure what to make of Vines' insistence on going it alone.

The water and the boat became decidedly darker as thick clouds moved in, obscuring the bright moon. Vines looked ahead, unable to make out Abby's boat. He checked his pocket for his small binoculars but realized he dropped them earlier when they started running. "Who's got night vision?"

Jeff pulled a small pair of binoculars from his belt and handed them over. Vines had him hold the wheel while he cranked up the brightness to accommodate for the sudden darkness. "There she is, clear as a bell." He smiled, moving in for the kill.

*   *   *

A light drizzle began to fall as Abby watched the agents' boat fade into the darkness behind her. *Thank you!* She allowed herself to feel a small bit of relief—luck was on her side, at least for the time being.

With the nose of the boat pointed toward hundreds of miles of open water, and the throttle open, Abby rummaged around in a bin looking for a rope or something to keep the wheel straight. She settled on a short bungee cord that she looped through the wheel and hooked to a cup holder directly under it. Satisfied that it would keep the boat pointed relatively forward, Abby turned her attention to her leg and foot.

The cut on her thigh didn't go too deep, and actually appeared to have stopped bleeding. She thought about tearing away some of the material around the wound to better clean it, but then figured the compression of the tight pants that surrounded the cut was probably helping, so she decided to leave it alone for now.

Instead, she turned to the pain in her foot, and after carefully taking off her boot, she was pleased to find only a flesh wound. The bullet had grazed the inside of her foot and drawn some blood, but otherwise, she was all right.

Abby next went through the glove box and found an emergency first aid kit. The alcohol stung and both of her wounds bled just a bit more as she cleansed them, but she was over it by the time she packed them with gauze and medical tape.

As she put the kit back, there was a tremendous thud as something slammed into the boat and the watercraft rocked to the side. Abby stumbled to her left, but her quick hands grabbed the wheel and she kept her balance. She immediately cut the power and looked around to see a buoy floating twenty feet behind the vessel as the increasingly steady rain made thousands of mini-splashes around it.

I must have hit it.

She realized that she should probably slow down at this point, looking back and seeing just a few twinkling lights on the shore. Then she heard something. At first she assumed it was just the gentle white noise made by millions of raindrops plunking into the massive lake, but then she realized it was something else. Something more powerful. Something man-made. The sound of another engine. Close by.

Ripping her night-vision monocular from her belt, she looked back to see the agents in their fishing boat gaining on her, and fast.

Abby turned over the key and gave the engine the full throttle as she looked back to see the boat barreling down on her. As the front of the boat pitched up, Bryce's body rolled backward on the deck and thumped into the row of cinderblocks lined up near the engine.

She wiped the rain from her eyes and looked down at the speedometer to see she was going sixty knots. She wasn't exactly sure how fast a knot was, but figured it was probably something like miles per hour. The rain was pelting her forehead hard enough, so she'd believe that.

About a mile a minute… she thought about this as she looked back again through her monocular and saw the boat even closer, continuing to close distance.

The senior agent was at the helm, looking through his own night-vision binoculars and waving.

She looked back at Bryce, face down by the cinderblocks. She was far enough out that she could dump him here, but not with a boatload of FBI agents one hundred and fifty feet behind her. She figured going a mile a minute, if she could disable the agents for just a couple of minutes, she could dash away and hide in the darkness.

Looking out at the lake, rain pouring down around her, she couldn't see more than twenty feet without her night vision. If the agents didn't have theirs, she would be fine, but she couldn't exactly jump in their boat, grab them, and chuck them in the water.

Think… think… think…

Abby was suddenly struck with an idea. She looked into her pouch and found her last flash-bang grenade. She pulled it out and realized it would do her no good. It had been crushed, probably during the fight, and was just a bag of powder and duct tape now.

Damn.

After securing the bungee cord to the steering wheel again, she ripped open the glove box. She tossed the first aid kit aside to look through the other contents. After chucking a couple of old compact discs, a book of matches, and some maps behind her, she realized she wasn't going to find what she had hoped for in there.

Her eyes darted around the boat until they settled on the bench seat at the rear of the boat, where Bryce lay face down next to the cinder blocks. She ran to the back of the boat and lifted the seat to reveal a storage compartment underneath. Her eyes quickly took stock: *rope, half a dozen life preservers, oars, inflatable raft… aha!*

Suddenly a large hand clamped around her ankle. "Bitch!" Bryce shouted as he ripped her leg out from under her, knocking her to the deck.

Despite being caught off-guard, Abby sprung up as soon as she hit the wet deck, whereas it took Bryce a moment to get to his feet. He was moving slowly and purposefully, having just regained consciousness.

He swung a big, lazy fist toward Abby, but she ducked and jabbed him in one of his cracked ribs. Bryce winced in pain, and like a wounded animal with a crazed look in his eye, jumped toward Abby screaming, trying to wrap his arms around her.

Twisting her body and throwing all of her weight behind her shoulder, she landed the first hit to his midsection, causing him to gasp as the air rushed from his lungs. Rotating her shoulders with each blow, she landed shot after shot to his body. Screaming and filled with rage, Abby unleashed a fury of blows to his body to his stomach and ribs, until he struggled to breathe, each gasp as painful as another punch.

As Abby ran out of air herself, her screaming stopped. She looked up at his rain-soaked face. Bryce wavered on his feet with the movement of the boat. Time stood still for a second as she took in the face of the monster she once saw as her ticket out of a horrible life.

He seemed in a trance as Abby threw a right cross to his jaw, snapping his head to the side with a knock-out punch as though she were a prizefighter. As his knees buckled, she grabbed the back of his head and smashed his face into the railing of the boat, breaking his nose. He collapsed face down on the deck in a heap.

Abby stood, staring down at the man, rain pouring down all around her, soaked to the bone and breathing heavily. She waited for him to move.

Nothing.

Only remembering the three FBI agents closing in on her broke her from her daze.

She grabbed the emergency boating kit and quickly found what she had hoped for. Making her way back to the front, she unhooked the bungee cord and steadied the boat. Looking ahead with her monocular she saw nothing but open water. To her right was the same, and to her left, twinkling lights that indicated the coastline. She estimated it was three or four miles away.

Looking behind her, she saw Vines at the helm, watching her through his night- vision binoculars and waving his arms, all the while shouting, "Stop the boat! Stop the boat!" The two younger agents on the bow held onto the rail, clearly ready to hop on her boat when they got close enough, likely within the next few minutes.

As the boats raced at full throttle into the blackness, she estimated they were only fifty feet away now. Much closer and neither would need their night vision anymore.

She examined the deck, Bryce hadn't moved, but the pool of blood from his broken nose had grown substantially larger.

She looked behind her with the night vision one last time to be sure Vines' eyes were still trained on her, and they were.

In one swift motion, she lowered the throttle, slowing her boat as she twisted her body around and shot the flare gun directly back at the fishing boat. The flash of light blinded Vines who was still looking through the night vision. He instinctively jerked the wheel hard to the right to avoid it, sending one of the junior agents into the water and the other toppling onto the deck.

Abby heard Vines scream and knew from experience that the sudden hot light had momentarily blinded him. She cut the wheel hard to the left and pegged the throttle forward, putting as much distance between herself and the agents as she possibly could in the little time she had. As she sped away, she looked back through her monocular to see Vines rocking back and forth, holding his eyes, and one of the junior agents throwing a life jacket out to the man in the water. The flare had landed on the far side of the boat and given it an eerie backlit glow.

She knew they would regroup quickly, so she turned her attention forward, concentrating on the shortest angle to the shoreline. She didn't want to reach the shoreline— just get within swimming distance. Abby glanced over her shoulder occasionally though all she could see with the naked eye was the glow of the flare, and that was beginning to fade, too.

26

ONCE ABBY SAW the flare go out, she cut the engine and listened. The rain had become a light drizzle and she couldn't hear anything, but some light drops around her. Raising the monocular, she looked back toward where the FBI boat should be, but she couldn't make out anything. It was too far away. She hoped that was mutual, but wasn't about to waste any time finding out.

A quick check of the clock showed that about four minutes had passed. Looking around and doing some quick calculations, she figured the FBI boat was about four miles behind her with no way of knowing where she was. The shoreline looked to be a mile off the left side of the boat.

That should be far enough, and close enough.

She gave Bryce a gentle nudge with her foot.

Nothing.

She pressed her fingers to his neck and felt a pulse.

Good. A quick death is too good for this piece of shit.

It made her feel evil and vile, but she wanted him to die in pain. Abby wanted him to feel the pain and terror that he had inflicted on her.

She unrolled and laid out a black plastic body bag next to him, a bag that had been intended for her. She rolled him on top of it and pulled the edges up around him.

As he lay there, she couldn't help but think that he almost looked peaceful.

Warm tears flowed from her eyes and spilled down her cheeks as she began to sob. She paced the deck, trying to get control of herself.

"Get it together, Abby," she muttered to herself. Taking a few deep breaths, she wiped the tears from her eyes and turned back to the task at hand.

Holding the two flaps together, she pulled up the heavy zipper from his feet until it reached the midway point of his chest, where she finally stopped to look at him.

Tears flowed down her cheeks again.

With bile in her stomach and adrenaline coursing through her veins, she slapped him so hard across the face that she drew blood.

"Fuck you, Bryce!" she screamed, staring down at his still body.

Suddenly, she wretched the contents of her stomach over the side of the boat.

"Let's get this over with," she said to him, wiping her chin.

She finished zipping the bag, rolled him to the bench seat at the back of the boat, where adrenaline and leverage helped her to push, pull, and maneuver him onto the seat, then onto the platform behind it.

Setting four of the cinderblocks on top of him, she quickly ran chains through them and around the body, pulling the chains taught and securing the whole package tightly with two padlocks.

Taking a moment to be still, she inspected her work, watching the two cinderblocks on his chest rise and fall slightly with his breath.

She could hear Ava's voice in her head, the last thing she said before Abby left her behind.

Abby spoke the words aloud to make them real: "Make sure he's dead this time."

The bag suddenly jerked as though he were awake, but not fast enough. Abby tore her knife from its sheath and plunged it into Bryce's stomach. A scream emitted from his lips below the fabric of the bag. She ripped the knife from the fresh wound and stabbed him again, drawing another scream.

As she felt the knife pierce him, she knew acid from his stomach would quickly spill into the wound, causing massive pain in addition to blood loss. One way or another, he would be dead within minutes, but not before experiencing the worst pain possible.

She wiped the knife clean on the bag before returning it to its sheath.

He groaned and whimpered as the bag moved slowly like a fat earthworm struggling under its own weight. He instinctively tried to get into the fetal position, but the cinderblocks at last kept him still.

*   *   *

He woke disoriented.

Where the hell am I?

Everything around him was pitch black, and he felt confined. He strained his eyes but saw nothing.

His head was throbbing, and it hurt to keep his eyes open, even though there was no light.

He tried to call out, but as soon as he moved his mouth, a searing pain shot through his jaw.

He tried to reach up through the darkness to feel it with his hand, but he couldn't move his hand either.

He tried to sit up, but without his arms it was a losing battle. It was as though a massive weight was crushing his chest, holding him down.

Bryce closed his eyes again. The throbbing in his skull only worsened with each movement. Even the thought of moving caused him pain. As he lay there, confused, he took stock of his facilities.

There has to be an option. How did I get here? Then he heard a familiar female voice speak, and it all came rushing back.

The voice said, "Make sure he's dead this time."

Bryce jerked forward upon hearing Abby's voice, trying to sit up, but he suddenly screamed as he felt the sharp tip of her knife slice into his gut and tear into his stomach. He screamed again as she repeated the action.

He writhed, trying to get into the fetal position as a searing pain spread through his abdominal cavity, but he couldn't move. His heart pounded at the walls of his chest as his breaths came in short gasps. Blackness enveloped him as consciousness escaped him.

*   *   *

Abby watched the movement stop, though the cinderblocks continued to rise and fall at a rapid rate on his chest. She smiled. *He passed out from the shock.*

With one foot on the deck and the other on the seat, Abby placed her hands on the side of the bag as the man inside shook with a tremor. She thought about all the pain Bryce had caused not only to her, but also to so many others. All the men he killed, the lives he ruined, the families he had devastated. She remembered her promise to Rosso just before he died: she would make Bryce pay for killing his son.

She hoped the pain he was in now was just a short taste of what was to come.

Abby leaned next to his head and whispered, "Burn in hell, motherfucker."

She heaved, pushing him over the edge of the platform and watched as he splashed into the water below, floating for just a moment before the blackness swallowed him up and he was gone from sight.

*   *   *

He battled to stay awake, but it seemed to be a losing fight.

As Bryce fought between consciousness and reality, he felt for a moment as though he were falling. The weight on his chest lifted for a brief instant. He was aware of the searing pain in his gut but couldn't recall how that had come to be or how long it had gone on.

Am I dying?

Suddenly he stopped falling, but only for a moment. The weight was heavier now, and he fell again, but more slowly. The weight was not only on his chest—but it was all around him, nearly crushing him. It was as though he were being enveloped in a cool embrace. It was almost a struggle to draw a breath, and when he finally managed to, he choked on... *water?*

A sudden rush of adrenaline brought a fleeting moment of clarity and realization. His eyes flashed open, suddenly aware of all around him. The next breath brought another mouthful of water, and he coughed and choked as he gasped for air while it burned his throat.

As the weight of the cinderblocks dragged him further into the crushing darkness below, he struggled against his own chains and thrashed with all his might, but there was no escape for him.

Not tonight.

Not ever.

With his final breath, Bryce let out a primal scream that no one would ever hear. He tried to hold his breath as panic embraced him as fully as the depths of the water around him. He could not hold it forever, though. His lungs forced open his airways to suck in precious oxygen though there was none left. As the water coursed through his throat and filled his lungs, it burned like acid as he crashed to the bottom of the lake with an inaudible thud.

Then, all was still.

27

ABBY LOOKED UP, the sound of helicopter blades chopping through the air in the distance waking her from her celebration. She saw nothing in the black sky, with or without her monocular, but she could hear it out there somewhere.

Looking across the water, she couldn't see Vines' boat either, but she knew it was looking for her. She'd be damned if she was going to be punished for doing what the law couldn't do: put Bryce away for good.

Moments later, the faint glow of searchlights in the distance dispelled any thoughts she had that they weren't out there for her. Though miles away, she could make out the flashing strobe lights of police boats cutting through the water.

She had to act fast. Still a mile out, she had hoped to pilot herself a bit closer to shore, but that wasn't going to happen now. Knowing they were searching for her both from the air and water, and that one, if not both, were bound to have heat imaging, she wanted to be as far from the boat as possible when they found it.

Abby did a quick check, convincing herself that she was up for a little swim.

She quickly wrestled the overhead canopy into place so that no one could see into the boat, then turned the key until the engine rumbled to life. Abby pointed the boat toward open water and secured the steering wheel in place one last time with the bungee cord.

Taking a deep breath, she pegged the throttle all the way forward and sent the boat surging ahead into the wide-open sea. After a moment, assured that this would work, Abby ran to the back of the boat and leaped off into the chilly water.

The sound of the runaway boat became a distant noise as quickly as the pain shot through her body when her leg wound hit the water. She hadn't counted on that, and as she started to kick, the mile or so distance to shore suddenly seemed insurmountable.

A few minutes later, she couldn't hear the boat at all. She turned and treaded water for a few moments to get her bearings, and saw that the police boats and helicopter appeared to be moving toward the boat, not her. By the time they figured out she wasn't on it, she planned to be long gone.

As she treaded water, she began to cry. All of the hurt, all of the pain, all of the terror that she had endured over the past decade were behind her now.

He can't hurt us anymore.

They were tears of joy.

Nothing was reversed, but the future was infinitely

more promising. She and Ava could live normal lives.

Struck by a sudden thought, she fished her disposable phone out of her back pocket and opened it in front of her face to find the screen black and unresponsive.

Damn it.

Abby would have to wait until she got to shore to call Donny and let him know everything was OK. She no longer had his burner number, but she remembered the name of the hotel, so that wouldn't be a problem.

Forty minutes later, what had been a searing pain in her leg when she first hit the water had eased to a dull stabbing, if there was such a thing. Her body shivered as she pushed onward. She had been swimming toward what appeared to be the closest point, a lonely light mounted on the end of a dock though she began to doubt she would ever make it there.

Her arms and legs burned from the exertion and were doing their best to lock up. It was only through sheer will that she had managed to keep moving at all. She knew if she didn't reach the shore soon, hypothermia would set in and she would drown. Abby estimated she only had a few hundred yards left, maybe the length of two or three football fields, but the distance felt like a marathon.

I just have to rest a moment.

Abby rolled onto her back and did her best to wrap her arms around herself in a fruitless attempt to keep warm. As she lay shivering in the water, she closed her eyes and thought of what it would be like to see Eric again.

*   *   *

As only a child can, Ava had passed out hours ago and managed to get a fair night's sleep.

Donny, on the other hand, was unable to do the same, not that he even tried.

Sitting up in the chair next to the door, he caught himself dozing off a couple of times, but otherwise spent the hours holding vigil for Abby and cursing his role as the babysitter.

I should be there with her. I should be helping her.

He looked through the window, then down at his phone. Finding nothing satisfactory with either view, he repeated the process no less than a hundred times over the past few hours.

The sky had begun to lighten, encroaching upon Abby's deadline.

Come on, Abby, come on…

To distract himself, he finally put on some coffee in the hotel supplied pot and flipped on the TV, quietly so as not to disturb the little angel who was still fast asleep in the bed just a few feet to his right. He surfed for a few minutes, finding his way to the morning news as the smell of coffee began to fill the room.

The young, pretty news anchor had a remarkably

serious face as she spoke into the camera. He turned it up a bit so he could hear.

"Tragedy on the lake last night…"

Donny's jaw dropped as the picture on the television changed to the front of Bryce's house, barely visible in the twilight, countless police cruisers around it.

The voiceover continued. "Authorities claim this was a domestic dispute that began in the middle of the night between a man and a woman believed to be his ex-wife though at this time their relationship is still unclear. The fight took a dangerous turn when neighbors heard shots fired around 2:00 a.m. and quickly called police. Authorities were unable to get to the scene before the dispute took to the water. The details are still coming in, but a little more than an hour later…"

As the picture on the television changed, Donny couldn't figure out what he was looking at right away, but the story quickly made it clear.

"… the boat that the man and woman had been on crashed into the small cargo ship you see here."

Choppy video showed two police boats and a helicopter following a smaller boat at high speed until suddenly the three pursuit vessels peeled off moments before the boat slammed into the side of the cargo ship and burst into flames.

"Authorities have said an official statement will come later this morning, but an investigator speaking off the record has said at this time that both parties are presumed dead. The speedboat was nothing more than a floating field of debris after the collision, and there have been no survivors found thus far."

Donny shut off the television as his heart sank to his toes. He felt as though he were going to be sick.

He looked at the little girl beginning to stir in bed. A little girl he was now somehow responsible for.

His mind began to race, thinking about keeping Ava safe. The heads of the family had been cut down, but the soldiers remained. They knew who Abby was, and he knew they had pieced together that he had helped her. They were surely out for blood.

But they're hundreds of miles away and don't know how to find us, right?

Yet Donny had no way to know if Bryce had told anyone they were here. For all he knew, half the family was on its way to this location right now, locked and loaded. He had to get out to protect Ava.

He also felt it was safe to assume they knew about Abby's sister, though he wasn't entirely sure if anyone in the family had helped Bryce abduct the little girl. Still, better to be safe and tell her to get the hell out.

Ava opened her eyes and read the concern on his face. "What's the matter?"

He did his best to offer a comforting grin. He wasn't about to tell Ava what he had just learned. "Nothing. Just tired. I'm going to step outside to make a call, alright?"

Ava stretched and rolled over. "OK."

Once outside, Donny paced, trying to decide what to do first. He looked at the phone and hit the speed-dial as Abby instructed last night.

A few thousand miles away, Robert looked down at his phone. He didn't recognize the number, but few people had his private line. Judging by the area code and the conversation he had yesterday, he ventured a guess at who was on the other line.

Her cheerily answered the line, "Abby, my dear. Please tell me that you're done with this nonsense and are coming home."

"This isn't Abby," Donny said sadly, recognizing the voice on the other side. "This is a friend."

Robert's expression quickly changed from his normal jovial state to concerned, then morose, as Donny relayed the events of the last twelve hours.

"Abby said to call you," Donny continued. "Ava isn't safe. I need to get her out of here. I don't think her sister Sarah is safe either. Abby said there was a plan in place for them."

"Yes, there is." Robert drifted away for a moment trying to process the news. He shook it off for the time being; there would be time to grieve later. "Let me make a couple of phone calls. I will contact Sarah." Robert thought a moment about what he and Abby had discussed.

"Are you still in Sandy Point?"

"Yes, in a ho…"

"It doesn't matter where," Robert said, cutting cut him off. "There's a small municipal airport about thirty minutes west in a town called Pearse. It's right on the lake. Can you get there?"

"Yes, sir. Should we leave now?"

"If you're safe where you are, sit tight but keep this line open and be ready to move when I call."

*   *   *

Donny stared blankly out the window of the private jet as they crossed the Canadian border for the second time that morning.

Robert worked quickly to make sure one of his planes picked up Ava and Donny within the hour. After his conversation with Abby last night, he had dispatched his jet to Chicago with a hunch that a get away vehicle would be needed. After a quick jump to Montreal, where they picked up Sarah and her few belongings, they were on their way back over the border en route to Los Angeles. Robert was there working on the preparations for the next season of *Trial Island*, and while he and Abby had discussed the scenario, they hadn't realistically entertained any details. He and Sarah would have to come up with a plan.

Donny wasn't even going to get on the plane, but Robert convinced him that Abby left her daughter in his care and he had a responsibility to keep her safe. Not only that, but he was in danger, too, and knowing all that he had done for Abby over the years, Robert insisted that Donny accept his assistance. He tried to say he could take care of himself, but Ava pleaded with him. Since he really had nowhere else to turn, he figured he would at least make sure they got to L.A. safely.

He rubbed his eyes and downed the rest of his coffee. It had been a long morning, with lots of questions from Ava, none of which he fully answered. For now, she was sitting on the other side of the plane next to her Aunt Sarah, mercifully distracted by the television. Both he and Sarah spent the morning in a state of shock and disbelief. They hadn't even begun to grieve yet, and certainly weren't going to do so in front of Ava.

As the plane began an obvious descent, Donny looked at his watch. He hadn't been expecting to touch down for another few hours. He asked the flight attendant if she knew why they were landing. She said she didn't know, but would ask the pilot.

Ava came over to sit next to him and to watch out the window.

His heart went out to the little girl. She had been through so much, and now losing her mother was almost too much to bear. He put his arm around her and pulled her close, mostly so she wouldn't see the tears welling up in his eyes. He made the mistake of looking across the plane and locking eyes with Sarah, at which point both of their eyes spilled over.

He quickly turned away to dry his with the back of his sleeve.

The pilot, an interesting character named Captain Frank who had greeted them when they got on the plane in a Hawaiian shirt and straw cowboy hat, came over the intercom system. "Make sure you're all buckled up back there. We'll be touching down in a few minutes to pick up one more passenger, and then we'll be on our way to the west coast. Just sit tight."

One more passenger? What the hell is going on?

As they neared the ground, Donny recognized the airport as the same one they had taken off from that morning.

As the plane taxied to a stop at the end of the small municipal runway, Ava beamed a huge smile and jumped up and down pointing out the window.

Donny turned to see a petite figure dressed in black walking up to the plane with a slight limp. A huge grin took over his face, and he raced to the front of the plane.

28

ABBY LAUGHED at the interviewer's comment as the director called a break. She touched the young girl on the shoulder as they stood. "This hasn't been nearly as bad as I thought it would be. Thank you."

The girl was speechless as Abby turned and walked away to chat with Robert.

Just yesterday, Liz Bennington had been a low-level intern at Robert's cable news outlet, and today she was conducting what could only be described as the interview of a lifetime. The established and celebrated news personalities she had spent the last six months fetching coffee for would have killed for this opportunity to sit down with Abby.

When she got a phone call from Robert, she was only told that she was the best choice for a special segment he was personally working on and to drop everything and prepare to be away for a couple of days. When the billionaire owner of your news outlet drops something like that in your lap, you do exactly what he asks. Though she was unsure at the time how her internship and her blog— albeit a popular one—qualified her to work with someone of his stature. But she wasn't about to point that out to him either.

Liz was then whisked away to some beautiful village in Italy and brought to a gorgeous villa, which had been taken over by the camera and lighting equipment. She tried to get information from the crew, hair, and make-up people about what exactly was going on, but none of them had a clue either. Of course, things made a little more sense once Abby entered the room. Liz had dedicated the last few years of her life to maintaining the most popular blog on the web about *Trial Island*, and specifically Abby: her disappearance, subsequent death, and all of the conspiracy theories surrounding it.

As Abby sat down, Liz smiled at her as though seeing an old friend. Abby had lost a little weight, showed a few more wrinkles around the eyes, and had shorter hair than her last known photo before she had been shot by the hitman in Canada, but it was definitely Abby.

Liz knew why she was chosen—it was because she could jump into this interview with zero preparation. It was an interview she had conducted a thousand times over in her head.

"So," Liz began, "where have you been?"

Abby laughed, and they chatted like old friends as Liz walked through the known events surrounding Abby over the past couple years. Abby revealed that she and Eric had spent time living in northern Canada. She teared up recounting the ranch they had lived on and the life they had together. She needed a change of scenery after his death, which is why she was now living in Europe with her daughter, though she declined to disclose where.

Authorities investigating the fire at Buena Sera quickly linked the restaurant back to the Rosso family. When viewed in light of the raid at the family compound the night before, the fight reported by neighbors and the high-speed boat chase ending in a fiery wreck a short time later, it made all too much sense. The owner of the restaurant was also quickly identified as former mobster Bryce Haydenson. The raid at Rosso's had not been solved when it fell off the news cycle though most people assumed it was the feds.

Dive teams scoured the bottom of the lake under the wreck for nearly two weeks searching for bodies, but with Bryce sleeping with the fishes fifty miles southwest of there, none were found. The helicopter team never saw anyone jump from the boat or otherwise leave the craft, though, so the occupants had to be dead.

Agent Eddie Vines never got to claim the headlines or the glory. When his two-man team reported to their director what happened—that the agents could have diffused the fight before it started if Vines hadn't given the command to stand down to increase his notoriety—news quickly traveled up the chain of command. The powers that be knew the story would be huge, and this would be another major black mark against the agency. A gag order was placed on Vines and the other two men, their reports sealed as confidential. Any party found to reveal details about what truly happened would be prosecuted, with the full force of the government behind it. Abby's involvement was never disclosed, though a rumor surfaced, which the feds quickly disproved. Vines lived out the last few months after his retirement on a small pension until dropping dead of a heart attack at a boat dealership.

There had been rumors and theories that Abby had been behind it all. Those rumors mainly stemmed from the claim of a young girl who was a hostess at Buena Sera. She claimed that Abby came into the restaurant and started the fire in a rage. Though she maintained her story, she, too, disappeared from the news cycle as quickly as she'd come on the scene.

All the while, Abby hadn't shown her face in public. After all, she was dead.

Until now.

The media was the last piece. Abby intended to live out her life quietly with her daughter. She didn't want to spend the rest of it looking over her shoulder, waiting for someone to find her, to figure out who she was.

Robert convinced her to address it head on. "Give them what they want," he said. It took convincing, but ultimately she agreed that it was best. If she sat down for an interview and put it all out there, the story would be over. There would be nothing left for anyone to chase after. It made sense.

So here they were in a remote village in northern Italy, laying it all out for everyone to hear.

As Liz wrapped up the interview, she folded her hands

ESCAPE
Dead End

on her lap. "It certainly has been a ride, hasn't it, Abby?"

She nodded. "One hell of a ride, that's for sure."

"You know, I'm sure the studios are clamoring for the rights to your life story. I certainly wouldn't be the first one to say it should be made into a movie, or at the very least, a book."

Abby chuckled and gave Liz a smile. "No one would ever believe it's all true."

*   *   *

Abby never saw the interview. Nor did anyone on her island, but Robert said it was a huge success. Also, the current season of *Trial Island* was a massive success. The extra media attention from Abby's story shot the show back to the top of the ratings and having been back for a couple of years, the island was populated with a sizeable cast that made for must-see viewing.

As she emerged from the well-beaten path that led from the market back to her beachfront villa on her little secluded island, the scene took her breath away, as it always had.

Slowly walking along the sand toward her home in the distance, she contemplated how much her life had changed since JJ found her here nearly three years ago. She had left paradise to explore her past, a past for which she had no memory.

She smiled as she watched her beautiful daughter in the distance hunting for shells along the shore with Ben, an activity of which neither seemed to grow tired. Ben had grown into a fine young man in the time since Abby and Eric had waved goodbye to him at the end of the dock as they motored away. Abby was hopeful that he and Ava would remain close over the years. She knew Eric would approve.

Abby felt close to Eric when she was here in the paradise that they built with their own two hands. She missed him, of course, but she always remembered a conversation she had with Robert.

"You loved Eric, right?"

"Absolutely," Abby sobbed. "With all of my heart."

"And he loved you, of that there is no question, my dear. Look at what he did. He sacrificed his own life to save yours."

Abby nodded with tear-filled eyes, recalling the final moments of his life.

Robert then turned to her and held her face in his hands, as Eric often had. "Do you believe that if Eric were here right now, he would want you to spend your life mourning him over what he did?"

She shook her head no. He'd want her to be happy.

"No, he would want you to live your life to the fullest. To celebrate each additional day you've been granted. To love and to care for your daughter. To be happy and live without fear. That's what he would want, Abby."

Robert sighed, arm around her as he continued. "I've been on this earth a great many years. I've amassed an absurd fortune, spent time with every world leader of any consequence, religious leaders of all faiths, leaders of the scientific community—truly the brightest minds in the world. Do you want to know what I learned? The single most important thing?"

Abby admired his confident smile, the look he got when he was about to impart some wisdom he was especially proud of.

"None of us—not a single one of us—has a bloody clue. When it comes down to it, we know nothing, and truly are nothing. All my money and power, it's meaningless outside of the relatively miniscule confines of our society. In life, I am a very powerful man. The instant I die, my money, my power, has no meaning. All that truly matters is the legacy we leave behind. We are nothing more than the lives we touch and the memories we leave behind.

"Eric gave you the greatest gift another human being can give another. So whenever you find yourself feeling down or bad for yourself, remember that final act of love. Cry because of its meaning if you must; sob at the thought of how beautiful a thing such an act of love truly is, but don't weep for his loss. As you live on, and Ava lives on, so he lives on in you."

Abby remembered that advice now as she sat on the steps and leaned back on her elbows in front of the French doors leading into her cozy villa. She found peace. Ava, in the distance, waved, as did Ben, but they weren't waving at her.

Abby looked to her right and smiled as Donny walked onto the beach with an armful of firewood for the evening's fire. Ben's father, Jay, and the rest of his family would be joining them for dinner later, and they would all sit around the fire enjoying each other's company until their eyes refused to stay open any longer.

Donny smiled as he sat next to her on the step and placed a hand on her knee. She laced her fingers through his and leaned over to give him a gentle kiss on the lips.

He reached down and caressed her stomach with his free hand. As she laid her hand over his, she watched his heart skip a beat when he felt a faint kick from their little miracle.

His eyes opened wide and he smiled. "That never gets old."

Abby nodded, beaming, glowing. "Little Erica has been very active today!"

She lay there, soaking in the sun, knowing that they were not only happy, but safe. Her life felt complete. She was right where she belonged.

Abby closed her eyes and smiled, letting out an easy breath as she enjoyed her tropical escape. "So this is what true happiness feels like."

THE END

Author's note

Thank you for reading my books! I would love to hear from you. You can email me from my website, www.Antocci.com, or follow me on Facebook and introduce yourself. I personally respond to everyone.

While this book is the end of the ESCAPE trilogy, it is no where even close to the end of my writing, so be sure to drop me an email or follow me on Facebook to hear news about future books!

I certainly hope you had as much fun reading the ESCAPE books as I had writing them. If you liked what you read, please tell a friend – or better yet tell the world by writing a quick review on the Amazon page. Even a few short sentences are helpful. As an independently published author, I don't have a marketing department behind me. I have you, the reader. So please, spread the word!

Thanks again so very much!

All the best - Dave

44154131R00175

Made in the USA
Lexington, KY
08 July 2019